Halley and the Mystery of the Lost Girls

Halley and the Mystery of the Lost Girls

Susy Robison

Copyright © 2024 Susy Robison
All rights reserved.
ISBN: 9798989104079
E-ISBN: 9798989104086
Big Sister Books
Pittsburgh, PA

Big Sister Books
Two Sisters Press

In loving memory of my parents
Dr. Harald Norlin and Frances Johnson

PA HUMANITIES
AUTHOR TALK EVENT
SUSY ROBISON

SUSY BEGAN WRITING HER DEBUT NOVEL WHEN SHE RETIRED IN 2019 AFTER YEARS OF DIRECTING VOLUNTEER PROGRAMS WITH SEVERAL NOT-FOR-PROFITS IN PITTSBURGH. LIVING IN INDIA WHEN SHE WAS A CHILD, HER MEMORIES FROM THOSE YEARS FLAVOR HER FIRST NOVEL, "HALLEY AND THE MYSTERY OF THE LOST GIRLS", A YOUNG ADULT HISTORICAL ADVENTURE SET IN INDIA IN 1952, 5 YEARS AFTER PARTITION.

SUSY RECIEVED A BA IN ENGLISH FROM THE UNIVERSITY OF CALIFORINA, BERKELEY AND LIVES IN PITTSBURGH WITH HER HUSBAND. THEY LOVE TO HANG OUT WITH THEIR ADULT SON AND DAUGHTER AND HAPPILY DOG SIT SEVERAL TIMES A WEEK,

**845 PHILADELPHIA STREET
DOWNTOWN INDIANA
WWW.INDIANAFREELIBRARY.ORG**

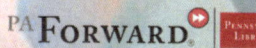

Prologue

I lived in India when I was a child.
An elephant walking along a dusty road, a steaming bowl of curry, the unique drone of a sitar, and the scent of sandalwood all swirl ☺ through my memories.
India flavors my life.
++ Susy Robison ++

1

Anchors Away - December 23, 1951

From the railing on the deck of their ocean liner, the RMS *Strathmore*, fifteen-year-old Halley Pederson and her father searched for her aunt's white hat in the throng on the pier below. All around them the boisterous crowd of fellow passengers was shouting "Goodbye" and flinging streamers at the well-wishers on the shore, amid gales of laughter.

"There she is." Dr. Karl Pederson pointed out his sister and threw a streamer at her. Halley pushed her unmanageable red hair out of her face and looked where he was pointing. She wanted to appear happy about this part of their voyage to India and tried to smile.

"Bon Voyage!" Her aunt tossed one back at them, shouting up into the din. They joined the horde in earnest, hurling and hollering. Halley held on to the ends of her streamers and watched each one uncurl, spiraling down toward her aunt, blending into a weaving of hundreds of thin paper strips that interlocked in the middle. Like a glorious, multicolored abstract tapestry, it linked them to the shore.

She tossed her last one and waved just as the ship began to move. A catch in her throat stifled her last goodbye. She blinked back a tear and felt the slow pull of the ship tug on the paper fabric, shredding it across the middle. It wafted up into the breeze like a cape. Halley grabbed the brim of her hat and waved it slowly until her aunt merged into the dots of color on the pier. She looked at the fog hovering over the wake of the ship behind them and shivered. The shoreline of England melted into the morning mist just as a sudden spritz of rain sent them scurrying away from the deck and down the stairs. *Oh darn,* she thought, *now my hair will be even frizzier.*

"I'm going to check out the game room," her dad said and wandered away.

Halley thought this ship looked larger than the one they'd taken from New York City to England and decided to go exploring. After a few bends in the corridor, she came to a stairway going up marked "Private." How could they have a private anything with so many people? She peeked into the beauty salon as she passed. Uniformed beauticians bustled around several ladies who were getting their hair washed. A few others sat under hair dryers. *Silly,* she thought. *We've barely left England and they're already getting their hair done.* She continued through the perfumed wave of steam billowing out of the doorway.

Just past the gift shop was the game room. Dad was leaning on a post near the billiard table, watching another man play; a puff of pipe smoke drifted toward her. She recognized the smell, warm vanilla. Several ladies were at a table nearby playing cards. A cigarette dangled between the fingers of one of the ladies, who coughed discreetly. The lady seated across from her clinched a cigarette holder between her lips, freeing both hands. She pulled a card from the ones fanned out between the fingers of her other hand, held it for a moment, then slowly set it on the table. A jazzy record hummed in the background, and the tune followed Halley down the corridor.

Around the next bend were stairs marked "Upper Deck." Up she went. At the landing, she paused at the door to the deck and peered at the gloomy mist through the door's window. She decided to take the hallway on her left instead. It looked like it might continue back over the one below.

This hallway smelled different, more exotic. Large doors marched down the corridor on both sides. A fashionably dressed woman came out of one, escorted by a tan teenager with straight, black hair. He was about Halley's age, but a little shorter. Halley walked by, looking at the floor. After a few more strides, she came to a staircase from below and realized it must be the one she saw downstairs marked "Private." She continued on.

Several yards ahead, a man slammed a door and grumbled, "I could kill her," as he stormed past Halley. A trail of men's cologne followed him down the stairs. Still hovering in front of that suite was a cloud of incense that circled around Halley like a trap. She stopped. From behind the door, she could hear a woman and several men arguing in Spanish. Thanks to all her Spanish classes at Chapman School in New York City, she understood what they were saying.

The woman's low, guttural snarl bristled up Halley's neck. "I don't trust him." A fist thumped on a table, and a wind chime of glass jingled. "He's an idiot, a baboon."

The sinister voice moved closer to the door, and Halley froze.

The voice turned away from the door with a swish of fabric and more clinking glass. "Remind me why we brought him, anyway," the woman demanded. Halley could almost taste the venom.

A man's shaky, high-pitched voice responded, "You'll need him when you get to Bombay."

"Don't make me regret this," the woman shrieked. "We never have room for mistakes."

Another man spoke, slowly and deliberately. "Madam, I vouched for him and know he's the best in the business. You will see."

A door opened farther down the corridor. Halley jumped. She moved back toward the stairway she'd passed and scurried down it, bursting into the passageway below, almost bumping into a large family.

She leaned against the wall, shaking. Who were those awful people? What was she doing there? She wished she'd never heard them. She felt like she was going to throw up and closed her eyes.

"Excuse me. Are you okay?"

Halley opened her eyes and recognized the dark-haired boy she had passed upstairs.

"I think so," she mumbled. "Must be something I ate."

"I'm Harin from New Delhi." He spelled out his name in his sing-song English accent. "To you it would sound like H-a-r-e-e-n." He paused. "Maybe you'd feel better if you went up on deck and got some air. It's just back that way."

"Good idea."

"Can you walk?" His cautious dark eyes lit up his kind, round face.

"Yes." She tried to smile. "I'm Halley. Rhymes with valley. I'm from New York City."

Harin turned out to be right. When they got to the deck, the mist was gone, and it was warmer outside. She took a deep breath.

"When you feel better, do you think you might like to play some shuffleboard?"

Halley smiled. She loved playing shuffleboard at her grandfather's club near Meadowcroft, his summer house north of Boston. "That would be nice."

They found the deck games near the swimming pool. A lifeguard paced around the deep end, watching several children dangling their feet over the edge while their parents hovered. A group of teenagers mingled nearby, including two blond girls who could have been twins. One waved.

"Hey, you guys want to play shuffleboard?" The girl's accent sounded Norwegian, like Halley's Grandmother Pederson's. "I'm Anne," the girl continued, "and this is my sister Ellie. We're from Oslo, Norway." Halley smiled, pleased that she'd guessed correctly.

After several games, one of the twins said, "Shall we meet up again after lunch?" They all agreed, and Halley headed for her cabin.

It had been three months since the evening her dad burst into their New York City apartment. She and her mom had just flourished the final notes of a piano duet. With a broad grin, Dad announced that the D.T. Bjerke Foundation had offered him a prestigious medical research position with the famous Dr. Gustaf Norlin in India. Halley remembered feeling like a mouse caught in a trap with peanut butter as the bait—excited but cornered.

Now, she closed her door, braced herself against it, and crumpled to the floor. A dim circle of gray light from a porthole played on the red-and-brown carpet beneath her feet. They had been so busy boarding the ship, finding their staterooms, and throwing streamers at her aunt that the awful images had slipped down the hallway of her mind. Flashes from that awful day last November now rushed back in. Halley leaned back, took a deep breath, and opened the gold, heart-shaped locket hanging around her neck. On one side was a miniature of her tenth-grade photo from last spring. On the other was her mother's beautiful face circled by her short, dark hair. Halley stared at it and was right back in the emergency room, holding her mother's hand. It was still warm, but they were too late.

Halley snapped the locket shut. Maybe if Dad hadn't signed that stupid contract just a few weeks before the cab hit Mom, they wouldn't be on this dumb ocean liner bound for India.

I should unpack, she thought and wiped her face with her sleeve. She yanked off her hat and leapt up. Flipping on the light above her, she dragged one of her suitcases to the bed. It opened easily.

Perched on top of the books piled inside was an ancient copy of *Graham's American Monthly* magazine. Its yellowed pages contained the Edgar Allen Poe poem she'd memorized for the Chapman School competition last spring. The final words jumped inside her mind, twisting her. "*That the play is the tragedy 'Man,' And its hero the Conqueror Worm.*"

For the millionth time, images from her mother's funeral tore into her. The hearse, the flowers on the casket, the limousine, her grandmother crumpled on the middle seat in front of her, cradled in her grandfather's arms, sobbing, gulping air, and moaning. Halley could still feel Dad's hand on her shoulder.

Her welling tears were interrupted by the chime of the lunch bell passing by her door.

******

Centered prominently between Halley and Dad on the lunch table in the dining room was an orange card "cordially" inviting them to three events in the Grand Room: the welcome party that evening after dinner,

Christmas Eve with Santa, and Happy New Year 1952, which was on the night before they were scheduled to land in Bombay.

Halley remembered seeing a vast, dimly lit room with a grand piano and a stage covered with drums and microphones just beyond the game room. Maybe that was the Grand Room.

Dad picked up the invitation. "When I got to my cabin before lunch, I found a card from the captain under the door inviting us to join him at his table for dinner tomorrow. It sounds like a nice offer." His voice had a hopeful lilt. "Shall we say yes?"

The last thing she wanted to do was sit at a dreary table on Christmas Eve with a bunch of adults making small talk. But both of them could use the distraction.

"Sure," she said, trying to sound positive.

Halley noticed Dad perk up when they overheard someone at the next table say something about billiards in the game room. When they finished eating, he pushed back his chair. "Shall we meet here for tea around three thirty? I'm going back to the game room, have a smoke, and maybe play some billiards."

A cool breeze was blowing off the water when Halley found Harin and the twins at the shuffleboard court on deck. She was glad she'd worn a sweater.

"There she is," said one of the twins. "Hey, Halley! We just decided to switch around. You and Anne will be a team, and I'll play with Harin. You two go first. Okay?"

The shuffleboard was a nice distraction, and before Halley knew it, the afternoon sun was dipping toward the horizon.

"That was fun," Halley said. "See you tonight." Then she headed off to her cabin to get ready for dinner.

At the welcome party that evening, Halley danced with Dad and played Monopoly with Harin and the twins. The teens all agreed to meet at the pool in the morning. At the end of the evening, Halley hooked her arm around Dad's elbow. Once they were in the corridor, he said, "Your new friends seem very nice. Did you have fun tonight?"

She remembered the others making silly jokes all evening and smiled. "Yes," she said and gave his elbow a squeeze.

When she was alone in her room, Halley dug deeper into her suitcase of books. She uncovered an almost flat, rectangular box. She closed her eyes and held it close like a baby, rocking, remembering her mother hunched over a piano in the window of Manny's Music Store, not too far from their apartment in New York. Several salesmen and a few customers were standing nearby, listening to her play.

Halley lifted the lid off the box. Nestled inside the pale-blue tissue paper was a new copy of piano music, Beethoven's "Tempest Sonata." She ran her finger around the delicate green border on the cover, lifted it to her face, and inhaled deeply a few times. Crisp paper, new ink, smelled like summer.

"Your father will love this music," Mom had said. "Let's give it to him on Christmas Eve on board ship."

Halley folded the tissue back over the music and closed the box.

By mid-afternoon the next day, she'd almost forgotten it was Christmas Eve. No snow. Blazing sunshine. Her hair smelled of chlorine and was dripping on her shirt when she flopped down on the deck chair next to Dad's. He was watching a steward wheel the teacart toward them. It was covered with ornate white-and-chocolate glazed cakes, a silver tea pot, and china plates and cups.

"Howdy stranger," he said, laughing. "You're just in time to pick out your own *petit fours*."

The steward stopped in front of them. "Good afternoon, sir, miss. Would you care for anything?"

They made their selections, and the steward added milk and sugar cubes to their tea, dished out their choices of cakes, and moved on.

"It looked like you were having fun in the pool," Dad said. "I saw your swan dive off the side. Not bad."

"Thanks, Dad."

"I met a guy from India in the game room, a petroleum engineer with a gas and oil company in New Delhi. He's returning home with his family after spending a year in Texas. He has a son that's about your age."

Halley wondered if it was Harin, but she couldn't ask. Her mouth was full of cake.

By the time they had each consumed several scrumptious little cakes, the sun had shifted. Rather than adding to the mass of freckles that had appeared on her legs, Halley got up. "See you at dinner," she said and left Dad with his book. She knew she'd have trouble with her hair and wanted to carefully comb through her kinky curls after a shower, so she could look her best when they arrived at the captain's table.

That evening after Halley and Dad had been introduced to the other guests around his table, the captain told them he was expecting one more person. "Mrs. Kaliya, the wife of an international businessman." He had barely finished speaking when Halley noticed an exotically beautiful woman gliding toward them. The subdued light from the flickering candles reflected off the jewels around her neck and the gold embroidery on her dark red *sari*. Long black curls cascaded around her shimmering earrings and over her shoulders.

When Mrs. Kaliya reached the table, all the men stood. She glanced at the captain and looked briefly at Halley's dad. But when her dark eyes rested on Halley, her lips almost curled up into a smile. *She seems nice enough*, Halley thought, *and so pretty*.

One of the waiters pulled out the chair next to Halley, and Mrs. Kaliya settled onto it, an alluring perfume hovering around her. The woman's graceful movements were accompanied by the chiming of glass bracelets that circled her slender arm.

The captain introduced her to everyone, and she nodded to each in silence.

During dinner Mrs. Kaliya watched while everyone else laughed and chatted. Halley's dad relayed some of the humorous moments in the *Twelfth Night* performance they'd seen in London. But the whole time he was talking, Halley grew more and more uncomfortable. Mrs. Kaliya was silent, watching her. Just as they finished dessert, the woman finally spoke.

"Halley, what did you think of the Tower of London?"

Halley shuddered. Tinkling glass bracelets. That viperous voice.

Goosebumps crept up her arms. This was the woman she'd overheard shrieking, "We never have room for mistakes!"

What do I think about the Tower of London? I hated it, she thought. The bloody tower. Stories of brutal murders and executions. She glanced up. Mrs. Kaliya was looking at her hair. Without speaking, her glass-bangled arm reached over, and she touched a curl on Halley's shoulder, sending a horrifying tremor over Halley's head. It spilled down her neck, and Halley suppressed an impulse to jerk away. "It was okay, I guess," she stammered.

How dare she touch me? Who is she?

"Look!" The captain pointed out the window. "The Rock of Gibraltar."

In the distance, Halley could see a massive rock at the end of the land, rising out of the ocean.

"On either side of the Rock," the captain continued, "is the United Kingdom territory of Gibraltar. The Rock marks the entrance into the Mediterranean Sea. During the second world war, the British stationed thousands of their troops in the caves within the Rock to guard the entrance to the Mediterranean."

Mrs. Kaliya's bracelets clinked, distracting Halley. What was the woman planning to do in Bombay?

Dad nudged Halley, interrupting her thoughts, and pointed at the Rock, "Pretty amazing, huh?"

The captain continued, "When we pass from the Atlantic Ocean into the Mediterranean Sea, you may notice that there's a distinct line. The bodies of water are different colors."

Halley draped her arm around Dad's neck, leaned on his shoulder, and shuddered. She hoped she'd be able to draw a distinct line between herself and Mrs. Kaliya. The woman gave her the creeps.

Once dinner was over and they had thanked the captain, Halley couldn't get away fast enough. When she and Dad reached her cabin, he said, "Sounds like everyone is going to the Christmas Eve party tonight. Santa Claus is expected to make an appearance. Would you like to go together?"

"Sure, Dad." His green eyes glistened, and she continued, "Let's meet at your cabin. I have something for you."

An hour later, Halley knocked at his door, hugging the thin, rectangular box to her chest. She had circled it with a red ribbon, but now she questioned herself. Maybe this was bad timing. Maybe she should wait until tomorrow when they weren't on their way to a party. But then Dad opened the door, and it was too late to turn back.

He seemed relaxed and almost happy. "What have you got there, milady?"

She had practiced what she would say many times since they left New York. But now she was stymied. "Dad…" His eyes sparkled. She knew he would love the music. Should she tell him that Mom picked it out? "Can we sit down?"

He pointed to a chair. "This suspense is killing me," he said and sat down in the other one.

Halley slid the gift to him and continued to hunch over her lap. "I hope you like it." He carefully untied the ribbon and opened the box.

"Holy cow. 'The Tempest!' This is great." He caressed the cover just as she'd done the night before. "There's that piano in the Grand Room. I'll sneak in there tomorrow and give it a go."

Halley was blinking. *No, no. Don't cry.*

Dad moved his chair next to hers. "Honey, what's wrong?"

She hesitated, groping for the right words. A moment earlier he looked so happy. How could she tell him? Finally, she blurted out, "Mom and I bought it for you together. She wanted us to give it to you tonight, together. I've been keeping it, waiting." Through her tears, finally flowing freely, she could see his face scrunching with sadness, then she felt his arm circle her. Nestled in the crook of his other arm was "The Tempest." Halley reached over, laid her hand on Mom's music, and closed the circle.

2

Tiny Hands on the Window

After spending a week navigating the Mediterranean Sea, the narrow Suez Canal, and crossing the Red Sea, their ship entered Bombay Harbour. Halley made her last visit to the gift shop to buy a box of English chocolates, the ones with the brightly colored foil wrappers. Ever since London she'd been collecting the small, shiny sheets. After popping the candies into her mouth, especially savoring the dark chocolate ones, she would press each wrapper flat with the back of her thumbnail until it shone like the paint on a new car. Then she'd add it to the stack in her diary and take them out from time to time to look at them in the light.

She hurried back to her cabin and settled down at the dressing table in front of the mirror just as a steward passed by, playing a warning chime. Oh, dear. She had less than an hour to write a letter to her best friend, Mary, before the final mail pickup.

The last thing Dad had said at breakfast was that she should make a final check around her room then get up on deck and watch for their head servant, known as their "bearer." Kashif would arrive on one of the tugboats and would be wearing a turban.

"Head servant?" she'd asked.

Dad nodded. "While we live in India, we are expected to support and provide housing for several servants. It's part of the economy. Once we move into our bungalow, Kashif will help me find a cook and a gardener."

Halley glanced into the mirror at her still uncombed curls and opened a sheet of airmail paper. Mary had been her best friend since the first day of third grade at Chapman School. Halley knew her friend would understand if she told her how unhappy and alone she was feeling, but she decided against it. Instead, she wrote about their whirlwind tour through London, the leather purse she bought from one of the boats that came out to their ship in Port Said, Egypt, and the camels they saw when their ship passed through the Suez Canal. She signed the bottom, gave her shoulder-length curls a few swipes with the brush, and pulled on her blue hat with the brim.

She pictured her mom's short hair. It had been so stylish. But the last time she'd seen her head, it had been shaved for surgery. She sighed and stuffed the brush and the box of chocolates into her new purse. A brief whiff of the leather reminded her of her favorite horse at her grandfather's. The smell of Lancelot's leather saddle and his head when he nuzzled her shoulder after their final ride along the beach near Meadowcroft. She felt an ache stir deep within her chest.

Oh dear, she thought. *Not now! I need to be strong.*

Halley straightened to her full height, lifted the purse strap over her head, and grabbed the letter.

Each time she stepped out of her room into the dim light of the musty corridor, she was reminded of the spooky Tower of London. She hurried to the mailbox, glad it was near the stairs to the deck, and slid the letter in just as she heard several passengers approaching from around the bend. She recognized one of the voices and gasped. It was Mrs. Kaliya.

Ever since she met the woman at the captain's table on Christmas Eve, Halley had dreaded running into Mrs. Kaliya on the ship. Rather than pass her in the dim passage, Halley darted up the stairs near the mailbox and out onto the deck, where she slammed into a wall of unbelievably hot air and bright sunlight. She blinked and immediately started to perspire. Hoping to catch some of the breeze from the movement of the ship, she made her way through the dense crowd of passengers to the rail. There, spread out before her, was Bombay Harbour, vast and teeming with ships, great and small. One of the tugboats was below her. Men dressed in loose-fitting white clothing were helping to secure the ship. Some wore turbans. She leaned on the rail and gazed out across the water. At the edge of the land directly in front of her stood a magnificent monument with an arch in the middle. The Gateway of India!

"Hey, Halley."

She turned back to see her friend Harin working his way through the crowd. Wisps of black hair peeked out from under his white cap. He was struggling with a large suitcase. "I was hoping I'd find you. Here's my address. You left last night before I could give it to you." He shoved a paper toward her, and their hands brushed. "Please write to me. Maybe we can get together when your dad takes you to Agra to see the Taj Mahal or something. New Delhi is not too far away from there. You and your dad are welcome to stay with us."

Halley smiled.

Standing right behind Harin was his mother. Her tan face and short black hair were surrounded by a large, yellow-brimmed hat. "Yes, Halley, it would be great to see you."

Before Halley could think of an answer, Harin and his mother were melting into the crowd moving toward the gangplank. "That would be nice," she hollered when they were almost out of earshot. The last thing she could see was Harin's white hat bobbing between the others.

A pang of loneliness grabbed at her again, and she turned back toward the water. But all she could see was an enormous blue-and-gold bird flying straight at her over the water. It flapped its gigantic wings a few times to slow down and landed on the railing right in front of her, causing a swish of air that cooled her flushed cheeks.

"Hello," it said in a disturbingly human voice.

"Well, hello to you . . .too," she answered, not daring to take her eyes off him.

A voice behind her said, "*Memsaab* Halley, Sundara won't hurt you." She turned quickly. A very tall, slender man wearing a blue turban, leather shoes that curled up in front, and what looked like pajamas was standing right behind her.

This must be our bearer, she thought.

He bowed. "I am Kashif."

Sundara flew over her head with another blast of air and landed on Kashif's shoulder. "Are you ready, *Memsaab*?" Kashif asked in a sing-song English accent.

She nodded, glancing down at his unusual shoes again and back up to his neatly trimmed beard. His height, his white, pajama-like pants, and the parrot on his shoulder were beyond anything Halley had ever seen before. "Yes, thank you," she said hesitantly, remembering her manners.

"Then let's be off," he replied and protectively placed his hand on her shoulder. The crowd approaching the gangplank ahead of them fell away, allowing them to pass. *Wow*, she thought. *He would have been a big help on the New York City sidewalks.*

"Halley, Kashif, over here!" Dad stood off to the side of the crowd.

"Dad," she called out. A deep wave of relief flowed through her. As always, he was carrying his old leather bag. His camera bag hung from his shoulder, and he was wearing a tan, broad-brimmed hat made of soft leather that almost hid his dark-blond curls. Halley thought his blue-striped summer suit made him look like a tourist. She laughed out loud and gave him a hug, then together, they followed Kashif and Sundara to the gangplank.

Halley grabbed the cords on either side of her and hesitantly started down the ramp with her dad right behind her. A large colony of gulls swarmed above them. She caught a whiff of something burning and looked down into the crowd on the pier. Hundreds of brightly dressed people were everywhere, walking, standing, cooking on small fires, and chatting away. As they descended the smells became stronger. Spicy and sweet odors almost covered the rancid ones. Finally, she reached the bottom of the ramp. When her feet touched solid ground, she paused. India surrounded her. But instead of feeling reassured after so many days at sea, she shivered in the heat.

Dad put his hand on her back and gently nudged her to follow Kashif toward a light blue station wagon a few yards away. Kashif gave the man guarding the car some money, and he disappeared into the crowd. After helping Halley into the backseat and waiting for her dad to be seated in front, Kashif climbed in behind the wheel on the wrong side of the car. Halley remembered Dad telling her that cars drove on the left side of the road in India. He also told her that along with his recently acquired piano, cases of powdered milk, Kleenex, and toilet paper, he had also shipped a car.

Sundara was still on Kashif's shoulder. Their heads almost touched the roof of the car, and Sundara's long tail trailed down the back of Kashif's seat right in front of Halley. "Please leave the windows shut until we get going," Kashif said.

That was an odd request. It was unbearably hot, and without even a little bit of breeze, it was stifling inside the car. She inclined her head back against the seat and had almost closed her eyes when something hit the glass next to her with a bang. She shrieked, then saw that several small hands had slammed into her window, followed by more on both sides of the car. Nearly naked children, barely tall enough to reach the windows, surrounded them pleading, "*Pice, pice,*" louder and louder. More children rushed toward the car, all hollering, "*Pice, pice.*" There was one small child standing in the midst of them with her arms hanging next to her sides, crying.

Halley threw her hands up in front of her face. "Who are these poor children? Please give them something."

"*Memsaab*, it's impossible," Kashif said. "If we give a *pice* to one, we have to give one to all of them, and we just can't." The car inched forward, and the children dropped away. Halley sank onto the seat with a groan, removed the hanky from her purse, and wiped away the sweat on her face.

As soon as they were clear of the children, Kashif said, "Now you can open your windows, if you're warm." Halley looked up at the parrot. He was watching her from his perch. Kashif was quietly talking about the brutal lives of the children, "They belong to very bad people. Every day they are sent out into the streets and are beaten if they don't bring back some money. It's awful."

She cranked down the window and used her hat as a fan. They were moving very slowly but there was enough of a breeze to cool her a little. She looked around. The street was noisy and filled with people: vendors shouting, horns honking, women in colorful *saris* walking with brass jugs on their heads, some squatting by the road nursing babies, and men on bicycles with long hair and beards and some with turbans. At almost every corner, a policeman stood in the middle of the intersection, signaling pedestrians when it was their turn to cross. The streets were jammed with cars and bicycle carts loaded with passengers. There were also carts drawn by large cow-like animals; water buffalo, she was told.

"There's a holy man." Kashif pointed at a white-haired, bearded man standing under a large tree, leaning on a sturdy stick. Several beaded wooden necklaces hung down over his naked chest, and his legs were partially covered by a thin white cloth that circled him. Some of it was pulled up between his legs and tucked into the front of his waistband.

At one intersection, they waited for a wedding parade to pass. First came the band, followed by a rider on a white horse. The rider was decorated with garlands of colorful flowers that started on top of his head, covered his face, and ran down his body and over the horse.

"That's the groom," Kashif said. "When he arrives at the wedding, he will greet his bride, who is also covered with flowers. They will sit side by side through the ceremony. When they are finally married, they will part the flowers and see each other's face for the first time."

"How peculiar," Halley said, scrunching her face. "What if he turns out to be the weird boy at the music school that she thought was ridiculous. What would happen then?" She pictured the scene and said, "Jimmy, what are you doing here?" Kashif and her dad laughed with her.

A large, colorfully painted elephant and more musicians brought up the rear of the parade. Halley leaned back in her seat and smiled. "Amazing. I can't wait to write Mary." She laughed again and glanced out her window.

Right beside them, going in the same direction, was a small, three-wheeled bicycle cart with garish paint. In the passenger seat under the canopy, Halley could see a woman and a man, but the cart awning hid their faces. The lady's arm was covered with glass bangles. Even though she knew that the possibility the woman could be Mrs. Kaliya was one in a million, Halley shuddered and slid down in her seat.

Dad was listening intently to Kashif talk about Indian weddings, unaware that their fellow ship passenger might be in the cart next to them. The street cleared a little in front of them, and they pulled ahead.

Halley had been so unnerved by the possible encounter with Mrs. Kaliya that she had missed part of the conversation and tuned back in when her dad asked, "Have you had your parrot very long?"

"Yes. The Maharaja gave him to me. Sundara has been with me for twenty years."

"That's fantastic. How long is he expected to live?"

"Sundara could live for at least fifty years."

The parrot appeared to know they were talking about him and nuzzled Kashif's neck. Suddenly, he stretched up tall and hollered, "Stop." A man was running into the street directly in front of them. Kashif slammed on the brakes and barely missed him.

Although the incident didn't appear to faze Kashif, Halley's dad exploded. "Idiot. What's the matter with that guy?"

Kashif explained, "He is one of the many tricksters who run in front of cars to get hit, hoping we'll pay them for their injuries."

"Are they nuts?" Dad was noticeably shaken.

Halley leaned forward between them. "Kashif, first it's children crying for money and now it's a man trying to get hit by our car so we'll pay him. Why? Can't anyone help them?"

"I'm sorry, *Memsaab* Halley. There are many good people in India who are desperate. They live and sleep on the streets of the cities and towns. Survival is very difficult." His voice trailed off and they drove on in silence.

Halley rested her head against the seatback and closed her eyes. What if Sundara hadn't squawked? Would Kashif have stopped in time? She pictured the man bleeding on the road. Then she drifted back to New

York, remembering the terror that overcame her when their cab inched through the traffic to get to her mother in the hospital.

3

The Girl Behind the Curtain

"Here's our hotel." Halley felt Dad tap her knee. She sat up and looked out the car window. They were entering a large plaza in front of the beautiful Taj Mahal Palace Hotel. Hundreds of pigeons scattered in front of them. In an instant, her grim reverie switched to delight. A central domed tower loomed over hundreds of ornate windows of varying shapes. Remembering a scene from *The Wizard of Oz* movie, she giggled, "Toto, I have a feeling we're not in Kansas anymore."

Her dad exploded with laughter and spurted, "We must be over the rainbow." Kashif slowed way down and only pulled up in front of the building when they finished laughing.

Several uniformed doormen opened the doors and helped them out. Kashif did all the talking then ushered them through a large entrance into the lobby. Halley looked around and took a deep breath. The vast room was filled with exotically dressed men and women, some standing around, some seated on intricately carved high-backed chairs or low, red-velvet couches, many greeting each other. Detailed carpeting covered the floors.

A man approached them. "*Sahib* Pederson, welcome to the Taj Mahal Palace. I am the concierge." Like Kashif's, his accent sounded almost British with a musical lilt. "Your trunks will be here shortly. Would you like us to show you to your rooms now or wait until after you've had some tea?"

"Tea?" Halley turned to look at her dad. They exchanged silly smiles. Tea on board their ocean liner had been a lavish affair. One of their favorite delights had been to stretch out on the deckchairs, reading or gazing out over the water at teatime.

Just then, Halley's stomach grumbled, and she remembered that she hadn't been able to eat anything that morning. "Sure," she and Dad said at the same time and smiled again at each other.

After Kashif and Dad exchanged a few words about the trunks, they followed the concierge. He led them past a grand staircase with carved banisters and lush carpeting that divided on the first landing. The staircases continued separately to the next floor and back again, circling up toward the vaulted ceiling. Halley looked back to see her dad's reaction, but his eyes were on a dark-skinned man in a Western-style blue suit who was heading toward them. Kashif was gone.

"Dr. Pederson?" The man smiled. "I am Anaka Gupta." He grabbed Dad's outstretched hand and shook it. "Dr. Gustaf Norlin apologizes that he is not able to get here until this evening for your welcome party. He asked me to greet you."

"Thank you, Dr. Gupta. I've been looking forward to meeting you." Dad paused and signaled for Halley to come over. "May I present my daughter, Halley?"

Halley looked up into Anaka Gupta's happy face and smiled. His brown eyes sparkled. But instead of shaking her hand, he took it in both of his, bent low, and kissed it. "Delighted," he said. She blushed and giggled.

Dad smiled. "Would you care to join us for tea? We were just about to sit down." He pointed at the concierge, who was waiting nearby. They followed him into an interior courtyard filled with brilliant pink, lilac, and yellow flowers shaded by tall, leafy plants. He seated them at a table near a large blue-and-green tiled fountain. Birds flew about in the branches above them. Several servers appeared with tea and a platter filled with small triangular and circular sandwiches. Halley noticed the crusts had been removed, just like afternoon tea in London.

While the men talked about Gustaf Norlin's work in Poona, Halley took a bite of a spicy egg salad sandwich and watched a huge fish with orange-gold scales circle in the fountain, just below the surface. She remembered her dad talking about Gustaf Norlin when they were on the ship. Dr. Norlin had lived in India for many years and was married to Maria Norlin, a doctor from Holland. They had two children. Their son was Halley's age and attended a boarding school near New Delhi. Johanna was a year younger and attended school in Poona. Halley finished her sandwich and sipped the tea. The server had added some milk and a little sugar. It was delicious.

Kashif approached. His pants flapped as he walked, and Sundara was calmly perched next to his head. Kashif stopped behind Dad and stood quietly. When the men had finished what they were saying, he spoke. "*Sahib,* your trunks are in your rooms."

What was Kashif's story, she wondered. *And why did someone named the Maharaja give him a parrot?*

Anaka Gupta and Dad stood up and waited for Halley to grab her purse. Then they parted with Dr, Gupta and followed Kashif into the lobby, where the concierge assigned a bellhop to take them to their rooms. As the elevator doors were closing, Halley saw a woman in a red *sari* enter the lobby. It was Mrs. Kaliya. Halley trembled. The memory of that moment when Mrs. Kaliya touched her hair shot through her. Just then Sundara started shifting back and forth on Kashif's shoulder and making a soft clicking sound. He settled down when they arrived at the door to their suite.

Their bedrooms were on either side of a beautiful sitting room with tall windows that looked out toward the sea. Kashif had seen to it that their trunks were in their rooms. Dad asked him about the unusual man sitting outside their door.

"He's one of the hotel servants," Kashif said, "your *chokadar*. He is assigned to protect you and your belongings from thieves." When he led Halley into her room, he pointed out a brown paper parcel on the loveseat at the foot of the bed. "That is a gift from *Memsaab* Johanna, Dr. Norlin's daughter." He bowed and withdrew into the sitting room, closing the door behind him.

Halley sat down next to the package. She untied the string, turned it over, and peeled back the paper. Inside was a two-piece garment made of light-blue silk. She unfolded the top. It looked like a short dress she might have worn for ice skating in the park. Around the neck, tiny mirrors sparkled from a border of colorfully embroidered flowers. More little mirrors circled the ends of the long, airy sleeves and along the bottom. The other piece was a pair of flowing pants of the same fabric. Underneath them, still in the package, was a pair of decorated dark-blue cloth shoes and a note.

Dear Halley,

Welcome to India. I can't wait to meet you. Mom helped me pick out this present for you. It is sometimes called a Punjabi suit. If it fits and you like it, maybe you could wear it to the party tonight. Mom bought me one too. Mine's pink. See you soon.

Sincerely, Johanna

Halley folded up the note and held up the blue top to get a better look at it. She was excited that she might have something new to wear. She looked around the room. A fan turned lazily above her with a gentle whirring sound. On the wall near the closet was a full-length mirror with a carved wooden frame. In it she could see the four-poster bed behind her. It had a dark red cover and lots of pillows. They reminded her of the red-velvet cushions on the dining room chairs in their New York City apartment.

One night, several weeks after Mom's funeral, Halley and Dad had just finished dinner, and he asked if she could go through her mother's clothes. Whatever she didn't want he would take to the Salvation Army.

The sorting had been hard. The scent of her mother's perfume still lingered around the jackets and coats. Every few minutes she had to stop and take breaths to hold back her tears. Some of Mom's things had fit Halley, including a simple black dress and a knee-length green one. She had been planning to wear the green dress to their welcome party, but now she might not have to.

On the other side of the room was a dressing table with three mirrors attached to the top. It had an inviting assortment of notions and a box of tissues. She went over to the windows that jutted out from a small glassed-in porch. They reminded her of the bay windows at Meadowcroft. She looked out the window on one side and noticed a similar glassed porch. It was part of the room next to hers. She was curious about the people who were staying there and sat down to get a better view.

Two women were standing near the window. One was much smaller than the other and appeared to be crying. It looked like the larger woman was yelling at her. Suddenly, there was a third woman. The smaller woman continued to cower. The first woman left the window. The light changed a little, and through the lacy curtains, Halley could now make out more details. She watched the third woman walk back and forth, waving her fist at the smaller one. Her red *sari* fluttered around her. Was it Mrs. Kaliya? Halley shrank back. That wasn't possible. This hotel had hundreds of rooms. How could Mrs. Kaliya be in the one right next to hers?

She was shaking and crept back to the little couch. A tap on the door startled her.

"Halley," said Dad. "We'll go down to the party in an hour. Okay?"

She took a deep breath and opened the door. "Dad, Kashif left me a package from Dr. Norlin's daughter." She showed him Johanna's note and held the top up in front of her.

"Wow, that's beautiful," he said, "and it brings out your blue eyes. Does it fit?"

"I'll try it on in a few minutes and show you." After he left, she pulled out her brush and sat down at the dressing table. Although muffled, she could hear a woman's voice coming from behind a brocade curtain on the wall beside her. She stood up and peeked behind it. The curtain was covering a door to the next room. Although she couldn't understand what they were saying, one of the voices was loud and angry. Was it Mrs.

Kaliya? Who was that young woman? Why were they yelling at her? She wished she hadn't heard them and let the curtain drop.

Halley inched out of her dress, pulled on the pants and the top, and slipped into the shoes. When she finished securing the last hook under her left arm, she stood in front of the wall mirror. The little mirrors sparkled. Everything fit perfectly. How did Mrs. Norlin know her size?

Then, seated at the dressing table, she picked up the brush and tried unsuccessfully to get it through her unruly curls. She felt an ache seep through her, and her head dropped into her hands. Even when she got to high school there were many days when her mother helped her with her hair. Her piano recital was on the Saturday before the accident. Mom came in to check on why she was taking so long to get ready and saw her choking back tears. Without saying anything, Mom picked up the brush.

Suddenly, Dad was at the door. "Are you decent?" Halley managed to peep out a response, and he came in quickly.

Wiping her face with the back of her hand, she tried to smile. It was hard enough for him without her blubbering away. "I'm okay, Dad." She blew her nose on her hanky. "It's just that my hair is impossible. You remember Mom always helped me, especially when we were going somewhere special."

He lovingly eased the brush out of her hand and began to brush her hair. He used his fingers to open up the knotted clumps, just like her mother did. "Before Margaret had hers cut into that short hairdo, I used to brush her hair before bed almost every night." His voice cracked and he continued brushing in silence. In the mirror, Halley saw the now familiar sad look in his eyes.

Through the door she heard Kashif answer the sitting room door. "Yes, *Memsaab* Johanna, they are here. Please come in." Halley stood up and followed her dad, twisting her finger around a curl that had fallen into her face.

Johanna was slender, almost as tall as Halley. She was wearing a pink Punjabi suit, her long blond hair tied back with a matching ribbon. She smiled, and Halley felt a warm bubble flow into her heart.

"Halley, it fits you so well," Johanna grinned. "Mom guessed right."

She turned to Dad. "You must be Dr. Pederson. Our family is so excited that you are finally here. Guess what? Our suite is just down the hall."

Halley's dad disappeared into his room to dress, and the girls sat down. After a moment of awkward silence, Johanna asked. "How was your trip from London? It can be so long. Did you meet anyone interesting?"

By the time Dad returned, they were chatting happily. Halley looked up at him with a smile and admired his neat suit. "Dad, you look great."

Moments later, with a big smile on his face, he descended the grand staircase with a girl on each arm.

4

A Tragic Message

Everyone was quiet when Halley, Dad, and Johanna entered the salon. All eyes were on a man seated at a long grand piano at the far end of the most beautiful room Halley had ever seen. The walls were covered with enormous paintings and tapestries. There were several larger-than-life-sized sculptures. Mythical gold figures peeked out from the corners of the room near the ceiling.

The pianist's back was to them. The gentle first notes were followed by ripples running up and down the keyboard; his head bowed over the keys one moment and flung back the next, his blond hair flipping around with the music. Johanna whispered, "I was hoping he'd play that Chopin 'Fantasie-Impromptu.' It's my favorite."

A woman standing near them breathed out, "Shhhh." Another smiled at them. From under her breath the lady whispered, "It's Dr. Norlin."

From where they stood, Halley could see his hands flying across the keys, not missing a note. Dad took her hand and squeezed it. Gustaf Norlin was playing the very piece her mother had been memorizing. A flutter of butterflies passed through her.

She glanced around. The room was full of silent, colorfully dressed people, some standing, others sitting on high-backed settees, all listening intently as the pianist's fingers flew over the keyboard with the final runs. She sighed quietly as he tenderly caressed the last few notes.

Dr. Norlin turned around on the bench and smiled as everyone applauded. Halley thought he looked like a blond version of the actor Cary Grant—lanky and ruggedly good-looking. He noticed them standing in the back and stood up, held out his hand toward them, and with a clear Swedish accent said, "We are here this evening to welcome my American colleague, Dr. Karl Pederson, and his daughter, Halley, to India. They arrived this morning on the *Strathmore* and are standing over there with our daughter, Johanna." Everyone turned toward them. When they waved, everyone applauded again.

By the time Gustaf Norlin reached them, a few friendly couples had placed several garlands of fragrant flowers over Halley's and her dad's heads.

"I see you've been properly greeted," Dr. Norlin laughed.

Halley bowed over the flowers on her shoulders and inhaled. She felt both elegant and silly; submerged in flowers, decorated with little mirrors, enveloped in silky pajamas. She giggled when several men draped Johanna and her father with flowers too. The girls smiled at each other.

A professional-sounding band began to play. Several servers walked around with trays full of delicious refreshments. Almost everyone introduced themselves; women in *sari*s or outfits like hers; men in long tunics with tight pants. Some of the guests wore European-style clothes.

"I think you've met everyone," Johanna said, pointing to a sofa beneath an angular window. "These shoes are pretty, but not very comfortable." They collapsed onto the cushions, sending a delicate floral scent swirling around them.

Halley looked to see if anyone was near enough to hear her, then said, "I'm worried about a young woman in the room next to mine. First, I saw her through my window. It tilts toward hers. The light wasn't good, but she was definitely cowering. Two women were yelling at her. One of them was wearing a red *sari*, but I couldn't hear what they were saying." Johanna looked at her intently, and Halley went on. "Later, when I was at my dressing table, I discovered a door in my room that's connected to hers and listened. They weren't speaking English."

Johanna said. "If they were speaking Hindi, I could understand what they're saying. My childhood *aiya*, the servant who took care of me, was Hindu and didn't speak any English. I'm pretty fluent."

I hope it was Hindi, Halley thought and said, "There's one way to find out."

When the party started to break up and their dads were thanking the guests by the door, the girls slipped out and went straight to Halley's room. Kashif greeted them at the door and helped them remove the flower garlands, draping the flowers over one of the chairs.

Once she and Johanna were alone in her room, Halley pulled the curtain aside. They both pressed an ear against the door. At first, everything seemed quiet. Then Halley heard a woman crying, and she looked at Johanna. Her new friend's eyes were wide. There were no other sounds or voices, just the sobs. Johanna pointed to the other side of the room. They put the curtain back and moved over by the mirror. Halley whispered, "What do you think we should do?"

Johanna looked back toward the door. "It doesn't sound like anyone is there with her. What if we knock on the door?"

"I don't know. It seems strange." Halley's stomach quivered.

"What's the worst that could happen?" Johanna seemed determined to make contact. "We could pull back the curtain, and you could say something like, 'Wow, look, there's a door here. I wonder where it goes.' Then we could listen to see if she stops crying. If there is someone else with her, they would probably say something."

"Well, okay." Halley said hesitantly. She went back and pulled the curtain aside. Again, she heard sobs. "Hey, look Johanna, there's a door," she said loudly. "I wonder where it goes."

Johanna came over and stood by the door with her. "Oh, it's just one of those two-way doors they have in the suites so they can make them bigger."

Halley followed up with, "I wonder if there's anyone in the next room."

They leaned toward the door. The crying had stopped. No one spoke. The girl appeared to be alone. Johanna knocked on the door and spoke aloud in Hindi, asking if there was anyone there. They listened again in silence. Halley heard footsteps approaching and the sound of someone pulling back a curtain. Then there came a tap on the door.

"Hello," the girl said in English. "I'm unlocking the door on my side." They heard a click. Halley was already unlocking their side. She pulled the door toward them.

Standing on the other side was a slender woman. Except for her eyes, she was covered from head to toe by a black garment.

"Oh dear," Johanna exclaimed in English. "You're in *purdah*. Are you going to be alone for a little while?"

The woman started to remove the black drape that covered her head. "Yes," she replied in English. "They'll be gone for about thirty more minutes."

Halley was really nervous. They should hurry, she thought, trying to calm the tightness in her chest. "We're sorry to interfere, but we heard you crying and were worried about you."

The woman released the last clasp and uncovered her face. The black fabric fell onto her shoulders like a large collar. Halley gulped. Although her face was puffed up from crying, the young woman standing before them was strikingly beautiful.

"I am Ganika Acharya."

They quickly introduced themselves and told her they would be taking the train to Poona in the morning.

"Poona?" Ganika asked, looking at them as though trying to decide if she could trust them. Then, she continued, "I need help. Could you please take a message to Padma Arya? She teaches tennis at the Royal Palm Club in Poona and is my friend." They nodded. "Tell her where I am and ask her to get that message to Rabar Chowdhury." She paused, took a deep breath, and went on, "He's my husband."

Suddenly, she backed away from the door. "I must go. They are coming back." Johanna swung the door shut. They heard the click of the lock and the rustle of her curtain, so they locked their door and let the curtain drop.

"Quick," Johanna said. "We need to write down the names right away." They found some hotel paper and a pencil in the dressing table drawer. Once they agreed that they had the right names, Johanna continued, "You'll be staying at the Royal Palm Club, right?"

Halley nodded.

"She is obviously Hindu, and Rabar is a Muslim name," Johanna said. "Judging from the *purdah* veil and the angry women, I think she and her husband must have fallen in love and run away to get married. Something their families would be absolutely against. We rarely hear of Hindu-Muslim marriages. Before Indian independence from Britain four years ago, many Hindus and Muslims were killing each other. It's still a problem." Johanna glanced back at the curtain. "Putting her in *purdah* in Bombay is the kiss of death. She will never be able to go outside without being completely covered. She's like a prisoner. No one will be able to recognize her."

"What will they do with her?"

"Because she married a Muslim man for love, she's like damaged property to her family. Her husband will never see her again."

They sat down on the little couch.

"Oh dear," Johanna said, jerking her hand to her mouth. "What if they're going to sell her?"

Halley trembled and clasped her hands together and was right back on the ocean liner in front of the door, listening to Mrs. Kaliya yell at the men. What did the one man mean when he'd said, "I vouched for him, he's the best in the business"? What business? Kidnapping and selling women? "That's horrible," she said.

"We can't let that happen," Johanna said. "We have to reach Padma Arya with Ganika's message as soon as we get to Poona."

"Definitely." Halley stood up.

At the door, Johanna stopped. "I'm thinking my dad wouldn't want to get into the middle of Ganika's family matter. It might not be safe.

We should probably keep Ganika's request to ourselves for now." Halley nodded.

When they entered the sitting room, their fathers were discussing their travel plans for the following day. Dr. Norlin said, "We'll be leaving on the midday train to Poona. Kashif will see to the trunks while we're at breakfast and meet us in front. He'll drop us at Victoria Station, then drive your car to Poona. He'll join you at the Royal Palm Club." Turning to Halley, he went on, "That's where you and your dad will be staying until your house is ready."

Halley looked at Johanna. Their eyes met, and they nodded at each other. She wondered if it would be very hard to find Padma Arya.

Dr. Norlin moved toward the door. "Kashif, will you bring their *chota hazri* at seven?"

"Yes, *Sahib*." Kashif's calm voice emerged from the corner of the room.

Halley realized that he'd been quietly standing behind her father throughout the conversation. She looked around for Sundara and found him perched on a stand next to the window, preening his feathers. Kashif gracefully crossed the room with just a few strides, opened the door for the Norlins, and held it until they were out in the hall.

Once the door was closed, Dad looked at Halley with a little grin. "It looks like you and Johanna made a nice connection today. Do you like her?"

"Very much." She ran her hand down her sleeve. The silky satin still felt cool on her arm. "Kashif, what is *chota hazri*?"

He stopped tiding up the room. "*Memsaab*, it's a little breakfast of tea and sliced fruit or toast. I will bring it to you when I wake you up tomorrow. Is that all right with you?"

She nodded and smiled. *Chota hazri* was a wake-up call she might be able to get used to. "That would be nice," she said. Kashif went into her room.

While they chatted about their day and the intriguing people they had met, Dad almost seemed like his old self. In a few minutes, Halley noticed Kashif move soundlessly past them to her dad's room. When he emerged, Dad leaned over and kissed the top of her head. "Goodnight, Halley Valley. I love you very much."

She got up and gave him a hug. "I love you too, Dad."

At her door, she turned and watched Dad head toward his room. When he stopped to say good night to Kashif, she noticed that although both men were tall, Kashif was several inches taller.

Kashif bowed low. "Goodnight, *Sahib*."

Kashif had closed the curtains and turned down the covers on her bed. She pulled back one of the curtains. Near the hotel, the Gateway of India monument shimmered beside the water, bathed in gold and blue light. A large party had gathered in front of the towering arch, and a band was playing.

Their welcome party had been so elegant. Most of the people she had met were either doctors or people closely connected with Dr. Gustaf Norlin and his research. Some were from Bombay, others had traveled a long distance to welcome them. She loved the trays of exotic treats—delicious puffy pastry triangles, spicy fried patties that went with a sweet sauce, grilled chicken, vegetables on a stick, and more. The mango juice was the best drink she'd ever tasted.

Halley dropped the curtain and went over to the dressing table. What about Ganika? Had she eaten anything? She imagined her sitting on a chair in the corner of the room all day, covered completely in black with those awful women scaring her to death. She listened at the door from behind the curtain but couldn't hear anything.

In the gloomy half-light from the windows, she changed into her nightgown and collapsed on the bed. It seemed so quiet, so still. After more than a week on the *Strathmore*, she was used to the subtle movement of the ship at bedtime. Now, a peaceful stillness flowed into her. The copper fan circled slowly above her, stirring the slivers of light that cut around the curtains and into the room. Shadows wove in and out behind the rotating blades. She noticed a sparkling point that flickered from each blade as it passed. Halley stared at it and blinked. Tears of wonder broke the sparkle into a circling rainbow of light that whirled above her.

5
The Little Man

"Good morning, *Memsaab*."

Halley sat up and watched Kashif open the curtains. In the middle of the tray on the table beside her was a steaming cup of tea and a small banana. "Thank you, Kashif." She carefully lifted the tray onto the bed.

"*Sahib* wants you to know that breakfast is in an hour. Do you require anything else?" He was peacefully standing by the door.

"Yes, could you knock on my door when Dad is almost ready to go?"

"Yes, *Memsaab*." He made a simple bow and left.

Halley sipped the steaming tea and watched a crowd of boats head out into Bombay harbor. Her mind turned to the previous summer when she and Mom had picnicked at the beach near Meadowcroft. After eating some great peanut butter and sliced-cucumber sandwiches, Mom told her a hilarious story about the time she and some of her college friends sailed around Cuba.

Halley peeled half the banana, broke off the top part, and gazed at the glistening crystals of light that bounced off it, just like light sparkles from fresh-fallen snow in the moonlight. She took a bite and breathed in.

Ah, my first Indian banana.

When Kashif knocked on the door, she had just finished packing her trunk and was somewhat content with her dress and the way her hair had turned out. "Come in."

Two spotlessly uniformed porters carried her trunk to a cart in the hall and put it on top of her dad's. She smiled when she saw that Sundara was back on Kashif's shoulder.

"Good morning Sundara," she said, smiling.

The bird inclined his head. "Good morning."

Dad was standing next to the cart. "How are you today, my dear daughter?"

She laughed at his dignified tone and responded in an equally refined manner. "Very fine, my dear father."

A man in a red jacket led them across the dining room, which was full of guests. From their dress, Halley thought they could be from all over the world. Attendants bustled around the tables in white cotton shirts and pants with wide red belts. Most had white turbans or boat-shaped hats.

While they waited for the Norlins, Dad updated her on their travel plans. Dr. Norlin had reserved a compartment for all of them on the Deccan Queen. It would probably take an hour or more to get to Victoria Station from the hotel.

When Johanna arrived, she gave Halley a knowing look, sat down, and jerked her head toward the lobby. "Halley, would you walk with me for a minute? I want to check out something." Halley followed her to the lobby. When their fathers could no longer see them, Johanna stopped.

"I think the woman you saw in Ganika's room just crossed the lobby," Johanna said, her voice urgent. "She was wearing a green *sari*. One of her arms was covered with glass bangles." Halley's stomach churned, and Johanna continued, "She was heading into the other dining room."

Halley glanced where Johanna was pointing, then looked away, whispering, "Did she look like she was leaving?"

"No, she wasn't carrying anything. But we must get word to Padma Arya in Poona as soon as we can. They may be planning to move Ganika."

A chill descended from the top of Halley's head. She grabbed Johanna's arm and backed up a few steps. "We can't let Mrs. Kaliya see us. Let's go back."

Johanna stopped. "First you need to pinch your cheeks or something. You look like you just saw a ghost." Halley followed her advice, took a few deep breaths, and glanced up. Johanna was looking at her strangely. "Did you say her name was Kaliya?"

Halley nodded.

"In Hindi, Kaliya means poisonous snake."

Halley shuddered and pinched her cheeks again. "It seems like a perfect name for her."

Johanna grabbed Halley's arm and started walking toward the dining room. "I wonder what Mr. Kaliya is like," she said.

Their fathers watched them sit down. Halley's dad looked concerned. "Ladies, is everything all right?"

Halley glanced at him with a weak smile. "Yes, thanks, Dad."

They had just finished breakfast when Kashif arrived with Sundara. He led them through the busy lobby and out to their car. Halley looked down the whole time, hoping that if Mrs. Kaliya appeared, she wouldn't notice them. Then she gulped. There was no way anyone would miss seeing them. They were following Kashif and Sundara.

Kashif opened the back door, and Halley and Johanna climbed in. Dad followed, telling Dr. Norlin he'd sit in the back with the girls.

Before Kashif could drive away, a swarm of screaming children circled the car. Halley braced herself. Right next to the window was a boy with a knife stuck through the middle of his tongue. "No," Halley gasped, covering her eyes. Children pounded on the glass.

Halley felt Johanna's arm circle her shoulders. She could hear the doormen clapping their hands, sending the children away. Kashif inched forward, beeping the horn.

She dropped her hands. "Does anyone ever give them any money?" she asked. "How do they survive?"

Gustaf Norlin looked back at her. "It's a tremendous problem. Some of the churches and temples have made heroic efforts to help them. But it's hard. The children are treated badly by their keepers and are so desperate to collect money some of them even pass up food when it's offered. It looks like that ghastly cut in the boy's tongue has healed just like an ear pierced for an earring, making it possible for them to slip in the knife when the children are sent out to beg."

"Children," Sundara said softly. The crest on his head was ruffed up, and his cheeks were pink. He was looking right at her.

"What's wrong with Sundara?" she asked.

"The begging children always upset him," Kashif explained, rolling down his window. "He is very sensitive to the pain of others. He is also concerned about you, *Memsaab* Halley."

Sundara bobbed his head up and down a few times. "You, *Memsaab* Halley," he echoed.

Halley smiled at him. "Oh, Sundara." Johanna gave her a hug.

While they waited at the next intersection, Johanna squealed and opened her window. "Look!" She pointed past her father at a man standing near the corner with a monkey on each shoulder and one on his head. "It's a Monkey Man." The man was playing a flute, and the monkeys were clapping their little hands.

The rest of the trip to the station was exhilarating. At almost every corner, one of them pointed out another spectacle. When they passed a small plaza, Halley shrieked and pointed at a turbaned man sitting cross legged in the dirt, playing a long flute. A large snake was uncurling up out of a basket in front of him.

"Here we are," Dr. Norlin said. They were approaching a large building with pointed towers on each corner and a massive one in the center with arched porticos and porches covering the front and the sides. "Victoria Station."

"It's gigantic," Halley said. "It looks bigger than the hotel."

Dr. Norlin said, "Thieves and pick-pocketers are particularly bad at the stations. Girls, please put your purse straps over your heads. We can't be too careful. It would be a shame to lose anything, especially on your first day."

"I only have my brush and a handkerchief in mine," said Halley. "Should I leave it in the car?"

"Keep it," Johanna said. "Your strap is longer than mine. We can put my deck of cards in your bag, and I can leave mine in the car. Is that okay, Dad?"

Dr. Norlin smiled. "Sure, honey. Kashif should arrive at the Royal Palm Club a little after tea. We'll be there by then."

A large, black limousine passed them. It stopped at the station entrance right behind an elaborately decorated red-and-gold horse trailer. The chauffeur got out and spoke to one of the guards.

"Hey, Dad." Johanna leaned into the front seat and pointed at it. "Isn't that the Maharaja's Mercedes? It looks like it's following that horse trailer." They watched as the chauffeur returned to the car and followed the trailer around the corner of the station.

"It looks like it," Dr. Norlin continued with a laugh. "I think they must have a special entrance for royalty and their horses."

They waved goodbye to Kashif and Sundara and walked through the ornate portico. Halley looked up into the vast space above them. "It's larger than Grand Central Station in New York City," she said, double-checking her purse strap. Dad put his hand on her shoulder, and she clutched her purse with both hands. They followed the Norlins past a majestic, blue-stone staircase. The scent of flowers, exotic spices, and sweaty bodies circled around them. From her height, Halley could see a river of colorful head scarves, turbans, and hats flowing ahead of them toward the trains. It seemed like she'd been walking for miles when they finally stopped.

"Good," said Dr. Norlin. "Here's our train car."

The porter punched their tickets and led them up the steps and down a narrow corridor with numbered doors on one side. Just beyond the windows along the other side was another train. Their compartment had two cushioned benches with a table between them. The girls grabbed the seats by the window.

"This is great, Dad," Johanna said. "Maybe we'll be able to see the Western Ghats from this side of the train." Her father nodded.

"What're the Western Ghats?" asked Halley.

"They're a mountain range," said Johanna. "Sometimes we drive there when it gets really hot."

Halley's stomach growled. "Will we be eating soon?"

Dr. Norlin laughed. "Once we're moving, we'll go to the dining car for lunch or, as they say in Hindi, *tiffin*."

It wasn't long before they heard the whistle. While the train rumbled slowly through the back streets of Bombay, Johanna pointed out some of the larger buildings and temples.

Dr. Norlin added, "In the ocean near Bombay there's a lush island. The famous Elephanta Caves are there. Around the eighth century, artists carved huge sculptures and panels in the rock of five caves. The most surprising is the Trimurti, a three-headed statue cut out of a single rock. It represents the three aspects of divinity. It's as tall as a three-story house."

Halley loved having *tiffin* in the lush dining car with crisp white tablecloths and crystal goblets. The waiters brought them fancy platters filled with saucy vegetables and bowls of rice. Johanna showed her how to eat with the large, soft, cracker-like bread she called a *chapatti*. Halley struggled to keep from getting the sauce on her dress.

The hills and valleys rolled peacefully past the windows. After they finished their lunch, the girls left their fathers discussing some of the health challenges of the Indian people and went back to their compartment.

When they passed through the first sliding door into the next car, Halley laughed. "It's funny that our dads talk about blood and guts while we're eating. We must have cast-iron stomachs." Johanna laughed too.

Halley slid their compartment door closed. In front of them, seated cross-legged on one of the benches, was a little bald man clothed in white. His eyes were closed, and his sandals were on the floor in front of him.

"*Dadaji*," Johanna exclaimed.

The man opened his eyes and bowed to them. "*Namaste*, Johanna," he said with a clear British accent.

His sudden appearance startled Halley. Her first thought was to run back into the corridor. But wait... How did they know each other?

The man stood up. "Johanna," he continued in the same calm voice, "where can I find your father?"

Just then the door slid back. "*Dadaji*," Dr. Norlin said with surprise. He put his hands together in front of his chest and bowed. "*Namaste*."

"*Namaste*, Gustaf. After *tiffin* in his private coach, the Maharaja lost his balance when he stood up from the table and fell, cutting his head. He tried to get back up but couldn't. His servants moved him onto the bed."

"Please take me to him." Dr. Norlin pointed to the black bag on the floor next to Johanna. "Honey, hand me my case." She moved quickly, and Dr. Norlin turned to Halley's dad. "Karl, you had better come with me."

Halley collapsed onto the bench as soon as the men were gone. A scent of flowers lingered. "Who was that little man?"

Johanna sat down across from her by the window. "My parents met *Dadaji* years ago after Dad recovered from another bout of malaria. They were guests at a special event held by the Maharaja at his palace. During the program, Iyengar, a famous teacher, spoke about the benefits of the ancient practice of yoga. Then he invited one of his students to demonstrate. The student contorted his body into impossible postures while the teacher explained the health advantages of each one. The student was *Dadaji*. That evening, *Dadaji* became Dad's yoga teacher. When I turned twelve, he became my teacher too."

"Okay. Who is Maharaja?"

"This Maharaja is one of India's royalty. Before Indian independence, there were many princely states. He and his ancestors ruled one of them. The maharajas are somewhat like the royals in Europe."

"But how did he know your dad was on this train?" Halley realized her voice must have sounded more anxious than she felt.

"Hmm," Johanna dipped her head. "Maybe the last time they met together they discussed that they would all be traveling on this train. Or maybe *Dadaji* noticed Dad and Kashif when the Maharaja's car pulled in ahead of us at Victoria Station. Once on the train, it wouldn't have been hard for *Dadaji* to find out which compartment was ours. But then again, maybe he just knew. He has incredible insight and often knows things. *Dadaji* is very mysterious."

"This is a lot to take in." Halley shook her head and looked through the glass. Johanna followed her gaze. A short distance from the train they could see a man leading two big cows with long horns. They were pulling a rickety cart filled with something that looked like thick plates of dirt.

"Those are water buffalo," Johanna said, pointing at the animals. "It looks like the man has a cartload of water buffalo manure."

"Yuck!" Halley made a face. "What could he possibly be doing with all of that water buffalo poop?"

The train continued, leaving the man and his cart behind. Johanna smiled. "When you see people cooking, they're probably burning dried water buffalo dung."

"You're joking."

Johanna shook her head. "Dried water buffalo manure or cow dung is a very accessible fuel for cooking. They carefully build a mound of the round cow pies so they'll dry. Bobbi, my *aiya*, lives with her husband in a place behind ours. When I was little, she often took me out there while she cooked her family dinner. Her fuel was cow dung. It didn't smell bad to me. Funny, don't you think?"

"It is funny," Halley said. "But I can see that this cow dung business is just one of the many things I'll be learning about." She went to the door and slid it open. She looked around, then closed it again and sat next to Johanna. "When we get to the Royal Palm, how will we get away by ourselves to speak to Padma Arya about Ganika?"

"We could say that I'm going to show you the tennis courts. Oh," Johanna paused, "do you play tennis?"

"I took lessons when I was at Meadowcroft, my grandparents' summer place."

"Perfect."

They heard voices. The next moment the door slid open, and their fathers stepped into the compartment. When Dad spoke, he sounded annoyed.

"He seemed like a nice enough guy. But I don't like the way he speaks to his servants."

"I know what you mean." Dr. Norlin sat down across from Johanna.

"Is the Maharaja okay?" Johanna asked, sounding concerned.

"He'll be all right. His head will heal from the fall. We think he might have eaten too quickly; nothing serious."

"Gustaf," Halley's dad interrupted. They all looked at him. He closed the door and leaned back against it. "It sounded like the Maharaja was serious when he invited all of us to join him in his box for the Poona horse races at the end of the month. What do you think? Should we plan on it?"

"Horse races!" Johanna clapped. "Is that true?"

"I don't know, Karl." Dr. Norlin tilted his head and looked down. "Do you think you and Halley will have rested up enough after your trip by then?"

From where she sat, Halley thought she could see the glimmer of a smile.

"Dad, don't tease us!" Johanna was across the compartment in a flash and pounced on him.

"I give up," he laughed. "He's taking his stallion to the Hyderabad track for a race this week and will be back in Poona after that. It looks like we've received a coveted invitation to watch his horse run the race from the royal box. Let's plan on it."

6

An Elephant-Headed God

The Western Ghats were in the distance when the engineer blasted the horn and the train slowed. Evidence that they were approaching the outskirts of Poona was everywhere. They passed a man balancing an enormous parcel on the handlebars of an old bicycle. Johanna pointed out three women dressed in pastel *sari*s walking together, each balancing a large copper pot on her head.

"It never ceases to amaze me when I see women carrying those jugs like that," Johanna said. "They're not light. How do they do that? I can barely walk with a book on my head. I've tried."

They passed a boy leading a large, white bullock pulling a cart filled with what looked to Halley like cow dung. "Hey Dad," she said, pointing at them. "Can you believe it? That cart is filled with water buffalo manure. Did you know that they use the cow pies for fuel? They cook with it."

Dad sat next to her, shook his head, and laughed. "It sounds like you were studying while we were gone."

"We'll soon be near Ganesh Mandir," Dr. Norlin said. "It's a temple to Ganesha, the most revered of the Hindu gods. He has an elephant head."

"How did he get an elephant's head?" Halley asked. She looked around and saw that Johanna was waving at Dr. Norlin, who smiled.

"Johanna, would you like to tell them about Ganesha?"

"Yes." Johanna looked around, smiling. "It's one of my favorite stories about the Hindu gods." She settled back.

"Up in the Himalayas, the Hindu god Lord Shiva lived with his beloved wife, the goddess Parvati. Parvati was very modest and preferred to bathe in private. One day, Shiva came in when she was bathing, which embarrassed her. To keep this from happening again, she decided she needed a guardian while she bathed. She had always wanted a son, so she collected clay and mud from the ground, scented bark from the trees, and valuable elements from the earth. She combined them and molded them into a boy. When she breathed life into him, he looked at her and called her 'Mother.' This made her very happy, and they immediately loved each other. She called him Ganesha.

"Parvati told her son to guard the house while she bathed and not to let anyone in. Ganesha was at his post when Lord Shiva came back. When he discovered a boy he didn't recognize standing watch at the entrance to his house, he demanded, 'Who are you?'

"Ganesha replied, 'I'm the guardian of my mother's house.'

"Lord Shiva bellowed, 'That's not possible. This is my house.' Ganesha stepped in front of Shiva to keep him from getting closer.

"Shiva stood tall over Ganesha and shouted, 'I am Lord Shiva. Let me into my house at once.' When he tried again to enter, Ganesha hit him with his wooden stick. Shiva became so angry that he cut off the boy's head and stomped away.

"When Parvati emerged from her bath, she found the headless body of her son and went into a rage. She threatened to destroy all creation unless the murderer confessed.

"Another god, Brahma, knew what had happened and tried to reason with her. She said she would only change her mind if her son was brought back to life and was worshipped first before all the other gods.

"Lord Shiva confessed. Parvati was furious. To calm her down, he told her that he would bring Ganesha back to life.

"Lord Shiva went with Brahma into the jungle, intending to remove the head of the first animal they saw and put it on Ganesha.

"The first animal they came upon was a powerful elephant. Shiva took the head and put it on Ganesha and brought him back to life. Parvati was very happy, and all was well."

Johanna stopped talking and looked around at them.

Halley had been totally entranced by the story. She knew nothing about Hinduism except that Jawaharlal Nehru, the prime minister of India, was a Hindu. "How many gods do the Hindus have?" she asked.

Dr. Norlin cleared his throat, and Johanna leaned back. "The Hindus believe there are many gods. Each one manages a particular part of the universe—the sun, the moon, the wind. If each god didn't do their job, everything would collapse. Lord Krishna, the god of everything, manages all of them."

"Wow, that's a lot of gods." Halley said. "At St. Bart's in New York we only had one god."

They were passing a wide river. Whole families were in the water; children playing, people bathing, some washing clothes. A rainbow of multicolored *saris* was spread out to dry on the rocks like a giant fan. They reminded Halley of the time her folks took her swimming at Falls River Gorge when she was a kid. Those rocks were covered with colorful towels, just like the *saris*. She remembered watching her mother's floppy red hat float on the water above where Mom had disappeared beneath the surface to save a child from drowning.

Halley looked uncomfortably around their compartment and back out the window. She scooted over next to her dad, slipped her hand into the crook of his arm, and laid her head on his shoulder.

Johanna's dad stood up. "We're almost to the Poona station." He pointed to a temple with a towering gold steeple in the middle. "There's a seven-foot-tall gold statue of Ganesha in that temple. Thousands of pilgrims visit it every year."

The horn blew and moments later the train hissed to a stop. "There's Sarin, our bearer," Johanna said, pointing through the glass at a tall, thin man who was walking swiftly toward their train car. He was wearing the now familiar loose-fitting white pants with a sleeveless gray jacket over his white shirt. A white cap covered most of his short black hair.

Halley felt her dad's hand cover hers. "Are you ready, Halley?"

Was she ready? She took a breath and felt her purse on her shoulder. "Yes," she said and followed the Norlins into the corridor and off the train.

Sarin led them to the Norlins' car in front of the station. Halley thought it looked like her dad's station wagon, except it was white. She got in the middle of the back seat next to Johanna and braced herself. A moment later, she heard children running toward them. She closed her eyes and took a slow, deep breath. Johanna grabbed her hand, and Dad put his arm around her as the shouting children banged on the glass.

Sarin inched the car away, leaving the begging children behind. Halley realized she'd been holding her breath. She sighed and unclenched the muscles in her face. They rolled down all the windows. The breeze was hot.

The streets were alive with more new sights, smells, and sounds. Johanna and Dr. Norlin pointed out the merchant booths and shops by the road. They passed musical performers, animals pulling carts, and women in bright-colored *sari*s.

"We're almost there," said Dr. Norlin. "The Royal Palm Club had a devastating fire a few years ago. You'll see that they've done a great job of restoring it." They passed a luxurious swimming area with low bath houses, palm trees, big flowering bushes, lounge chairs, and children splashing around in a wading pool just beyond a larger one with a diving board.

He pointed at it and continued, "Johanna and Hans learned to swim in that pool when they were little. The club also has great tennis courts. Do either of you play?"

"Yes," said Dad. "We both do and brought our rackets."

A guard waved them through a high metal gate. Sarin parked in front of a long, pink building with an orange-tiled roof. Over the porch was a sign that read, "Royal Palm Club: Members Only." Behind it were more buildings with orange tiles. Lush green trees towered over some of them. Manicured gardens were everywhere. Several white-gloved doormen opened the car doors, and Halley got out behind her dad.

"Dad, look." Johanna pointed at a smooth, gray animal resting in the shade of the veranda. Its long tail curled around it.

"Good eye. It could be that mongoose we saw here last week."

"Wow, a mongoose," said Dad. "It almost looks like a pet just lying there like that. I read that they kill snakes."

"Yes," said Dr. Norlin. "People are really fortunate when a wild mongoose adopts a house or a building like this."

Halley looked at its rounded ears and short nose. "It's cute. Kinda reminds me of one of my grandmother's cats with that tail. But wouldn't the venomous snakes kill them?"

"That's what's so amazing about the mongoose," said Johanna. "They're resistant to snake venom. We have one that lives at our house. Just the other day, I saw her kill a snake near our servant's quarters."

They crossed a wide veranda with lots of high-backed chairs and potted palms. A doorman ushered them into the lobby. As Halley watched their dads walk ahead of them toward the registration desk, she stopped, and so did Johanna. It seemed like the perfect moment to break away to find Padma.

"Hey, Dad," Johanna said, "if you don't need us right now, can I show Halley the tennis courts?"

"That works out fine," Dr. Norlin replied. "Don't take too long. We'll meet you in the lounge for tea."

Johanna pointed at the doors on the side of the lobby. They hurriedly crossed another veranda and a flower garden and entered a small building next to the tennis courts. A young man looked up.

"Good afternoon," Johanna said. "Can you tell us where we can find Padma Arya?"

He pointed to a door behind him. "She just finished teaching a lesson and is out there near the courts."

Once outside, they spotted a young woman sitting on a bench in the shade of a flowering tree. A boy was walking away from her and toward a waiting car. Halley pictured Ganika Acharya imprisoned in Bombay. Would anyone be able to get there in time to rescue her? Even in the intense heat, Halley felt a shiver run up her back.

When they got closer, Halley could see the woman's profile. She had light skin and a petite nose. Her straight black hair was tied in a long ponytail. She appeared to be lost in thought. When they got close enough, Johanna cleared her throat and said, "Are you Padma Arya?"

The woman turned to look at them, and they both took a quick breath. She would have been considered beautiful, but on the other side of her face she had a huge, red burn running down her cheek. "Yes," she said. "Who are you?"

The girls gave her their names, and Halley went right to the point. "Yesterday, my father and I arrived in Bombay from America. When Johanna and I were in my room last night, we heard a woman crying in the one next to mine. We unlocked the connecting door, and so did the girl. She was in *purdah*." Padma gasped. Halley had noticed that Padma's expression had softened while she spoke. Padma now leaned forward, listening intently. Her large brown eyes were almost brimming over. Halley continued, "The girl uncovered her head and said, 'I am Ganika Acharya.'"

Padma jumped up and threw her arms around the girls. "Oh, thank you." She grabbed their hands and started striding toward the sports office. "We must contact her husband, Rabar Chowdhury, immediately. There may still be time to save her." Padma led them into her office, closed the door, and began dialing the phone on her desk. Halley caught herself biting a nail and noticed that Johanna was gently rocking back and forth in her chair.

"Rabar, are you free to talk?" Padma paused. She tapped her fingers on the desk. After what seemed like forever, she went on. "There are two girls here." Padma's eyes sparkled. She struggled to speak. "They . . . they found Ganika." Between gasps, she handed the phone to Halley. "Please talk to him."

"Hello, this is Halley Pederson." There was silence at the other end. "Are you there?"

She could hear a man sniffing. "Yes, I'm sorry. I had almost given up hope." He took a breath. "Please tell me where I can find her."

Halley gave him Ganika's room number at the Taj Mahal hotel. She also related the details about her captors. She described the door between the rooms. Her last words to him were, "Please hurry."

Padma sighed. "Thank you, girls. Now all we can do is pray he gets there in time."

When the girls returned to their fathers, Dr. Norlin was telling Halley's dad about a special music society dinner the following evening at the club. "My wife has reserved our seats at the dinner. She's planning to leave the hospital early to get home with time to dress."

The waiters pulled out chairs for the girls. "Did you hear that, Halley?" Dad asked when they were seated. "The Norlins have invited us to a special dinner here tomorrow."

When neither of the girls spoke, Dr. Norlin took a closer look at his daughter. "Are you girls all right?"

"Oh, sure." Johanna glanced at Halley. "Dad, we met the new tennis coach. Do you know how she got that awful burn on her face?"

"That's Padma, right?"

She nodded.

"You might ask your mom. She treated a Royal Palm Club employee at the hospital a few days ago."

Just then, there was a commotion in the lobby. They could hear laughter.

"That's Mom." Johanna smiled.

Halley was facing the lobby, so it was easy for her to see Dr. Maria Norlin enter. Johanna's mother looked glamorous in a delicate orange dress. The full skirt swirled around her, and her fashionable light-brown hair bounced as she walked. She was accompanied by a handsome dark-skinned man in a tan suit. Both men at the table stood up.

"Gustaf, darling," she said with a distinctly Dutch accent. "Look who I found."

"Anaka Gupta," Dr. Norlin laughed. "Two days in a row. Thanks for being the welcoming committee for the Pedersons yesterday. Please, join us for tea." The men all shook hands.

Maria Norlin gave Johanna and Halley each a hug, then sat between them. "So, girls, tell me all about the trip."

Halley thanked her for the outfit. "It's lovely and it fits perfectly."

Johanna told her about the welcome party and about eating on the train. "And," she dropped her voice, "can you believe it, *Dadaji* was in our compartment when Halley and I returned from *tiffin*. Dad was right behind us. *Dadaji* told him that the Maharaja had fallen. A moment later they were gone. Halley's dad, too, and guess what else? The Maharaja invited all of us to the races at the end of the month. He even had one of his racehorses on the train." The conversation remained light through tea.

They had almost finished when Kashif and Sundara walked through the lobby doors. Halley's dad waved to him. "How was your trip?" he asked.

Kashif looked relaxed considering his long, hot drive. "Uneventful," he said. Halley was happy to see them.

Sundara dipped his head toward Kashif, ruffled his feathers, and echoed, "Uneventful." Halley smiled at him.

After some brief instructions from Dad, Kashif bowed and left to arrange for their luggage to be delivered to their quarters.

Johanna pulled her mother aside when they reached the doors. "Mom, we met Padma Arya at the tennis courts today."

Maria Norlin's smile disappeared. "Oh my, how was she?"

"When we arrived, she appeared to be really depressed. How did she burn her face?"

Maria Norlin looked first at her daughter and then at Halley. "It wasn't an accident," she said. "But she didn't tell me how it happened. She was really upset. I had to give her a sedative to help her rest. We kept her in the hospital overnight."

Halley blinked back a tear. She wanted to scream. Who could be so mean to hurt Padma like that?

Johanna's face went red. She clenched her fists, looked down, stomped her foot, and growled. "That makes me so mad."

Maria Norlin turned to Halley. "I suspect this has been a big day for you. We'll head off now and see you tomorrow."

Halley put her hand through the crook of her dad's elbow, and they walked with the Norlins to their car. After watching them pull away, they returned to the breezy shade of the veranda and flopped onto the nearest chairs.

"Halley," he said. He looked almost happy for the first time in months. "Tomorrow we'll get settled and enjoy the dinner party. Then on Tuesday we'll go to St. Anne's Classical Academy to get you registered and pick up your uniforms. Okay?"

"Sure. I know we decided on St. Anne's, because it's in Poona, but now I have another reason to want to go there." She paused. "It's Johanna's school too."

Kashif returned and escorted them to their quarters. The main door opened into an elegant front room with couches, chairs, and a few tables. When they looked into the convenience kitchen, Kashif pointed through it to an open door. "My room is just back there."

From where she stood, Halley was happy to see Sundara in the back room preening himself on his stand by a sunny window. Kashif showed them some of the other first-floor features, then led them upstairs. The doors on either side of the landing were open. "As you instructed, *Sahib*, we moved your trunks into the rooms."

Dad walked into the room on the left. "Hey, Halley, you have the other room. My trunk's in here." He leaned back out the door. "Kashif, please make a dinner reservation for us at eight, and thank you for everything today." Kashif bowed with a wisp of a smile and retreated down the stairs.

"Okay, Dad," Halley said. "See you then."

She glanced around her room and went outside to test the balcony. From the railing, she could see the back garden illuminated by a parade of light posts that meandered away into the dusk. Maybe this would be a good time to write a letter to Mary. .

She was about to go back inside when a gardener emerged around the corner of their building. He kept glancing around, watering plants. Twilight seemed like a peculiar time to be watering. He stopped at a flower bed right below her that circled an unusual tree. The man splashed each plant around it until he stopped at a flowering bush. He bent down, pulled an envelope out from under the bush, and haphazardly spritzed a few more plants before disappearing back the way he came.

Halley thought that receiving mail from under a bush at dusk was even stranger than watering at nightfall and decided to find out more. She crept down the stairs. Kashif was gone. She opened the front door, saw no one, and slipped out. When she peeked around the corner, the gardener was rolling up the hose near the spigot. Then he walked away toward the tennis courts and disappeared into the gloom.

She hurried back to her room and flipped on the light. What in the world was she thinking? She dived onto the bed. What if he'd seen her? The ceiling fan stirred the air above her, and she shivered.

It's not like I don't have enough to worry about.

She got up, locked the balcony door, and started to get ready for dinner.

7

Sundara's Feather

Two nights later, Halley realized that so much had happened since she mailed the letter to Mary from the ship, so she took her airmail paper onto her balcony to write again. Shimmering moonlight filtered through the trees and, ruffled by a cool evening breeze, scattered away the dark shadows around her. She stretched out on the bench. There was enough light from the windows for her to write. She described the begging children, the welcome parties, and her visit to St. Anne's that morning to register and pick up several light-blue uniforms. She described the self-centered girl who showed them around the school and smiled when she remembered the face her dad made when their guide wasn't looking. When he asked the guide where the students ate lunch, instead of answering him, she talked about what a great actress she was, that she gave the best audition for the part of Lady Bracknell in the spring play, *The Importance of Being Earnest*, and that she was sure she'd get the part.

Halley stopped writing. She had already turned to the backside of the paper and realized there was not enough space to tell Mary about Ganika or *Dadaji*, or even Padma.

After she signed the letter, she went into her room to find a stamp. The past few days had been exciting, filled with new tastes and smells, surprising encounters, and a new friend, but the thought of going to St.

Anne's the next morning turned her stomach. She swallowed and tried to remember her first day at Chapman School. What had it been like? Mom was with her. She'd seen a photo of them in one of the family albums labeled "Halley's First Day at Chapman." They were both smiling. She was wearing the Chapman elementary uniform—a white blouse under a dark-blue plaid, sleeveless jumper. Her mother looked so young and pretty. Then she pictured what it would be like if Mary was with her and they were starting St. Anne's together. They would definitely have joked about the stupid uniform. Mary would have said something funny like, "Too bad the skirt is so long. It almost touches our knees. If the stupid white collar was any longer, we'd look like we'd dressed up as Pilgrims for the Thanksgiving play."

"Oh no," Halley said aloud, slapping her hand to her forehead. She hadn't been worried about the English class, but what about the other ones? How would the first half of her eleventh-grade physics class at Chapman compare to this one? Would she be way behind? What about math? She took a few quick breaths and swallowed again. A knock on the door and Dad's calming voice broke through her increasing panic.

"Are you ready for dinner?"

She emerged a few moments later with the letter in hand.

"Oh good," he said. "We can drop that off before we eat. Okay?" When she nodded, he took a closer look at her and put his arm around her. They walked in silence until they reached the reception desk.

The uniformed clerk looked up. "May I help you, *Sahib*?

"Yes," Dad replied. "We'd like to leave this letter with you. Can it go out in the next mail pickup?"

"Most assuredly, sir." The clerk took the letter and bowed.

The next morning, Halley sat next to Kashif and Sundara in the front seat of the car and set her school bag on the floor. Before they had driven through the gates, Sundara began to shift his weight from one foot to the other and back, turning his head to look at her at the same time. He didn't stop. They'd only gone a short distance before she asked. "What's bothering Sundara?"

"He's nervous." Kashif said.

"Why?" She resisted the urge to reach up and touch him.

"He knows you are troubled about something."

Sundara ruffed up his crest feathers, tilted his head toward her, and said, "Troubled."

She tried to smile. "Yes, Sundara, I'm really nervous about starting at St. Anne's today. I've gone to the same school all my life. I don't even know what to expect or how to act. At dinner last night, Dad told me to just relax and be myself. But it's not that easy. I'm afraid some of the girls will be mean to me since I'm new and an American. On top of that, I couldn't sleep last night and only ate a little breakfast." Halley realized she'd started to bite down on a fingernail. She moved her hand away and sat on it.

"*Memsaab*," Kashif said, "Sundara and I would like you to have this." Without taking his eyes off the road, he held out his hand and opened it. In his palm was one of Sundara's downy, gold feathers. "Please take this feather and put it in the little pocket beneath your belt. If at any time during the day you are feeling scared or nervous, put your finger in your pocket and touch it. It will help you."

Pocket? She felt around and was surprised to find a little pocket under her belt on her right side. She carefully picked up the feather and held it for a moment. It was bright gold and so soft. She tucked it into the pocket. The feather was beautiful, but how could it help her handle the problems she was dreading?

Kashif stopped in front of the main building, "*Memsaab*, Sundara's gold feather is special. Touching it will calm you and give you strength."

Sundara echoed, "Strength."

"Thank you, Sundara." She looked at him and attempted to smile.

While Kashif and Sundara walked around the car, she put her finger into the pocket and closed her eyes. When she touched the feather, she felt a pulse of cool energy flow up her arm to her head, and she took a deep breath.

Kashif opened her door. "We'll be here when you come out after school."

"Thank you both." She took her lunch basket.

Sundara turned his head around. "Hello," he said.

Directly behind them, Sarin was helping Johanna out of their car. She was also carrying a lunch basket. "Surprise," she said walking toward them. "Great timing!"

"Oh, Johanna, am I glad to see you." They gave each other a quick hug and started walking. "Our tour guide yesterday was more interested in talking about herself than in giving us any answers. I don't even know what to do with this basket or where we go for lunch."

Johanna laughed. "Did your guide happen to be Martha Miller?"

Halley nodded.

"Let's drop off our baskets first. Where are your morning classes?"

Once Halley went over where her morning classes would be—Halley was excited to discover she and Johanna had drama together—and where they'd meet for lunch, Johanna left Halley outside her first class: physics with Mr. Rossi. Three girls were walking toward her. They looked at her shoes and then at her hair. One of them scoffed *"Laal Baal"* as they passed. This sent a cold shudder up her neck. She remembered the feather and put her finger into her pocket. Just as she touched it, she noticed a short, round man walking quickly toward her. His straight, graying red hair peeked out from under his boat-shaped black hat. He looked up at her through thick glasses.

"Are you Halley Pederson?"

"Yes, sir." She smiled. He had pronounced her name correctly.

"Did you happen to be named after Halley's Comet?"

"Yes, sir."

"Excellent." He looked down with a subtle smile.

She followed him into the room and glanced around. Tall, sunny windows lined the opposite wall. Mr. Rossi left her standing awkwardly by the door and went right to an oversized desk. Behind it was a large blackboard covered with formulas and a diagram. Several rows of girls were all staring at her. Behind them was a cluster of high-topped lab tables. She looked back at Mr. Rossi.

"Good morning, class." The moment he started to speak, the girls slid back their chairs and stood up.

"Good morning, Mr. Rossi," they said in unison.

"Thank you, class. You may be seated." Their chairs scraped the floor again. He moved behind his desk. "This is Halley Pederson. She just arrived here from America." He looked around. "Aabroo." A girl in the back row slowly raised her hand. "I'd like you to be Halley's lab partner today." The girl looked like she'd just eaten a lemon. Mr. Rossi continued, "Halley, you can sit next to her."

Halley wanted to be invisible. Instead, she had to walk through a brilliant beam of sunlight pouring through the windows. She felt like a deer that had just wandered into a clan of hyenas, marked for the kill. Some of them appeared to be licking their lips. She looked down and kept moving.

Mr. Rossi waited until she was seated, then pointed at the drawing on the board. "Can any of you identify this diagram?" Halley looked at the board, took a breath, and thought about the feather.

She recognized the diagram from her physics lab last fall. It showed how an ammeter measures the current in an electrical circuit. She tucked her head down and smiled. How could she ever forget what it was? Her physics teacher at Chapman had been unsympathetically annoyed when she and her lab partner accidentally mis-wired their ammeter and blew it up. She scrunched her nose when she remembered the awful smell of the burnt wire and equipment.

The class was silent. Mr. Rossi looked at each girl. They shifted nervously, no one answering. Finally, he looked at Halley. "Miss Pederson! Do you know what it is?"

She wanted to say, "No." Giving the answer during the first moments of her first class would be the scent of blood to the hyenas. She'd never escape them after that. But her finger moved into the little pocket. She looked around the class, then at Mr. Rossi's kind face, and nodded sheepishly. "It's the diagram of an ammeter."

"That's right," he responded with a grateful smile.

She could see Aabroo's nails dig into the wooden table. She heard the girl on her other side whisper to the girl next to her. A murmur went through the room. They were all looking at her.

She caressed the feather and exhaled.

Mr. Rossi explained the diagram and the electrical current and then spent the rest of the class going over the homework they were supposed to have covered. When the bell rang, he asked Halley to stay for a minute. He gave her a copy of the textbook and the assignment sheet. His final words were, "Welcome to St. Anne's."

She had survived the first hour. Next class: drama.

When she entered the theater, Johanna pulled her aside. In an excited whisper she blurted, "Guess what? The girl who was going to play the part of Jack broke her leg. Sister Jane has to choose someone else for the part. If you'd like to try out for it, let's go talk to her right now. Oh," she smiled, "and she cast me as Lady Bracknell."

Halley felt a happy twinge and followed Johanna. Oscar Wilde's humorous farce, *The Importance of Being Earnest*, was one of her favorites. As a tall student in an all-girls' school, she was used to being cast as a boy. Most recently she played the part of Romeo in *Romeo and Juliet* at Chapman. If she got the part, she'd be thrilled to be the witty Jack Worthing. "Yes," she said. "That'd be great"

Halfway down the center aisle, she almost stopped. Johanna was heading toward a large, dark-skinned woman in a full black nun's habit with a wimple covering her head. She was standing in front of the stage holding a clipboard, talking quietly with a group of students. Halley recognized one of them: her tour guide, Martha Miller, who'd been hoping for the part of Lady Bracknell that Johanna had gotten. Even though Halley had heard that Sister Jane was the most popular teacher at the school, her formidable presence was startling. She remembered the two nuns she met at her mother's funeral. During the reception after the service, they told her about the day her mother began to volunteer at their church soup kitchen and about her kindness to the homeless. This gentle thought lingered until she caught up with Johanna.

Sister Jane noticed them. "Hello, Johanna. It looks like you're bringing me our new student." She looked at Halley. "I understand you've had some acting experience. We're presenting *The Importance of Being*

Earnest this spring. Would you be interested in auditioning for the part of Jack?"

"Yes, Sister Jane."

"Are you familiar with the play?"

Halley nodded.

"Very good." Sister Jane handed Halley the script. "I've opened it to the part in Act I when Lady Bracknell is interviewing Jack about his family to see if he's acceptable enough to marry her daughter. She thinks Jack is Ernest Worthing. I'll read her part. You read Jack's. Okay?"

The rest of the class sat down in the first few rows of seats. Martha Miller whispered something to the girl next to her and made a face. Johanna smiled encouragingly. Halley looked at the script and tried to keep her hand from shaking. She sensed Sundara's feather through her belt.

"Okay, Halley, let's start."

Halley held up her hand, signaling for a momentary delay and looked down. What would Jack be feeling at that moment? *Forget about Halley*, she thought. *You are Jack, a clever, confident young man. You are not intimidated by Lady Bracknell. There is no audience.*

She brought her hand down and nodded to Sister Jane.

"You can take a seat, Mr. Worthing." Sister Jane's throaty British-Indian accent set the tone.

Attempting to imitate a deep English accent, Halley became Jack. "Thank you, Lady Bracknell, I prefer standing."

Their banter continued. The others giggled at the appropriate times. Finally, Sister Jane's Lady Bracknell took a few steps away with her nose in the air and concluded with indignation, "Good morning, Mr. Worthing!"

No one spoke. Sister Jane started scribbling on her clipboard.

Halley sat down in the closest empty seat, grateful for the quiet. The audition had been both exhilarating and draining. She had become Jack and loved it.

After a few minutes of writing, Sister Jane looked at the class. "Would anyone else like to try out for the part?" Several students raised their hands. The auditions continued. The uncomfortable silence that followed each audition was broken only by the scratching of Sister Jane's pencil. After recording her last notes, she spoke to the entire class. "You all did very well. I'll let you know my decision in a few days."

Johanna walked partway to the gym with Halley. "I think your audition was the best."

"Thanks." She looked at Johanna, "I'm wondering if you could help me. When I was heading into physics, a girl said *'Laal Baal'* in a nasty tone as she passed me. Do you know what that means?"

"Yes, *Laal Baal* means red hair. I'm sorry they were mean." Johanna patted Halley's back. "I hope your tennis class goes well. See you at lunch."

Halley felt miserable and was relieved that none of the students were around when she found the locker room. The attendant assigned her a locker and showed her where to pick up a gym uniform and towel each day. She pulled her tennis shoes out of her school bag, set them on the bench, and started to change. From the next row of lockers, she heard several girls arrive.

One said, "Have you been to the Royal Palm this week to play tennis?"

"Yes."

"Did you see Padma?"

"No, she wasn't there."

"You should see the ugly burn she has on her cheek. It's awful."

"Sounds like a nasty accident." A locker door slammed.

"It doesn't look like an accident to me." The voices were moving away. "Kavita was furious when she heard that Padma was seen talking to her boyfriend, Radhesh. He's the gardener at the Royal Palm."

That was the last thing Halley heard. She wondered if Radhesh was the gardener she saw the other night. She finished tying her shoes and hurried into the hallway. Was the girl suggesting that Kavita had something to do with Padma's burn? Two girls exited through a side door. Once outside, Halley saw them join a group of girls under a grove of bushy trees that shaded the tennis courts. They were clustered around a handsome young man wearing a white sports visor and a whistle around his neck. *This must be Coach Sing*, she thought and stepped into the shade behind the others.

"Pair up for doubles. Use the first three courts," he said, pointing at a large cart filled with rackets. Then he noticed Halley. "Ah, I see our new student. While they rally, I'd like to hit a few balls with you. Okay?"

"Yes, sir!"

She took a racket and followed him. He was carrying a wire basket full of tennis balls. For the next half hour, she was all over the court. Each time he hit another ball to her, she had to work harder to knock it back. It was obvious that he was testing her. Perspiration rolled down her face and back. Finally, when she was beginning to think she couldn't get any hotter, he called for her to meet him at the net.

"That was good. How long have you played tennis?"

"I started lessons during the summer when I was five, sir."

"Well, we're done for today. Please pick up the balls. I'll take your racket."

Halley was relieved that the rest of the students were all gathered around the coach and weren't looking her way. Picking up the balls by herself gave her a chance to cool off and not have to face them.

By the time she finished, everyone was heading back to the locker room, and the coach was nowhere to be seen. Three girls dropped behind the others and waited for her. They looked familiar, but she couldn't remember where she'd seen them. The largest one spoke first.

"Hey, Red. You think you're so smart."

"Yes," one of the others chimed in.

"And," the first one went on, "you look stupid in that uniform."

Halley glanced quickly at them, looked down at the ground, and kept walking.

"And," the girl continued, laughing, "You're a sweaty mess."

Halley caught up with the other students at the door. The last one held it open for her and stepped between her and the annoying students. She was as tall as Halley.

Halley smiled at her. "Thank you."

"Looks like you've played tennis before," she said. "Are you really from America?"

"Yes. My father and I arrived in Bombay a few days ago. I'm Halley."

"It's nice to meet you. I'm Karuli."

When it was time for lunch, Halley grabbed her basket and breathed a sigh of relief when Karuli asked if they could sit together. They were soon joined by Johanna and several of her friends. One of them had been in their drama class.

Two of the three girls who had insulted her after tennis were in her choir class. She was relieved when they sat on the other side of the room. In English, she was assigned to a small group that included one of Johanna's friends from lunch.

The last bell rang at the end of math, and she headed toward the central hall to pick up her lunch basket. She thought about lunch with Karuli, Johanna, and her friends and smiled. What had she been afraid of?

She turned a corner. The next corridor was empty. Where did everyone go? She could hear the clump of her own shoes echo. It was very hot. She passed a door into another hallway. Was that where she should turn? Maybe it would take her outside. She pushed on the door. It was locked. A shiver shot through her. When she turned to retrace her steps, she saw several shadows bounce along the wall. A group of girls she didn't recognize came around the corner.

The one in front spoke. "Well, what do you know, it's Miss Know-it-all."

Halley froze.

They circled her, laughing, moving closer. "Think you're so smart."

She felt helpless and paralyzed by fear.

"Yuck! You stink." The girl was so close that Halley could smell her breath. Was she going to touch her?

She remembered the feather. When her finger brushed against it, the girls backed away, turned, and scattered quickly down the passage.

Wow, she thought. *What just happened?*

Worried that she might get lost again, Halley followed them at a distance until she saw the room where she left her basket. She was relieved to see that Johanna was there waiting for her.

"I just saw Maya and her gang speed past. Did you have a run-in with them?"

Halley smiled at Johanna and said, "Sort of."

8

A Helpless Prisoner

Kashif and Sundara were waiting for them outside the main doors. "*Memsaab* Johanna, your father asked me to pick you up too. Sarin will get you later at the Royal Palm."

The girls smiled at each other and got into the back seat together. Sundara watched Halley roll down the window. "Hello," he said.

The girls laughed and chimed back, "Hello, Sundara."

Halley continued. "Thank you for your feather."

He sat calmly on Kashif's shoulder and replied, "Thank you."

Halley lifted her hand. She had a tremendous urge to run it down his brilliant, blue-back feathers.

"Kashif. Would Sundara let me touch him?"

When he said, "Yes," she reached up, placed her fingers on Sundara's head, and moved them slowly down his feathers. They were soft but sturdy, and they glistened. Sundara stirred under her touch, and she felt a cool strength travel through her. He turned and looked at her. "Thank you," he repeated.

When they reached the club, Kashif took her school bag and basket. "Would the *Memsaab*s be taking tea on the veranda?"

"That's a great idea, Kashif, thank you," Halley replied. "Could you arrange it for us?"

"Certainly."

They stepped into the cool shade just as the club manager emerged through the front doors. "Good afternoon, Miss Pederson. Please stop at the desk. Someone left a message for you."

Who could that be? Johanna followed her into the lobby. Kashif waited inside the door while the desk clerk gave Halley a small envelope. She pulled out the note.

Halley, please come to my office. It's urgent. Thanks, Padma.

Halley showed the note to Johanna and turned to Kashif. "Please hold off on tea. We need to go see the tennis instructor."

A minute or two later, Padma jumped up when they entered. "Thank you so much for coming right away," she said, motioning toward a handsome young man seated near the window. "This is Rabar Chowdhury, Ganika's husband." The man stood up.

From the troubled look on his face, Halley knew immediately that he hadn't found Ganika. "Oh dear," she said.

"You've guessed right," Padma said. "Rabar, tell them what happened."

They all sat down.

"I arrived at the Taj Mahal Palace Hotel yesterday afternoon. They booked me into the room you had. I listened for a while at the door between the rooms and watched their window from mine, but I didn't see or hear anyone. Eventually, I went back to the registration desk and asked if anyone was in that room. The clerk looked in the book and said that the room was available." Rabar's voice cracked. "The previous occupants had checked out that morning."

Halley jumped up. "Oh no. This is terrible." Rabar motioned for her to sit back down.

"The clerk noticed my alarm, so I told him I had hoped to meet with one of them. He said he'd been on duty when the three women emerged from the elevator. Two of them stood near the lobby doors. One was in *purdah*; she was shaking. The other woman held her by the elbow. The third one came over to the desk to pay for the room. He described her as extremely unpleasant with lots of glass bangles that clinked when she moved. After the women were gone, the doorman told the clerk that he had helped them into a cab. He was also concerned for the girl in *purdah*. The clerk suggested that I speak to that doorman." Rabar dropped his head into his shaking hands. "My precious Ganika . . ."

When he had collected himself, he stood up and continued. "I checked out of my room and went to speak to the doorman. He'd heard one of the women tell their taxi driver to take them to Victoria Station. I asked him if he remembered which driver took them. For a moment he stared blankly at the row of cabs in front of the hotel then pointed. 'That's the one,' he said and signaled for that cab to pull up to the door. I thanked him for his help and asked the driver to take me to Victoria Station. During the trip, he related what he remembered about the three women. He said they were planning to take the train to New Delhi. He was particularly concerned for the girl who was crying."

Rabar stopped and walked to the window and back. "The driver was sure she was there against her will, that it sounded like she was being disowned by her family and was in danger." Rabar crumpled into his chair. "When I got to the station, the train to New Delhi had already left."

Halley sensed the depth of Rabar's agony. There was no hope for Ganika. He had lost her all over again.

Johanna cleared her throat, and they all looked at her. "My mother's cousin's husband is in the police department in New Delhi. I could ask him to keep an eye out for Ganika. Is that a good idea?"

"Yes, thank you." Rabar said. He turned toward Padma.

Halley had been so focused on Rabar that she hadn't really looked at Padma. She noticed that the burn on her face was still blistered and red.

Padma must have read her expression. "This burn hurts both physically and emotionally. It was not an accident. But I'm afraid to talk about it before the situation is resolved."

"Of course. It just looks so painful."

"It is. After it happened, I went right to the hospital. Johanna, your mother was my doctor. She was very kind to me. I'm going back again on Friday."

They could hear talking in the outer office and then a knock on Padma's door. She stood. "That'll be my next student."

They followed her outside. As he walked, Rabar rubbed a hanky over his pinched-up forehead and blotted his eyes. He stopped when he reached his car and looked at the girls. "Thank you for your help," he said, his voice shaking. Then he climbed into the back seat of his chauffeured sedan and pulled away.

The girls walked back in silence. Halley's mind was churning with images of Ganika, Mrs. Kaliya's helpless prisoner. The situation was beyond awful, and there was nothing they could do.

When they reached the lobby, Kashif was still there. Sundara was on his shoulder, shifting his weight from one foot to the other. She remembered his feather and ran her finger over it. The great bird stopped moving and looked at her.

Once they were seated for tea on the veranda, Kashif bowed and left.

Halley said, "This is horrible. Poor Ganika. Poor Rabar."

"I know," Johanna groaned. "There are over a million people in New Delhi. Even if Uncle Andy can help, how would he ever find her? This is so awful."

Several waiters arrived with plates of tiny sandwiches and cakes. One of them poured tea into delicate china cups. Halley watched the vapor swirl up out of hers. "It seems so strange to be drinking steaming tea when we're so dreadfully hot already."

Johanna tried to smile. "It is pretty peculiar."

A cloud of gloom hung over them as they munched and tried to talk about school. When Sarin arrived, they agreed to meet for lunch the next day.

Kashif opened the door when Halley reached their bungalow. Sundara was on his stand in the front room. She stopped just inside.

"Kashif, could you sit down and talk with me, please?"

"Yes *Memsaab*."

"First, I want to thank you and Sundara for the feather. Every time I was troubled today and I touched it or thought about it, things were not as bad. But I'm confused. How is that possible?"

They were silent for a few moments. She looked into his face, full of compassionate gentleness, and felt safe.

"*Memsaab*, look at Sundara and tell me what you see."

"I see a magnificent, blue-and-gold parrot with a long tail. He's preening himself."

"Now, think his name."

When she thought, "Sundara," the parrot raised his head and looked at her.

Kashif continued. "Ever since I was first around him, he has surprised me many times. Remember when he warned me about the man who was going to throw himself in front of the car in Bombay?" Halley nodded. "This morning when we were waiting for you at the car, he plucked the feather and dropped it into my hand. When you asked what was wrong with him, I realized he knew you were worried and had plucked it for you."

Halley touched her belt above the pocket and thought about her encounter with Maya's gang in the hallway. Then her mind flitted to the other times she had touched or thought about the feather that day.

"I will always wear it," she vowed. Then she remembered that some of her clothes had no pockets.

Sundara squawked and flew through the kitchen to Kashif's room. A moment later, he returned with a tan-leather cord dangling from his beak. He landed with a flourish on the table in front of them and dropped it. In the middle of the cord was a little cloth pouch.

Kashif laughed. "Of course. Great idea." He opened it. "Let's see if the feather fits in here."

Halley pulled out the silky feather and Kashif delicately slipped it into the pouch. When he set it on the table, it lay perfectly flat. "Try it on around your neck."

There was a small knot on one end of the cord. Halley picked it up with both ends, held it around her neck, and fit the knot into the loop at the other end. When she tucked it under the front of her uniform, it wasn't visible.

"Thank you, Sundara," she said and lifted her hand as though to pet him. He strutted to her and put his head into her hand and whistled a few notes, sending a thrilling vibration through her fingers.

Halley was still laughing when her dad came through the door carrying his old leather bag. Kashif stood up.

Dr. Pederson removed his hat. "May I join you both?" He motioned for Kashif to sit back down. Sundara was still on the table and gave another whistle. They all laughed.

"So, Halley, how was your first day at St Anne's?"

"It was okay." She searched for something nice to say. "I auditioned for the part of Jack in *The Importance of Being Earnest.* The girl who had the part broke her leg. Sister Jane, the drama teacher, was great."

"Did you see our tour guide?" Dad's eyes twinkled.

"Yes. She made a face right before I began my audition. Then I remembered what our director at Chapman said when we were rehearsing for *Romeo and Juliet.* 'Empathize with your character. Become your character.' I imagined Jack, clever, confident, and forgot about that girl and the audience."

"Excellent."

"Tennis class was exhausting, especially in the heat."

"How did you do?"

"I survived."

He patted her hand. "That's my girl. Anything else to report?"

"I had lunch with Johanna, and she came back here with us after school. We had tea on the veranda."

"Sounds delightful. How about homework?"

"Mr. Rossi, my physics teacher, gave me the textbook and the assignment schedule. And guess what? He's a light-skinned Indian man with red hair. Isn't 'Rossi' Italian for red?"

Dad nodded.

"The English teacher put us into groups. We have to read "The Man Who Would Be King," a longish short story by Rudyard Kipling, write an essay about it, and discuss it in our group. Then we're supposed to present our ideas to the class. One of the characters refers to some Biblical passages. In our essay, we're supposed to write about their significance. Have you read it?"

"Yes, it's an interesting story. When are you expected to make the presentation?"

"In three weeks."

Halley watched Dad pick up his bag. His expression had changed. Something was troubling him. He pulled out a few papers. The top paper was a map. He spread it out on the table, and Sundara hopped onto Kashif's shoulder.

"Gustaf came to my office this morning," Dad said. "He'd just received a call from a Dr. George Fischer, who told him there's a wounded spotted panther terrorizing villages in the jungle near Jaipur, south of New Delhi. It's already killed three people and a dozen animals. Dr. Fischer said the government is forming a team of experienced marksmen to stop it and asked Gustaf to join him and bring another hunter. He's been called to help in the past. You might remember that he helped me get the permits I needed to bring my hunting rifle and my handgun with me into India. He knows I can shoot and asked me to go with them. Kashif would go too. It would mean taking the early train tomorrow morning, but I couldn't leave you here without us."

Halley glanced at Kashif and realized that he'd already been told. She thought about school, about missing the rest of the week and maybe missing out on the part of Jack, if she wasn't there. Why was it always about what *Dad* wanted? What *he* needed? Was Dad going to wreck what little she'd been able to start for herself? She looked at her father. His bright, green eyes sparkled with both excitement and worry. He wouldn't go if she didn't. She felt manipulated, miserable. A tear slipped into her eye. She blinked it back. He waited.

She thought about the times he took her to the firing range, how he hit the bullseye over and over again, how prepared he was when he went to Africa on safari. She remembered how heavy the gun had been when she fired it at the target, how the force threw her back and almost knocked her over.

They'd asked for his help. The people in the villages needed him.

Sundara was moving around on Kashif's shoulder. He kept looking at her, then away. She felt the cloth pouch on her chest and took a deep breath.

"All right. I'll go."

9

Jungle Calls

When Kashif brought *chota hazri* at 5:30 a.m., Halley was already up, dressed for travel. Since she'd packed another dress, her jeans, hiking boots, and khaki shirt the night before, she had time to write a letter to Harin, her friend from the ocean liner. She took paper, pen, and her tea onto the balcony. It was still cool and the light from the window was enough for her to see the paper. The first birds were beginning to chirp. Pre-dawn light hovered behind the garden trees, and the gardenias poured their fragrance onto the breeze. She thought about Harin and closed her eyes. He was so funny. She pictured him singing "When You Wish upon a Star" at the talent show on the boat and smiled, remembering how his dark hair shone in the spotlight.

She wrote to him about Johanna, the audition for the play, and that they were taking the train to Jaipur to hunt for a wounded panther that was killing people and animals.

Halley finished addressing the envelope just as a bird landed on the rail in front of her. Above the yellow splash of feathers on its head, she saw the morning star peeking through the lacy silhouettes of the trees and drew in a breath. *Someday*, she thought, *I wish I'll see Harin again.* The little bird darted away. She whispered, "Dear God, please be with us." Just then, the first beam of sunlight burst over the garden.

She realized she needed to hurry and jumped up.

When Kashif and Sundara came for her bag, she was ready. Dad was right behind them. "Good morning, darling daughter." He was wearing his field clothes—high laced boots, khaki pants and shirt—and was holding a broad-brimmed, weather-beaten hat. He reminded her of the time they saw Groucho Marx sing and dance the African explorer song at the beginning of the movie *Animal Crackers*. Big game hunter! She giggled.

Gustaf Norlin and Sarin were already at the Poona station when their taxi dropped them off. Dr. Norlin shook Dad's hand, pushed his glasses up his nose, and smiled at Halley. "Thank you so much for coming," he said.

Again, he reminded her of blond Cary Grant, only this time as the big-game hunter in the movie *Bringing up Baby*.

Since the train would take almost thirty hours, Dr. Norlin had arranged for the Pedersons to have a sleeping compartment next to his. Kashif and Sarin would share their own, and one of them would guard their baggage every time they left their compartments.

By the time the train rumbled out of the station, they were on their way to the dining car. Halley was ravenous. The waiters brought coffee and fruit. She sipped on mango juice and watched the city streets slide by. Her thoughts drifted away from their conversation. She pictured her letter to Harin sitting on top of the outgoing mail at the reception desk and wondered how long it would take for it to reach New Delhi. And what about Ganika? What had happened to her?

Dr. Norlin was in mid-sentence. ". . . then we'll meet up with George Fischer at the Maharaja's hunting lodge. It's less than an hour past the Amber Fort. He's covered all the details. We'll stop by the police station in Jaipur so you can sign out your bullets before we head out. We should get to the compound by teatime."

The waiters arrived with cereal, hot biscuits, and guava jam. Halley reached for a biscuit. "Why does Dad need to get his bullets at the Jaipur police station?"

Dr. Norlin said, "India gives us permits for the guns we bring into the country. They understand that we need them to collect animals that are carrying viruses for our research. Whenever there is an animal that is a danger to people, like the wounded panther, the government asks hunters with guns to help. But to keep track of gun use, they hold our ammunition at the police stations and only let us remove a certain number of rounds at a time. I picked up my bullets in Poona yesterday. Last night the police station was closed when your father called about joining the hunting team, and our train left before they opened. So this morning, George Fischer made arrangements with the Jaipur police for your father to sign out some of his ammunition."

Between meals, Halley read the Kipling story for her English class. When they returned from dinner, she was happy to see that the porter had already pulled their beds out of the walls and made them up with fresh sheets and covers. She got ready for bed and climbed into hers. Dad was standing in the middle of the compartment.

"Do you think you'll be able to sleep tonight?" he asked.

"I think so, Dad. What about you?"

He was looking out the window into the dark night. She could see from the tightness around his mouth that he was struggling. She wanted to ask if he was thinking about Mom, but she didn't think that was her business.

He ran his fingers through his hair. "I hope so," he said. "We'll need all the rest we can get. We may not be able to get much sleep tomorrow night in the jungle, and the next morning we'll set out early with the Indian hunters, known as the *shikari*. They'll know where the panther was last seen and how to draw him out."

She knew that his African safari experience had not been rugged or scary. They slept in elevated, luxury tents and ate their meals on china dishes with white table linens. They killed big game from platforms or from the jeep. The closest they got to the wild animals was when the monkeys found them eating dinner in the outdoor dining area. Like enormous bugs, they surrounded the hunters, picking at their hair and at the food on their plates. Dad hadn't been afraid then. But would the idea of hunting for a crazy, wounded panther interfere with his sleep?

He'd shown her a picture of a large, golden panther with shining black rose-shaped spots and said it was also called the Indian leopard.

Should *she* be afraid? She'd be going into the jungle with him. Would she be in danger? A snarling panther circling her rushed into her thoughts. His menacing eyes glinted. She shivered and touched the little pouch with Sundara's feather. The drooling panther disappeared, replaced by the gentle rocking of the train and the rhythmic clickety-clack of the steel wheels against the rails.

Halley didn't know how long she'd slept when she felt the train stop. She peeked around the curtain at a dimly lit station platform and could see the silhouettes of several men and a few women in *sari*s. They were boarding one of the cars behind them. Where was Ganika right now? Was she awake? Within a few minutes, they were moving again. An almost full moon revealed sparse nearby trees and distant hills. She closed her eyes.

After lunch the next day, they reached the outskirts of Jaipur, and Kashif arrived to help with the bags. Halley smiled when she saw Sundara. Her father had just finished briefing Kashif on the schedule when they heard Dr. Norlin and Sarin in the corridor.

George Fischer's driver met them on the platform next to their railcar and helped Kashif and Sarin load everything into an old jeep wagon. Halley got in back between her dad and Kashif, and they rumbled away, stopping briefly at the police station to pick up the ammunition before heading north.

Halley loved traveling with Dr. Norlin. He seemed to know something about almost everything. They hadn't gone very far when he pointed to a large building perched on the crest of the hills above Jaipur.

"That's Nahargarh Fort. It was built in the eighteenth century by the Maharaja for a retreat palace and to protect the city from attack. He became the ruler of this area at the age of eleven when his father died. 'Nahargarh' means 'tiger abode.'"

Halley imagined this maharaja and his court all dressed in ornate clothing, listening to music, watching exotic dancers, and eating large chunks of juicy mangos.

They passed two elephants ambling along with a driver sitting on top of each of the animals' heads. Dr. Norlin explained that the platforms on their backs were called *howdahs* and that the large pile of cloth bags on each of them was probably stuffed with vegetables and bananas. The elephants reminded her of the ones they used to visit at the Bronx Zoo in New York City.

A large lake loomed ahead. For a moment, Halley thought she was seeing things. It looked like there was a palace or something in the middle of the lake. When they got closer, Dad pointed at it. "Wow. Is that the Jal Mahal?"

Now she could plainly see a beautiful, orange palace with towers and arching doorways. It had a garden with trees on the top and was surrounded by water.

"Yes," said Dr. Norlin.

They slowed down and crawled past a horse that was pulling a flat wagon with a dozen seated men, legs dangling over the edge. Directly beyond the wagon was a decorated gate that opened into a garden filled with palms and other trees. Halley noticed a black and white bird hovering in one spot above the wall, like a hummingbird, only larger. His long, black bill stuck out in front of him.

Dr. Norlin saw it too. "Look! There's a Pied Kingfisher. I've only seen them over by the coast." He pointed over the wall. "This garden palace was built by the same maharaja who built the Nahargarh Fort." A minute later, he pointed out the opposite windows of the car. "That citadel up there is the Amber Palace. Parts of it are over a thousand years old."

The rutted road took them on and on through struggling villages. Naked children watched them pass, and craggy hilltops towered over them in the brilliant sunlight.

When they rolled into the shade, Halley felt the jungle close in around them. Brightly colored birds flew across the road; monkeys dangled from branches, chattering at them. One swung down and almost landed on the jeep. Halley felt Dad flinch.

"Hello," Sundara said. Halley smiled.

They turned onto a narrower dirt road and pulled through a gate into a large compound. The driver stopped in front of an elegantly rustic lodge, stirring up a cloud of dust that almost overpowered the delicate aroma emanating from a cascade of white flowers on the veranda. There were numerous low buildings on either side. At the far end of the compound, three almost-naked men were washing a large elephant. One man had his long hair tied like a tail behind his neck.

Kashif was opening the rear compartment of the jeep when Halley noticed two men walking toward them from the lodge. Dr. Norlin introduced them to the tall, burly one. "Karl, this is Dr. George Fischer, our host and director of the chemical laboratory in New Delhi."

George Fischer greeted them warmly in a thick German accent. His laughing eyes matched his close-cropped gray hair.

Dr. Norlin waved to the man behind him. "And this is his colleague, Dr. Jalil Rabek." Then he turned back. "Gentlemen, this is Dr. Karl Pederson and his daughter, Halley. They arrived here from America last weekend."

Halley noticed that unlike the khaki outfits on the other men, Jalil Rabek was wearing a long white shirt, white pants, and very dark glasses.

Soon they were seated in the shade of the veranda, munching on small sandwiches and sipping tea. Kashif and Sarin had disappeared inside with the baggage. The men agreed that they would set out early in the morning with the *shikari* hunters. Halley learned a group of men called beaters would whack sticks together to move the panther toward them. She kept glancing at Dad. He seemed mesmerized, especially by Jalil Rabek, who had removed his dark glasses and periodically interjected hunting stories in his deep, Indian-British accent.

"Once, Gustaf and I hunted a rogue panther in Dehu District. It turned out to be a nursing female. Hey," he looked at Dr. Norlin, "do you still have her cub that the *shikari* brought to you?"

"Ah, yes." Gustaf Norlin smiled and looked at Halley and her dad. "That cub had been injured when the dogs carried all the cubs out of the panther's lair by the scruffs of their necks. Johanna named her Maria, after my wife." Everyone laughed.

After tea, George Fischer guided them through the lodge. Their private quarters circled a cavernous front room. Mounted over a huge, stone fireplace was the head of a snarling tiger. On the other side of the room stretched a long wooden table with high-backed chairs, surrounded by the heads of other animals along the walls. Kashif and Sundara and joined them.

"This is your room, *Memsaab*," Kashif said, pointing to the door behind him. "Your father has the one next to yours. You'll have several hours before dinner."

Voluminous yards of white mosquito netting were suspended from a wooden frame that circled her bed. She opened her bag, pulled out her boots, arranged her shirt and jeans for the morning, and sat down at the dressing table.

The gentle fragrance of the flowers on the veranda drifted in through the windows. She looked out. The sun had dropped down behind the trees and the craggy cliffs above them. The light was beginning to fade, and the compound gate was closed. Several men were seated around a table across from the lodge, smoking. She wondered if they were the men she'd seen washing the elephant. One of them had long dark hair. A flock of small birds gathered in the trees above the wall. She laughed at herself, remembering the image she had of what their primitive jungle camp would be like. Now, here she was in a Maharaja's elegant hunting lodge.

Kashif and the other bearers served dinner at the long table in the main room. George Fischer was seated at the end, with Halley on his right. Dad was next to her.

"How do you like your room?" she asked him.

He laughed. "I really didn't expect the accommodations in the jungle to be quite so ample."

10

Hunted

The jeeps were all packed when the *shikari* arrived after breakfast. Halley sat in the back between Kashif and Dad, while Sundara stayed at the lodge. They headed up the dirt road, farther into the jungle. The beaters and their dogs were already at the clearing when they arrived. George Fischer went over the plan again, and Jalil Rabek translated for the *shikari* guides. The *shikari* gave the instructions to the beaters and they left. The hunters loaded their guns and waited. The silence was electric.

Halley had been instructed to stay behind the hunters and move into the jeep if she felt she was in danger. *Ha,* she thought, *I already feel the danger. Maybe I should just get in now.* Instead, she moved near Kashif, who was holding her dad's ammunition. They were all gathered at the bottom of an open incline, with the vehicles behind them. For what seemed like an hour, all she could hear was the chatter of the birds. She watched a small flock of sandy-colored pigeons searching through the grass nearby. In the distance, she could see a large black bird circling above the craggy cliffs and the high stone walls of an old fortress or temple.

Suddenly the sound came, a hollow, wooden whacking. "That's the beaters," Kashif whispered.

At first it seemed like the beat was circling them. Halley realized that they were at the far end of a circle, and the clatter was closing in toward them. Animals burst out of the woods into the open area at the top of the incline before rapidly scattering in all directions. An antelope swerved back and forth down the hillside toward them and bolted away. It seemed like the beaters were almost at the top of the clearing.

Then, with golden fur glistening between angry black spots, the panther stepped magnificently into the glaring sunlight at the top of the hill. The men were ready, rifles poised, all aiming at him. The great cat hesitated, took a few skulking steps away from the beaters, then, lunging ahead, sprinted straight down the slope toward them. Halley heard explosions from two of the guns and watched the snarling beast continue hurtling on. Another crack! The beast roared. He was almost on top of them. Halley froze, terrified. The panther would land on her in less than a second. She felt the blast of her father's gun next to her. The deadly panther flipped over and landed on his feet right in front of her. His eyes blazed and his legs crouched under him, ready to spring again.

Instead, he tipped to the side and collapsed in a heap.

Everyone had been holding their breath. Their collective exhalation was followed immediately by jubilant shouts. The *shikari* appeared and joined the circle around the lifeless panther. It stared blankly at their feet. Everyone converged on her dad, slapping his back, laughing, and hollering.

Still holding his rifle, Dad looked around at them, smiling like a young boy after a home run. A wave of joy mingled with receding terror swept up Halley's chest and into her throat. She blinked back tears and threw her arms around him.

"Hey," Dr. Norlin said, "It's a female."

Sarin produced a camera. Without moving the panther, they gathered around it for pictures. The men stood in back, leaning on their rifles. The *shikari* and the beaters held the dogs. Halley knelt and touched the panther's regal head. It was warm and soft. She shuddered, then ran her fingers over it, petting. The wild, raw power had vanished in an instant. "She's so beautiful." Her gaze shifted to its enormous teeth, and she remembered the terrified villagers.

On the way back in the jeep, Dr. Norlin said, "Karl, yours was the kill shot. You can keep the hide. There's a good taxidermist in New Delhi. He makes great lined rugs with the skins. For just a little bit more, he could mount the head with glass eyes."

Halley's dad patted her hand. She leaned her head on his shoulder, thought about her letter to Harin, and giggled.

I'll get to New Delhi before my letter.

During lunch they accepted George Fischer's invitation to stay with him in New Delhi.

"If we leave soon, we should be able to get to my house before dinner," he said. "My wife, Geeta, will be so excited to meet you."

In less than an hour, their jeeps rolled through the gate. Just outside the compound, they passed several men standing beside a jeep, engrossed in a heated argument. The drivers maneuvered around them and retraced their route back through the jungle toward the main road.

"Say, Gustaf," said Dad, "these female panthers usually have a mate. I bet there'll be an angry male out there in this jungle tonight, wouldn't you think?"

"Yes, I wouldn't want to be out there after dark. That's for sure."

Halley looked down at the strand of white flowers she had picked from the veranda, held them beneath her nose, and breathed in their exotic aroma. What was Harin like when he was at home? She imagined surprising him. He would meet her at the door, maybe even give her a big hug. His black hair would fall into his brown eyes. He would laugh. "How wonderful," he would exclaim. She closed her eyes and continued to think about him, his voice, and his silly jokes. She drifted off.

Harin invites her to stay for lunch, shows her his room, and plays a recording. They dance and laugh.

Halley was groggy when she woke up. Their driver had stopped on the side of the road a little way behind the other jeep. The sun was dropping behind a hill.

"Where are we?" she asked, rubbing her eyes.

"Looks like their radiator overheated," replied Dad.

Steam was gushing from George Fischer's jeep. All the men got out and walked into the swirling cloud. She heard one of them say, "We'll have to wait until their engine cools off."

Halley started to doze off again.

The door opened. *Wow, that was quick*, she thought. Then she felt a hand over her mouth. Several men were there. One grabbed her legs, and the other two hauled her out. Halley was now completely awake, her heart pounding. Who were these men? Where were they taking her? There was another jeep idling next to theirs. She struggled, but they were too strong. Within a few moments they had surrounded her in the back seat and were crunching out onto the road. She felt the hand on her mouth release.

"Dad!" she screamed. The man on the other side slammed her in the face, and she crumpled back onto the seat. Hot pain shot through her head.

I can't faint, she thought, and panted. *Need oxygen*. Through a blur of gushing tears, she tried to focus on the driver. He looked familiar. Where had she seen him before? The men were too close—the foul smell of their bodies, the stale cigarette odor. So close. Was she going to throw up? They were yelling at each other. She didn't understand what they were saying.

Have to look out the window, she thought. *Have to see where we're going*.

The jeep turned left onto a side road. They were entering the jungle again. The men next to her were still yelling.

The driver turned around. Everything became quiet for a moment. She started to look down, but before she did, she noticed his hair, tied at the back of his neck. Her scalp prickled. He was the man she had seen washing the elephant in the compound. They must have followed their jeeps. But why?

His angry voice rambled on. At the end of his tirade, she distinctly heard him say, "*Memsaab* Kaliya" and "*laal baal*."

What? Panic pierced her. How could they possibly know Mrs. Kaliya, that horrible woman? Why would they be talking about red hair?

When he stopped yelling, both her guards reached up and fingered her curls. A shiver raced down her spine. "Stop that!" she hollered and pushed at their hands.

Their fists came back hard against her head. They were yelling again. She wiped away tears of pain and anger. Did they kidnap her because she had red hair? Had Mrs. Kaliya told them about her? Why would Mrs. Kaliya have anything to do with them?

She remembered looking through the hotel window at Mrs. Kaliya when she was yelling at Ganika. At the time, she assumed Mrs. Kaliya was from Ganika's family. But maybe it was more sinister than that. Halley trembled. Had Mrs. Kaliya already been in the process of purchasing Ganika?

The full weight of her own situation suddenly dawned on her. The dreaded question surfaced: Were they kidnapping her to sell her? She covered her face with her hands. Her heart paused, her skin twitched, her lungs grabbed several panting breaths, and a torrent of tears washed through her fingers.

The jeep stopped next to the ruins of an old temple. In the fading light, she could see long vines circling up the crumbling pillars. A huge elephant was tied to a stone tiger. No one else was around. The driver yelled at the other men, took a large flashlight from the jeep, and turned it on. In his other hand he had a long stick with a sharp point at the end. One of the other men brought over a ladder and leaned it against the elephant. The driver climbed up and sat behind the elephant's head. The others pulled Halley by both wrists to the ladder. *I can't let them take me,* she thought, and pulled backward, trying to anchor her feet in the dirt. One of them slapped her hard on the back of her legs until she started to climb. The animal let out a rumbling, purring sound.

She crawled onto a woven jute mat tied to the top of the elephant's back. Hard twists of fiber stuck out, scratching her palms. She dug her fingers through the loops in the matting to keep from falling and winced. Once her guards climbed up and sat in front of her, the driver prodded the elephant with the stick, the ladder fell away, and they lumbered onto the road. Except for the flashlight pointing ahead and the moon hovering just out of sight, it was completely dark.

Dread slid in. Her scalp prickled. Where were they taking her? Why were they on an elephant? She looked frantically from side to side. She could see the silhouettes of the two men in front of her. They were still angry and loudly hissed at each other, but they were not paying any attention to her. She looked down into the black pit below. They must be at least ten feet off the ground. What could she do? How could she save herself? Panting short inhales, she felt panic seethed up inside, ready to overwhelm her.

Sundara's feather! She rested her hand above it and decided that no matter where the men were taking her, staying with them was more dangerous than the jungle. She grabbed the edges of the mat, lowered herself into the darkness, and dropped into the void, landing silently on the soft loam of the forest floor. She crouched there taking short breaths and watched the elephant plod away. How long would it take for them to realize she had disappeared?

The sharp hoot of an owl startled her. She frantically glanced around. The full moon was beginning to peek through the lacy trees. It cast eerie shadows all around her, but she could see the narrow road. Should she retrace their tracks? The men would undoubtedly come back this way when they realized she was gone. She pictured the driver trying to turn the enormous elephant around on the narrow road and almost smiled. Another owl hooted. In between the moonlit shadows around her, she saw the entrance to a footpath, took a gulping swallow, put her hand over the feather pouch, and stepped into the woods.

After walking for a while, the path split. *Dear God*, she thought, *which way should I go?* She heard a rustle in the grass to her left. Could it be a snake? When another owl hooted over the other path, she followed it instead, walking quickly. Animal eyes reflecting the moonlight watched her from every side. The trail was climbing. When it finally leveled out, she sat down on a rock to catch her breath.

Arching over the path in front of her was the shape of a doorway without a door or walls, just trees on either side. A doorway in the woods? How odd. She took a closer look. On a small ledge attached to one side of the frame sat a little statue. Carved letters ran down both sides of the doorway. Was this the entrance to a holy place? When she looked closer at the statue, she felt a sense of deep peace. A cool breeze circled her, inviting her to enter.

The path continued on the other side almost as though the doorway in the woods hadn't even been there. A few yards past it, the path ended abruptly. There was nothing in its place, only darkness. A cliff? She lay down on her stomach, crawled forward, and peered into the black chasm. With the help of the moonlight, she saw little ledges jutting from the rock wall below her. Were they steps? The wall disappeared into the blackness a few feet below. She knelt on the edge, reached down with one foot until she felt the first step, then, hanging on to the top with her fingertips she groped for the next one. Moments later she was standing on a narrow rock landing. Off to one side was the outline of a hut. Abandoned? Near it a glimmer of water slid by in the moonlight. Pain from her cheeks and head and total exhaustion were creeping in. She could barely keep her eyes open. Feeling along the ledge toward the other end of the rock wall and hidden in the dark, she found a patch of grass and lay down.

11

The Teacher

Halley was startled awake by the sound of shuffling feet. It was still dark. The moon was very low. What was left of the light was diffused by the trees. She held her breath and watched several furtive figures climb down the rock wall and move quietly away from her. They passed the hut and disappeared. She was sweating and shaking. They had no lights. How had they tracked her? She had to get farther away, but where?

The moon was setting. Billions of stars twinkled from the dark dome above her. She sensed movement below her and looked down. In the first glow of dawn, she could see that she was perched inches above water that was moving by like the blackest obsidian.

Suddenly, a deep, hollow sound rolled toward her. She pulled her knees to her chest and slid closer to the rock, barely breathing. The sound was so low it had no bottom. What was that? She shivered. To get away she would need to climb back up the rock. But what was making the sound? She felt drawn to it and got to her feet.

Crouching low, she crept toward the hut she'd spotted last night. But the sound was coming from beyond it. She stepped onto a narrow wooden pier that jutted out over the water. In the dim light, she could see another hut and inched toward it. The boardwalk turned and continued up the river, toward the sound.

She passed another dark hut. Dawn was hovering just below the horizon, and fingers of mist danced across the water toward her. She squatted on the walkway and watched the red and orange beams of light shoot up into the sky and over the river, backlighting the silhouettes of a small gathering of people seated on a floating platform just a few yards ahead of her. They were facing the sunrise. The deep sound was coming from them. They were repeating one low note—maybe one word—over and over. The moment the sun crested the horizon, the sound abruptly stopped, and the vibration echoed out into the silence. Halley sat down right where she was and crossed her legs. What were they doing?

The early light sparkled on the water. Several tiny, singing birds darted between nearby branches. Directly below the platform, a large, oval turtle slid into the darkness with a small splash. A loving energy was coming from the silent figures, and Halley felt a swelling quiver in her heart.

A long-legged gray bird was standing in the water near the opposite shore. It reminded her of the blue herons she saw when she went fishing with her dad. Dad! Where was he now? Did he hear her scream for him? She imagined how frantic he must be. How would she reach him?

After what seemed like an hour, she heard a delicate bell ring three times. When the last note stopped vibrating, the figures stood, brought their hands together, and bowed straight ahead. Then they turned and began walking single file, away from the platform and directly toward her. Halley quickly crawled onto the little bridge that led to the hut right beside her. They walked on by. When she was alone again, she got up and continued onto the platform. Only then did she notice a small man seated on the planks facing her. In the early light she could see his shoulder-length hair, thin gray beard, and balding forehead.

"Come here, child," he said in English, pointing to a cushion in front of him. He smiled gently. She bowed her head, walked slowly toward him, and sat down. She felt safe.

"Do you have a question?" he asked.

Halley sat quietly for a few moments. The first question that came to her was "Who are you?" The second was "What was that sound they were making?" But finally, she asked, "Can you help me find my father?"

"Where did you lose him?" When he spoke, the wrinkles on his face melted into a kindly smile.

"Yesterday. We had been following our friend's jeep to New Delhi when it overheated. My father went with the other men to fix it. While they were gone some, bad men dragged me out of our jeep and into theirs."

"How did you lose the bad men?"

Halley told him that although she didn't understand what the men were saying, she heard one of them say *Memsaab* Kaliya's name. She told him about meeting her on the ship, about watching her yell at Ganika through the curtain, about the moment in the jeep when Halley realized the men had either kidnapped her for ransom or were planning to sell her, and the moment that her fear gave her the courage to jump off the elephant when the men were distracted by their fighting. She described finding the path and following it in the moonlight to the rock.

When she stopped talking, she saw tears glisten in his eyes. "Yes," he said, "I will help you find your father. But first you must wait. The car will come back tomorrow morning with supplies. Until then you will be safe here. This is my *ashram,* and no one can harm you." He went on to explain that the other people were his students. Most of them lived in New Delhi. "They are here for the weekend to meditate." He stood up, crossed his arms, and slipped his hands into the sleeves of his thin robe. "Now it is time to eat."

Halley stayed right behind him. Each of his steps was slow and deliberate. She tried to walk like he did and almost fell off the walkway. She followed him into the hut near the rock. Most of the students were seated on the floor next to a long low table. Several others were serving them cups of tea and bowls of rice, *chapattis,* and vegetables. No one was talking. All the women had scarves covering their hair.

The little man sat down and motioned for Halley to sit beside him. One of the women moved over next to her on the other side. After they finished eating, the students left, and Halley was introduced to the woman, Sully. She spoke English and would be her guide. When Halley turned to thank the teacher, he was gone.

While Sully wrapped Halley's hair in a wide band of cloth, she said that everyone would be gathering in a few minutes at the boathouse. They would meditate until *tiffin*.

"How do you meditate?" Halley asked.

"When we meditate, we practice being in the present moment as much as possible. *Babaji* is our teacher. Until he gives you your own word to use, choose a short word of your own such as love, peace, or God. When you are meditating and you realize that your mind has wandered, notice your word and sink back into the silence with it. Don't strain."

"Do you meditate with your eyes open or closed?"

"*Babaji* encourages us to close our eyes to avoid visual distractions. Our thoughts are distracting enough. When we come to the *ashram* for a retreat, we try to be as aware as possible, even when we're eating, walking, or doing yoga. We don't talk unless *Babaji* asks us a question. Every evening he gives us a *dharma* talk."

"What's a *dharma* talk?" Halley was beginning to feel overwhelmed. Was she going to have to sit quietly with everyone until lunch? That seemed impossible.

Just outside the hut, she saw a man on the walkway hold up a short rope. From it dangled an ornate brass bar that curled up on the ends. When he struck one of the ends with a wooden stick, it sent a low sound vibrating out over the water.

"You will understand what a *dharma* talk is when you hear *Babaji* speak tonight."

Sully put her finger to her lips, and they fell into line behind the students. The boathouse was the large hut at the turn of the walkway. When the students entered, they sat down on cushions set up in rows facing two large doors that opened out over the river. Small, colorful flags attached to a cord fluttered above a low altar. Candles and incense were burning. *Babaji* was seated on a cushion next to it, facing the students. His eyes were closed.

The rest of the day went on forever. They sat. They walked. They ate. After dinner, *Babaji* talked about selfless love; love that doesn't ask for anything in return. Halley thought that this *dharma* talk sounded like a sermon she heard at St. Bart's last spring about the Good Samaritan, a man who stopped to help someone who had been beaten, robbed, and left to die by the side of the road. Someone he didn't even know. She wondered about *Babaji*. He was going to help her even though he didn't know her. That seemed like selfless love to her.

Babaji stopped speaking and closed his eyes. Halley did too.

In the silence that followed, Halley remembered a conversation she had with a woman at her mother's funeral. The woman told her that she was walking to lunch with Halley's mom after the museum board meeting when the cab sped around the corner. It was heading right for both of them. Without hesitating, Mom shoved the woman onto the sidewalk just before the cab crashed into her.

"If she hadn't pushed me, I would have been hit too," the woman said. "She saved my life."

Halley's thoughts flitted to some of the times she saw her mother help someone else; a man who needed directions, a lady who dropped her groceries, the child who fell in the river, their apartment building neighbor when he was sick.

The bell rang, jolting her back to the present. She opened her eyes just as a large, white bird flew past the boathouse in the fading light.

Halley followed Sully to the women's quarters, a low, flat room in the woods. It overlooked the river near the top of the rock wall. She had walked the same path last night within a few feet of the women's building and hadn't seen it. Three women smiled when they entered and silently brought Halley a bedcover and pillow. Sully unwrapped the cloth on Halley's head and gently brushed her hair, sending a shimmer down through her head and into her heart. Once they were all in bed, Sully extinguished the lantern.

Through the screen window next to her cot, Halley watched the moonlight on the river and thought about her dad. He must be so worried; two nights without a word from her. She pictured him hovering near George Fischer's telephone, hoping for news, and tears slid onto her pillow. Dr. Norlin would have alerted the police. Maybe they reached the policeman Johanna mentioned, the one who was married to her mom's cousin.

It was still dark when Sully nudged her awake and helped her cover her hair again. There was just enough light from the moon for them to climb down the rock and make their way along the walkway to the platform without falling in the water.

She sat down on a cushion next to Sully and waited. *Babaji* sang the deep note, alone at first, then the note sank deeper. It surrounded her, filled her, was coming from her. All the voices were swelling as one. The rising sun shot out a thin arc of light and the sound stopped, leaving the note suspended both in and around her.

After breakfast, Halley followed Sully and a group of students up the rock to the solitary gate in the woods. In the morning light she could see ornate carvings on both sides. The little statue had an elephant's head. Ganesha? They passed through it and took a path away from the river to a clearing. Within a few minutes, she heard a car crunching through the woods, and a brightly painted jeep van bounced around the bend and stopped in front of them just as *Babaji* arrived. Sully gave her a hug and began helping the students unload supplies from the jeep. Then she picked up a few bags from the pile and quietly disappeared back down the path with the others.

Babaji finished speaking with the driver, then turned to Halley and smiled. "I've instructed the driver to take you directly to Sergeant Patel at the main police station in New Delhi. He'll help you find your father." He put his palms together. "*Namaste*," he said and bowed toward her.

She remembered Johanna telling her that the word *Namaste* meant something like, "I bow to the divinity within you," and she instinctively bowed back. "*Namaste*," she replied, blinking back tears. "Thank you for saving my life," she whispered, letting his loving smile wash through her.

"You are an exceptional girl to have made it through the jungle to us and then to wait a whole day in silence, knowing that your father was worried about you. When you are alone and can meditate, or when you are troubled, remember the light that filled you with joy while you were here."

She climbed into the jeep and it lurched onto the road. Halley looked back and waved. The teacher waved back.

They rumbled on in silence. *Babaji*'s words continued to echo. "Remember the light." She pictured the sunbeam that burst through the open boathouse doors, showering the fluttering flags with light. She recalled the first light flareup over the hills and the sparkles on the water. Then she remembered Sully's words about meditation. "*Babaji* gives you your own word." She breathed a deep sigh and closed her eyes.

Light.

Joyful goosebumps spread over her arms. *Light. that's the word he has given me.* Light. A gentle wave washed through her.

The jeep slowed down suddenly, and Halley sat up. What was happening? Adrenaline gushed through her. She shuddered, remembering her father walking away from her toward George Fischer's steaming jeep, the horror of the painful ride into the jungle, the smell of the men, the shock that surged through her when they mentioned Mrs. Kaliya and when they touched her hair. She hugged herself. Hot tears shimmered in her eyes. She felt a bump under her wrist—the little cloth pouch with Sundara's feather. Kashif had said, "Touching it will calm you and send you strength." She touched it when she was on the elephant and then jumped off into the unknown. Had it given her the courage to jump, or had it just punctured a hole through her fear, providing a channel for her own bravery to gush out? Whatever it was, she realized that she needed all her strength and brains right now. Thanks to *Babaji*, she was heading for New Delhi.

The driver turned onto the main road, and they passed several men leading an ornately decorated cow toward a new house. The cow was covered with orange and gold shawls and garlands of flowers. One man was playing a long instrument that looked like an enlarged clarinet. Families with children were gathered into a crowd in front of the musicians.

Halley hoped that if anyone noticed her they saw the turban Sully had wrapped around her hair, instead of her face. Although she was obviously white skinned and tall, people such as Mrs. Kaliya and her goons might not recognize her with her hair covered. But she couldn't be too careful.

If Mrs. Kaliya did bring Ganika to New Delhi, Halley might be the only one who could find help for her. Her own kidnapping proved to her that even though she was an American, she wasn't safe. Poor Ganika.

She pictured Mrs. Kaliya. Besides her glass bangles and her *sari*, how would she describe her to the police? She had a nose ring, but unlike many of the women at the welcome parties, she had no mark on her forehead. In fact, her skin was very light. Her dark hair was long, but it was not the lush black of the Indian women. It was really dark brown. Actually, she looked more like her mom's friend, Carmen Lopez, in New York.

Halley's jaw dropped and she gasped. If Mrs. Kaliya was not from India, she must be married to an Indian man. She remembered Johanna saying, "Kaliya means poisonous snake in Hindi," and shuddered.

They appeared to be coming into the outskirts of a city. *Maybe this is New Delhi*, she thought. They passed a crowd of children standing amidst piles of garbage. In the next block, she saw a small boy sitting on the steps of an old building, holding a naked baby on his lap. They came into busier streets, passing colorful buses, cabs, carts, vendors with bananas and mangos, and crowds of pedestrians. They turned at a noisy intersection and approached a crowd of men who were listening to a man speaking from the platform of an open truck. A colorful sign was stretched out above him. "Vote for Daljit Singh." Other signs were everywhere; black and white or colorful, some in English, some not. A line of women in *saris* waited in front of a brick building. The sign above the man at the table on the landing said "Vote Here" in English and in several other languages. Everything seemed peaceful and organized.

They came to a small gathering of men in uniforms. Police? Her driver stopped the van in front of the building next to them, came around, and opened her door, signaling for her to follow him inside. He spoke to the officer at the counter, who jumped up and disappeared into the room next to him.

Her driver bowed to her. "*Namaste*," he said.

She bowed to him as he backed away. "*Namaste*," she replied. "Thank you." In less than a moment, he was gone.

The officer returned with a muscular, uniformed man who greeted her warmly with a lilting Indian-English accent. "I am Sergeant Patel. Your driver said that *Babaji* told him to bring you to me and asked me to help you find your father. Please come into my office."

She followed him through a dark wooden doorway. "Sergeant Patel" was written in large English letters on the glass. "Please sit down." He was pointing at a chair near his desk. "Would you like a Coke?"

"Yes, please."

He smiled at her, ordered the Coke, and sat down at the desk. "Now, how may I help you?"

"I lost my father on Friday when some men kidnapped me and took me into the jungle."

He held up his hand. "Do you have red hair?"

"Yes," she said. When she began to unwrap her turban, he picked up a paper from his desk. "Are you Halley Pederson?" he asked with genuine concern. She nodded, and he grabbed his phone. "Get Dr. Fischer!" he bellowed. "Tell him that Halley is here."

Relief swelled in her chest. *How did Babaji know to send me here? How did Dr. Fischer know to call him?* she wondered.

An officer came in with the Coke.

"Halley, you have had a lot of people frantically searching for you." The phone rang and he handed it to Halley. "It's your father."

"Daddy." She burst into tears.

"My baby!" She could hear his voice catch. "I've been so scared. We've been so worried. All the Norlins are here with me, even their son, Hans. They all arrived yesterday. None of us knew what to do." He took a breath. "Are you hurt?"

"I'm okay, Dad." She sniffed. "It's such a relief to hear your voice." Cheers were coming from behind him.

Sergeant Patel stood up and pointed to the phone.

"Dad, the officer wants to talk to you." She handed Sergeant Patel the phone.

"Dr. Pederson, we can get her there in ten minutes. Would that be all right?" He paused, listening. "Good. We're leaving now."

He led Halley quickly down the station steps to a waiting police car.

Sergeant Patel helped her into the back seat and handed her the Coke then walked around to the other side and got in next to her. She took a sip and the familiar taste bubbled into her. While they worked their way through the streets, he told her that he was married to Maria Norlin's cousin.

"Oh, wow, you're the officer Johanna told me about."

He said Gustaf Norlin had called him on Friday as soon as they could get to a phone. "They heard you yell, 'Dad!' I dispatched officers all over that area, hunting for you. But you had disappeared."

Halley settled back into her seat and took a deep breath. She pictured the sun rising over the river and the large, white bird gliding past the boathouse doors at dusk and felt her heart swelling with gratitude.

12

Searching

Everyone was on the veranda of Dr. Fischer's sprawling bungalow when Sergeant Patel pulled the car into Dr. Fischer's compound. Dad was already down the steps, racing toward the car. Halley jumped out, and his arms enveloped her.

"Dad, I was so scared!" Her tears flooded his shirt.

He kissed the top of her head. "My precious Halley Valley." He put his hands on her shoulders and stepped back to look at her, then hugged her again.

Halley looked around, drying her eyes on the back of her hand. Johanna moved in and hugged her. Maria Norlin stretched her arms around both of them and gently squeezed. Above the babble, Halley heard Sundara squawk, "Hello," followed by a peal of laughter from the others. He was with Kashif near the steps.

"Hello, Sundara." Halley noticed Kashif's expression of concern and relief. She stopped in front of them, pressed her hands together and bowed. "*Namaste.*"

Kashif bowed and replied, "*Namaste.*"

She reached up and stroked Sundara's lower back, recalling the moment when she was on the elephant. "Thank you," she whispered to them both and touched her shirt above the pouch.

Just then she noticed a handsome teenager coming down the steps, and she took a quick breath. Was this Johanna's brother? His blond curls circled his face like a halo. Her knees wanted to buckle under her. Johanna appeared beside her. "Halley, this is my brother, Hans. Dad called him on Friday and told him that you'd been kidnapped. He caught the first train to New Delhi."

"Hi." She smiled shyly. "Thank you."

He flashed a big smile. "Johanna told me about you. I've been wanting to meet you." His kind blue eyes twinkled.

She felt her dad's hand on her shoulder. Standing next to him was a slender, gray-haired lady in a pale green *sari*. Halley smiled when she noticed that on the delicate chain around her neck was a small gold cross.

"I'd like you to meet our hostess, Mrs. Geeta Fischer," Dad said. "George is at church. He was on the schedule to assist with communion and was already there before Sergeant Patel called. She left a message for him in the church office. He'll be so relieved. I don't think he's stopped praying for you since you disappeared."

Praying for me? Halley mused, glancing at her dad.

Mrs. Fischer must have noticed her quizzical expression. "Yes, Halley. We've all been praying for you."

When everyone was seated on the veranda with glasses of iced tea, Sergeant Patel asked Halley to tell them what had happened. He took out a notepad and pencil and leaned back. She looked around and noticed with relief that Kashif and Sundara were standing nearby. Everyone was silent. Beetles sang in the nearby trees.

Clearing her throat, she began. "I closed my eyes after I watched you guys walk toward Dr. Fischer's jeep. The door opened again, and I thought you were back, but several men jumped in. Before I realized what was happening, one of them covered my mouth with his hand. They lifted me up and dragged me to another jeep idling next to ours and shoved me into the back. Just as they were pulling away, the hand on my mouth dropped away. That's when I screamed for you, Dad." She could see tears hovering in Johanna's eyes and felt the warmth of her dad's hand on hers. "At one point the driver turned around to speak to the men, and I recognized him from the Maharaja's hunting compound."

When she described the violence, her dad gasped. She saw Johanna clench her fists when she heard that the man mentioned "*Memsaab Kaliya.*" There was a murmur among them when they learned that one of the men touched her hair when one of them said "red hair" in Hindi.

Finally, Halley stopped her story and said, "Johanna, I need to tell them about Ganika." Her friend nodded.

Halley relayed the story of Ganika and Rabar Chowdhury. She described her dread on the ship when she found herself outside one of the staterooms and overheard Mrs. Kaliya yelling at some men in Spanish. She recounted her escape from the elephant and how *Babaji* rescued her. When she finished, she saw Kashif bow his head.

Sergeant Patel was the first to break the silence. "You're a very lucky girl." He looked around at the others and continued. "During the past two years, many families in India have reported the disappearance of their daughters. You are the first one to be found alive." He glanced at his notes. "Halley, we'll need to get all the details you can remember about the men. You mentioned seeing the driver when you first arrived at the Maharaja's compound. It is possible that someone there may know who the men are. What else do you remember?"

"After they kidnapped me, they didn't go very far before they turned left into the jungle. They continued on that dirt road for maybe an hour. It was almost dark when they stopped at the ruins of an ancient temple. There was an elephant there tied to a stone tiger."

When she finished describing Mrs. Kaliya, Dad exclaimed, "Wow! Come to think of it, she did look like Carmen Lopez."

"What you have said is very helpful." Sergeant Patel pocketed the pad. "If you think of anything else, please call me at the station." He shook hands with her dad, thanked the Fischers, and drove away.

Dr. Maria Norlin turned to Halley. "Would you like to get cleaned up before lunch?"

Halley looked down at her jeans and boots and laughed. She had been wearing them for more than two days. "Is there time for a bath?"

Mrs. Fischer gave some instructions to a maid, and before long, Halley was soaking in a large tub, soothed by the aroma of jasmine bath salts. It was heavenly to shampoo her head and tilt it into the water. After rubbing her hair with a towel, she sat in front of the mirror. She thought about the loving kindness that permeated the women's quarters at *Babaji*'s *ashram* and Sully's gentle touch when she combed her hair. Then, dressed in her favorite black capris, a blue plaid shirt, and the socks that matched, Halley slipped into her loafers and found her way back downstairs.

Lunch was served in the solarium shaded by a few tall trees just outside the windows. A ceiling fan turned slowly above them. Halley was glad that Geeta Fischer seated her between Dad and Johanna with Hans across from her. Just the thought of engaging him in light chatter seemed impossible with the butterflies churning up her chest.

After a delicate dessert, Johanna led her to a screen porch on the side of the house. Hans was already there. Even glancing at him made her heart do flip-flops. "We can talk here," Johanna said. They settled into the white wicker chairs that looked out over a pond. "Hans thinks that Mrs. Kaliya may be staying in New Delhi. If Kashif were to help us, we could ask about her at all the fancy hotels."

Halley glanced at Hans and then at the lotus blossoms floating on the pond. She pictured Kashif leaving them in the car in front of each hotel while he spoke to the doorman. "Actually, that is a good idea. Rabar found out what happened to Ganika because he spoke to the clerk and the doorman at the Taj Mahal Palace in Bombay." She jumped up. "We have no time to lose. Let's go talk to Kashif."

They found him with Sarin and a few of the Fischers' servants in the back of the house.

"Kashif," Halley said. "Could you help us?" They went back to the screen porch and invited Kashif to sit with them at the table near the windows.

Hans spoke first. "We think we know how we might be able to track down Mrs. Kaliya." He described the plan and suggested that they leave right away. Halley said she'd talk to her dad, and Kashif went to get the car.

She found Johanna and Hans on the veranda. Kashif was standing near the car. "I told Dad about our plan. He agreed that they might be more willing to help if they were talking to Kashif." She patted the scarf tightly wrapped around her head. "He also suggested that I cover my hair."

After stopping at four luxurious hotels with no luck, they parked near the front of the fabulous Vivanta. Kashif stayed to talk to the doorman while the teens went inside for a minute to cool off. They found a cozy sitting area away from the entrance and collapsed into the large, overstuffed chairs.

"This is so frustrating," Johanna groaned.

Halley groaned too. "It's worse than searching for the proverbial needle in a haystack, and we still have another four big hotels to check."

Hans was staring at the list. "It looks like the next hotel is not too far from here."

Suddenly, Halley felt faint and shrank down in her chair. "Don't look now, but Mrs. Kaliya just stepped off the elevator. She's wearing a red *sari* and is talking to a large, bearded man in a white suit."

"They don't have any luggage, and they're heading outside," Hans reported. "They're not looking this way."

Halley jumped up. "We need to follow them." Johanna and Hans were right behind her.

At the hotel entrance, they stopped and looked through the doorway. Mrs. Kaliya and the man were getting into a black limousine. Kashif was already in the driver's seat of their car. When the limousine began to inch through the maze of cars in front of the hotel, they ran out. Halley climbed in first, then Johanna. Hans sat in front next to Kashif, and they pulled away.

"The doorman was just telling me that he didn't think she was at the Vivanta when she walked right past us to their car. Odd," Kashif said. "We can try to follow them, but it would not be smart to get too close."

"Yes, please follow them," Halley said. Kashif entered the traffic a few cars behind the limousine.

"I wonder if the man is Mr. Kaliya," Johanna mused. "He looked pretty ominous too."

"Definitely," Hans said. "I wouldn't ever want to run into him, especially on a dark night."

"Mrs. Kaliya wasn't afraid of him," Johanna said. "She's so creepy. I'm guessing there isn't a kind bone in her body."

Halley quivered and touched her shirt above the pouch. "I agree. She's very dangerous."

They rode on in silence. Every eye was on the limousine. After several turns, they passed a fenced-in park. Inside, they could see numerous ornate tombs.

"Kashif, do you know anything about that place?" Halley asked.

"Those are the *Lal Bangla* Mausoleums."

The limousine slowed to a stop in front of the gate to the mausoleums. At first it looked like they were going to drive in. Instead, they idled there while a fat, casually dressed European man with wild white hair shuffled across the street and got in. They immediately drove on.

"I wonder who that was." Hans said.

The street got a bit wider, and the limousine was moving a little faster. Kashif matched their speed. Halley didn't take her eyes off them. Where were they going? Her heart beat faster. Why did they pick up that man?

The vehicles moved into an industrial area. They approached several large factories separated by a row of houses. She could see the glint of water beyond them. A river? The limousine slowly came to a stop in front of a rundown little house. Kashif pulled over.

"We'll have to stay back here, or they'll notice us."

The factory closest to them was set back from the road. There were a few old trucks in the parking lot. Mrs. Kaliya and the others got out. They spoke briefly to several men standing near the door, then disappeared inside.

"What should we do?" Halley whispered. She wanted to follow them. "If only there was some way we could alert Sergeant Patel." She looked around. To one side of the factory, a handful of emaciated old men were squatting on the ground or sleeping in the shade of a few bleak hovels. Tattered blankets hung limply in the stagnant air. There were no women or children.

"Oh dear," Johanna whimpered, pointing toward the house.

The fat man emerged through the door, holding the arm of a terrified-looking young girl. Sinister delight oozed from his fleshy face. Mrs. Kaliya was right behind them. The guards remained at the door, but the man in the white suit didn't reappear.

"It's not Ganika," Halley gasped and reached toward the front seat. "Kashif, we must get word to Sergeant Patel. As soon as they leave, please drive as fast as you can to the police station and bring him here."

She looked at her friends. "I'm going to stay here and keep an eye on things. Will you stay with me?"

Johanna and Hans immediately agreed.

"*Memsaab*, I don't like leaving you here," Kashif said.

"We'll keep out of sight. They won't know we're here."

"As you wish, *Memsaab*."

Moments after the limousine drove away, Kashif turned the car around and left the teens standing beside the dusty road.

"That poor girl," Hans said. "What a ghastly man. What horrible people."

Halley felt a twinge from the bruise on her neck and clenched her fists. "Mrs. Kaliya has to be stopped." She glanced toward the factory near them and froze. One of the old men was hobbling toward them. Oh no, a beggar. Bad timing. What should they do?

When the man was close to them, he stopped. "Can I help you?" he asked in easily understandable English. His wrinkled face crinkled sadly. "You were following those people. I saw your reaction when they took the girl away. I have lived here for months now and have watched them drag terrified young girls into that house. When that woman brings a man with her in that black car, one of the girls leaves with them. There are always a few guards in front."

Halley looked him squarely in the eye, wondering if he might be paid by Mrs. Kaliya to watch out for suspicious onlookers. "How do we know we can trust you?" she asked, thinking that he looked much younger than he had when he first approached.

He scratched the back of his neck and glanced toward the road. When he looked back, his eyes met hers. "A few nights ago, I noticed a truck arrive. In the shadows of their flashlights, I could see them drag out a girl in *purdah* and take her to that door. I was disgusted. These people must be stopped."

Halley wondered if it was Ganika and turned to Johanna and Hans. "What do you think?

"Maybe we should wait for Kashif to return," said Hans.

"That makes good sense," added Johanna.

"Of course," the man said. "But you may want to move away from the road. That woman might return at any time, and she would see you here." He pointed toward the arched portico in front of the factory. "That area is shaded, and she wouldn't see you there. I'll take you." He started to limp toward the building.

Halley looked inquiringly at her friends. When they nodded, she said, "Okay," and followed him along the tall grass at the edge of the parking lot. Small clouds of dust circled their feet. The guards in front of the house were sitting on the steps, smoking. They didn't appear to see them. When they were passing the old men along the path, Halley noticed a strange odor coming from a low wall of round brown mud. It smelled slightly sweet, like dried grass mixed with dirt. Cow dung?

In a few minutes, they reached the cooler shadows next to the building. There were spider webs dangling around the main doors, and a jumble of weeds grew between the cracks below the arch. The factory was abandoned. The man waved for them to move farther into the gloom. There was only a wide driveway between them and the back of the house. Halley could hear the men talking but couldn't understand what they were saying. She watched Johanna creep a little closer to the edge of the shade. Did she understand them? Halley followed Hans until they were next to her.

Johanna whispered, "I can't understand every word they're saying, but I did hear one of them say 'Mrs. Kaliya' and 'back soon.'"

Halley turned around to see if the man had heard what the guards were saying, but he wasn't there.

13

Shivering Heat

A chill rippled through Halley. Her voice caught in her throat. No words slid out. She tapped her friends, pointed to where the man had been, and shuddered.

Only part of the compound was visible in the fading light. Through the gloom Halley could see what looked like the roofless ruins of a stone hut in the back of the house and signaled for Hans and Johanna to follow her. Before they got to the corner of the house, she looked toward the street. The man was in front, talking to the guards. Her scalp prickled. She was shaking. They reached the doorway to the hut and ducked inside, brushing away a tangle of spider webbing. From inside the entrance, Halley could see the man leading the guards toward the spot where they had just been. One of them had a flashlight. The beam of light swept from side to side over the dead shrubs.

"We can't stay here," she whispered. "Too obvious."

On the other side of the hut was another doorway. She inched toward it, crouching low over the rubble from the collapsed roof. Johanna and Hans followed her out into an abandoned garden.

Must find a place to hide, she thought, brushing away a mosquito. She touched her shirt above Sundara's feather and her thumping heart.

A faint glow emanated from under a porch on the far side of the house, giving them just enough light to see a dirt path. Each step stirred up thick dust that stuck to her sweaty legs. Had Kashif reached the police yet?

They ducked under the porch. A bare lightbulb dangled just inside the dirty window of a dilapidated cellar door. Cobwebs hung limply over the dust piled in front of it. Halley brushed them aside and peeked in. The room was completely empty. She turned the knob and the door swung into the room. Looking back at the others, she could see that the color had left Johanna's face. Hans had his hand under his sister's arm. There was no time to think about it. The muffled voices of the guards were near the stone hut. In a moment they would be coming around the house.

They slipped in, closed the door, and inched across the room to a low door in the wall near a cluttered stairway. Halley opened it, and they scrambled into the empty cramped chamber and closed the door just as they heard voices outside. From the fraction of light that filtered in through the crack in the door, Halley watched one of the guards push the outside door open, look around, and close it again, barking orders at the others.

"He said, 'They aren't here,'" Johanna whispered. "'They must have continued toward the street.' Then he shouted for the others to follow him. How can I be shivering this much when it's so hot in here?"

"Take a few deep breaths," Hans murmured.

"That's hard when it stinks in here," Halley whispered. "We'd better get out of here."

Johanna's voice was weaker. "But where can we go?"

Halley cracked the door and air rushed in. "Let's retrace our steps past the hut to the front of that abandoned factory. Maybe they won't think to go back there. From there we should be able to see what they're doing and watch for Kashif and the police."

She pushed the door open a little more and was about to crawl out when the door at the top of the stairs opened. They heard voices, and Johanna translated again. "They're yelling to get all the girls out to the truck. The police are coming."

Heavy feet started down the stairs. Halley quickly shut their cupboard door again. There was more yelling, and several men clumped into the cellar. One of them barked more orders. Keys clanked, and a lock clicked from across the room.

Another cupboard? The crack didn't point that way. All they could do was listen.

Girls whimpered; one yelped. Halley felt her whole body shake. Stumbling feet on the stairs. Crying.

"*Chup raho*!" one of the men hollered. "Shut up."

Halley tried to count the stumbling steps that were passing their hiding place. How many? Ten? A tear trickled down her cheek. Oh no. More shuffling feet struggled by them, heading up the stairs.

Dear God.

She felt Hans's arm around her shoulders. He was holding both of them.

The door at the top of the stairs slammed shut. More thumping pounded across the floor above them.

Hans murmured, "Let's get out of here."

They crawled out and shut the cupboard. Then they crept to the outside door, quietly opened it, and looked around. The moon, still almost full, was creeping up over the trees behind the house. It seemed like they'd be able to see their way past the hut to the entrance of the abandoned factory. *Here goes*, Halley thought. *We have no choice*.

When Hans closed the basement door behind them, she heard yelling and could almost see out to the street. Blocking a straight view were several stacks of large round cans under the porch. Were they paint cans? They moved silently the other way. Halley emerged from under the porch, looked around, and started toward the back yard. She could sense the others right behind her. Loud voices coming from the front of the house vanished when they rounded the corner. Icy blue shadows from the abandoned hut hid parts of the path until they reached the opposite corner of the house. She was sure there was no way they could cross between the buildings in the full moonlight without being spotted. Her heart dropped.

Hans touched her arm and pointed to the shadows along the side of the hut. It was also dark beneath the trees behind it.

It took only a few minutes for them to run all the way to the trees and back to the portico under the shadow of the factory wall. From there they could see the guards loading the girls into a large windowless truck. They seemed so small and helpless next to their jailors. Halley's hopes sank.

A man shouted, "*Jaldi.* Hurry." His voice reverberated toward them. Halley looked up the street, hoping to see Kashif or the police. Instead, she gulped. The lights of a large, dark car were moving quickly around the bend. Was it Mrs. Kaliya's limousine? She realized the headlights might flash toward them and signaled to the others. They all crouched behind the shrubbery.

There was more commotion near the truck. A girl cried out. The car stopped behind the truck and several people emerged, shouting. Halley could see the silhouette of a woman. Mrs. Kaliya? Her fear was overshadowed by anger, and prickles of adrenaline coursed through her. What kind of a woman was she? The woman's *sari* spilled out behind her, flowing into the light from the car. It was blood red.

How could they stop them? If they just had something, they could move in front of the truck to stop them or at least slow them down. But what? Was there anything in the hut? Maybe some of the boards from the collapsed roof?

The moon shadows had shifted and were falling over the clearing to the house. It looked like they could get back directly across the space to the house without being seen.

"We have to try to put something in front of the truck to slow them down," she whispered.

Hans said, "Did you see those cans by the basement door? Maybe we could stack them just tall enough between the headlights so the driver couldn't see them."

Johanna leaned closer. "That's a good idea. But I'm afraid he'd knock them over and just keep going."

Right now, we have her red handed, Halley thought. But if the police didn't get there in time, Mrs. Kaliya would get away and they'd never be able to prove that she had anything to do with this.

The voices in front were getting louder. Mrs. Kaliya screamed, "Find them."

Halley's hair bristled under her scarf. She could see several men rush along the clearing toward the back of the house, flashlights crisscrossing in front of them.

Hans tapped her arm and signaled for her to follow him away from the house. Ducking low behind the grass, they moved quickly toward the decrepit encampment they'd passed earlier. Hans and Johanna darted around the far side of the factory ahead of her. She was only a few steps behind them when the stench of human waste wafted toward her. She stifled a gag and covered her nose. Just before she reached the corner of the building, the beam of a flashlight caught her. A man shouted, "*Riken.* Stop!"

She turned away from the building toward the street and broke into a sprint. She was almost back to the place where they had last seen Kashif when she heard a man barreling down behind her. She kept running. When he was almost on top of her, she slowed to a stop, certain he was about to crash into her. The other men were right behind him.

Halley was on the verge of tears. One of the men grabbed her, yelling. Another put a hand under her arm. Her legs buckled beneath her, and they began dragging her down the road toward the truck. Her face felt red hot, prickles coursing through her. *I must be brave*, she thought. She had to protect Hans and Johanna.

The truck engine started. Mrs. Kaliya shouted orders and climbed into her car. By the time the men reached the truck with Halley, the car had pulled onto the road. One of the larger men lifted Halley like a sack of potatoes, tossed her into the back of the truck, and slammed the doors.

It was pitch black inside, and the heat was brutal. Halley could hear the other girls breathing. Some were crying softly. She stayed where she had landed and pressed her hand on Sundara's feather pouch. Then she remembered why she was there. "Ganika, are you here?" she said softly.

From somewhere deep in the truck, she heard a gasp, then rustling. "Yes."

Halley sat up and swallowed. "Ganika, this is Halley. I met you in the Taj Mahal Hotel in Bombay." She was shaking. What could she do to help? She was now in the same predicament.

Through the darkness she could hear Ganika moving toward her. It sounded like the others were scooting back to let her pass. "Halley, what happened? How did you get here?"

Halley would have laughed if her lips weren't trembling violently. The week since she'd met Ganika seemed like a year, like a dream. What was she doing here?

"Ganika, Rabar got to the hotel shortly after they took you away. He even found the cab you were in. But when he got to the station, your train was gone."

"My precious Rabar."

Halley felt a hand on her leg and reached out. Their fingers touched.

Ganika was crying and gasping, "I had...given up hope."

Halley wrapped her arms around the quaking girl and felt Ganika's wet cheek on her shoulder. The *purdah* shroud was gone. "Did you hear anything they said or where they might be taking the truck?"

Another voice spoke up in halting English. "I heard lady say, 'Take them to jungle.' Sounded like she not going with them."

Several other girls said something, and Ganika sat up. She told Halley they wanted to know what was happening and went on in Hindi. There was a murmur among the other girls. Ganika translated, "What else can you tell us?"

Halley told them what she said to her dad and friends that afternoon and what the police said about the disappearance of so many girls. "Since my friends weren't captured, they'll wait at the house for the police. Could you ask the girls if any of them were ever taken to the jungle before?"

There was some chatter and then Ganika said, "One girl was in the jungle briefly."

"Did they take her on an elephant, and if so, why didn't they go all the way by truck?"

More chatter.

"She said she was with some other girls. They were taken into the jungle in a truck. When it stopped, they were transferred onto several elephants that carried them across a wide river and up a steep road to an abandoned fort where they were shoved in front of a large, scary man. He pointed at several of the girls and they were taken away. The rest of the girls were forced back onto the elephants and transported back down to the truck. That was when they were taken to that house."

She could feel Ganika shaking. How strange and horrible. Who was the man in the fort? How was he connected to Mrs. Kaliya?

"Ganika, did Mrs. Kaliya take you right to the house?"

"No. A car picked us up at the train station and took us to a fancy house. She left me there with that other woman I was with in Bombay."

"Who is she?"

"She works for Mrs. Kaliya and is really scared of her. It's almost like Mrs. Kaliya owns her. They both scare me." Ganika continued to shake, but she continued, "She told me to take off my face covering! Mrs. Kaliya came back a few nights later. She had me put the covering back on and took me to that house."

The brakes squealed under them, and the truck made a sharp turn onto a rutted road. The girls slid around and cried out in pain when the truck bumped into holes and over rocks. Halley put her hands down on either side and braced herself on the bed of the truck. It felt like they were heading into the jungle.

"Ganika, the only chance we have is for one of us to escape. If they do move us to some elephants in the dark, you and I could create a distraction. Ask the girl who was in the jungle before if she would be willing to try. She knows more than any of us."

There was chatter between them, then Ganika translated. "She's terrified by the idea but will try. She wants to know what she should do if she does get away."

"Tell her to wait in the forest until the elephants leave. When she doesn't hear anyone anymore, she should walk back down to the main road and try to find help. The moon will give her some light. She must tell whoever she finds that she was kidnapped and held with some other girls and she needs to contact Sergeant Patel at the New Delhi police station. He is looking for all of you."

Halley heard Ganika's intense whisper but only understood three words. "Halley" and "Sergeant Patel." How could the girl find anyone once she reached the main road? Who would believe her and be able to help? *Think*! She pressed one hand against her chest above the pouch.

She thought about her trip to New Delhi with *Babaji*'s driver. After they turned onto the road from Jaipur, they passed a decorated cow. But what else? Oh, yes.

"Tell her to go left when she reaches the main road. After a while she'll come to a house. She needs to go there."

The truck slowed, then turned around and stopped. Halley's heart twisted.

"What is your name?" she whispered.

A man's voice hollered. The door handle turned. She grabbed Ganika, and they scooted away just before it opened. She felt a tap on her arm. "*Main hoon* Lavi." My name Lavi.

Men with flashlights were there immediately, pulling the girls out, shoving them past the front of the truck. Ganika grabbed Halley's hand and held onto it. Lavi was just ahead of them when one of the men shoved Halley right into her. He dropped his flashlight, and the beam shot off into the sky, immersing them in total blackness. She nudged Lavi to move away from them into the dark. When she sensed the girl was far enough from them, she squeezed Ganika's hand, and they began to cry loudly. Almost on cue, the other girls started crying. Men hollered.

The circling flashlight beams flashed past the eerie silhouettes of the struggling girls and right at several massive elephants that loomed ahead of them in the shadows. The girls were being pushed toward a ladder on the side of one of them. Ganika let go of Halley's hand and started to climb up. Halley looked back. Did Lavi get away?

The man behind her yelled and slammed his flashlight down on her shoulder. Halley shrieked and staggered forward into the ladder. She dragged herself up onto the *howdah* tied to the top of the elephant, made mostly out of scratchy gunnysack cloth, and collapsed onto her side, dizzy, tears burning. The guards' commands disappeared beneath her throbbing pain and sweating shivers. She clenched her teeth. Thoughts swirled. *I hate you. You're horrible. I'm going to die. Dad, I love you.*

An earthy animal odor mixed with a whiff of stale cigarette breath drifted in through the cracks of her budding hysteria. A man grunted. He was only a foot away. In front of him was the elephant's head. She jerked away.

A loud call rolled through the darkness. The animal shuddered and jerked forward, sending her skidding across the *howdah*. Miserable pain shot over her; panic pulsed. She was panting, gasping, grasping for something to stop her from falling off. *Oh God, help me.*

A cool hand stopped her slide and held on. It was Ganika.

"Halley." Ganika's urgent whisper broke through to her. "Sit up and hold on." They were both sliding toward the edge. Ganika was bracing her. Halley lurched up with a wince and grabbed at the rough burlap under her legs with both hands, twisting her body into a painful ball. Her right shoulder and arm throbbed mercilessly. She held on, slowly inching herself upright, moving one hand up and then the other. She was finally sitting up straight, facing out into the woods. The gloomy light from their driver's lamp flickered between the passing trees.

"What's that?" Halley whispered. She was looking into the dark jungle.

Ganika was facing the same way. She had barely uttered, "Where?" when she gasped.

Two large, shiny eyes were turning forward then back at them, keeping pace with the elephant. Moonlight flashed through a break in the trees. "It's a panther," Ganika gasped. "They don't usually go near the elephants. He must be stalking us."

Panther? Halley stared, paralyzed, at the angry eyes. She wondered how far they were from the Maharaja's hunting compound. Was this a parallel road? Her dad's panther was a female. Was this her angry mate, thirsty for blood?

The elephants were moving faster. Halley felt like her eyes were bulging out of her head. She was panting short, fast breaths, shaking, every muscle knotted, holding on with locked fists. She thought of the hunt.

It's very hot, impossible to get away from the roaring creature charging down the hill right at her. She can't move. A gun blasts next to her. The cat flips and lands, crouching in front of her, ready to spring.

She moaned, then felt Ganika's gentle nudge on her arm. "Shh."

Get ahold of yourself, she thought. *Hang on. Stay alert.*

The panther was soundlessly sliding between the trees. All she could hear was the thump of her heart and the crunch of twigs under the huge feet beneath them. *Need to focus.*

Halley took a deep breath and pictured the pouch on her chest rising with it and imagined pulling Sundara's golden feather out into the sunlight. "Remember the light" echoed through her mind. Light. With each breath, calmness floated down through her, finally settling just above her trembling heart. Light.

Must breathe and be watchful. Light.

A glint from one of the panther's eyes flashed into hers. *We'll never be able to stop. How can we lose him?*

Take a breath. Think of the light.

The crunching twigs became splashes. Flashes of moonlight shot up. Sparkles on black water were swirling swiftly toward them, crashing steadily into powerful legs propelling them onward.

They were crossing a wide stream. The panther was not.

No wonder they needed elephants. There might be a panther, and the trail stopped at a river. A prickly feeling circled her head. Where was the panther when she was hurrying away from her captors the other night? She shuddered, realizing that Lavi was probably still trudging the other way down the same road. What would have happened to her if the animal hadn't followed the elephants?

No longer obstructed by trees, a million stars glistened over her. Downriver the moon was chasing Jupiter toward the horizon. There was enough light for her to see the river's edge behind them and the dark form of the panther as it turned away and skulked back into the jungle.

14

The Edge of the Cliff

Halley closed her eyes and listened to the elephant's colossal feet crunch the branches beneath her. An image of the ancient forts perched above the Jaipur Road to New Delhi whirled uninvited into her thoughts.

She's back in the cupboard. Barking men force crying girls up the stairs. She can't breathe. Sweat pours down her back. Hans's hand is cool on her shoulder.

"Look up there," whispered Ganika, jerking Halley back. A girl near her whimpered.

A dark mountaintop loomed above them; ominous pillars silhouetted by the vaulted sky stabbed up between craggy cliffs. A torrent of fear rushed through her. The sinister mountain slid in front of the moon, snuffing some light. Jupiter was sinking. They were beginning to climb. Halley sensed a solid wall of rock beside them. On the other side, a deep, black well sank into the abyss. The path had narrowed. She shivered. Her fingers dug deeper into the rough fabric. She looked into the distant stars and remembered the evening their ocean liner entered the Suez Canal.

"That's Jupiter." Her dad was pointing at a bright star rising over a swath of barren desert in the twilight.

A hand grabbed her arm.

"Halley, I'm slipping." It was Ganika.

"Hold on," Halley gasped. Ganika's grasp tightened on her arm. They inched their way across the *howdah*, struggling together until they reached the center, then stopped, panting heavily. What if she didn't have Ganika? She would be lost completely.

Halley looked ahead. In the slate blue-black moonlight, she could see up the path. The lead elephant was passing under a tree that jutted out from a jagged rock. When her elephant was almost beside the tree, she saw a commotion in one of the upper branches, followed by an ear-splitting shriek. The girls gasped. With glistening black wings thumping loudly, a large bird rose from the branches. It turned in the air and with wings spread open, bombed toward them with more shrieking chatter. Before she could duck, a solid wing crashed hard against her face, dislodging her grip, flipping her off the rear of the elephant.

Falling. *Oh God, no.*

Going over the edge. *Gonna die. Mom, I'm coming.*

She was soaring into the void below them.

Pain. She crashed heavily onto the hard path and kept going, rolling, clawing frantically in the dust, grabbing for something solid to stop her. Her fingers touched a steady rock. She dug in, stopped sliding, and held on. Her burning knees were pressed into sharp rocks with her face in the dirt. *Can't breathe.*

She started to turn over and tried to push off with her feet, but there was nothing under them. She gasped and dug her fingernails deeper into the rocky path, pulling and pushing, inching forward. One foot felt solid ground, then the other. She pushed upward on her hands and looked up the hill just as the last elephant disappeared around the bend. She collapsed into the dirt, gasping, heart pounding with horror and relief, and burst into tears.

She heard scratching a few feet from her head and held her breath, afraid to move. A throaty clicking was coming closer. She breathed out with a rush, pushed up, and looked toward the sound through her watery eyes. Emerging out of the darkness was a large black bird, walking slowly toward her. Its sharp dark eyes reflected the moonlight. With a creaking-door voice, it spoke. "*Hailo.*"

Halley smiled faintly and whispered, "Well, Bird, are you friendly?" She tried to sit up and fell back. "Ow." A sharp rock was cutting into her knee. She moved her leg over. "Maybe you didn't notice, but I'm in kind of a tough spot here." She leaned on an elbow, winced, then pushed with her other hand until she was sitting upright. She wiped her eyes and rubbed the bruises on her arms. Her head throbbed. The collision and crash landing had partially unwrapped the scarf that covered her hair. She grabbed the corner that was trailing over her shoulder and twisted it back in. While she was doing this the bird side stepped, fluttered its wings, and leapt a few feet up the hill. Its head swiveled to look back at Halley. It flutter-jumped again with more guttural chatter. Halley managed to push herself into a painful squat and stood up, still slightly hunched over, hands ahead of her. When the bird took a longer hop, Halley struggled after it, relieved that she was moving farther from the edge. In a few more flutter-hops and staggering steps, they were beneath a gnarly old tree.

"Hey, wasn't this the tree you flew down from?"

The bird chattered, spread its wings, and flew to the top of a formidable rock beneath it. "Down from" it said, followed by more laughing chatter.

I'd better get off this path, she thought, looking up at the bird. She could see his eyes.

"It looks like I need to follow you."

"Follow," he echoed.

The rock was as high as a doorway. She found a sturdy root jutting out near the bottom and stepped on it. Another one was above it. Her fingers found more, and moments later she was at the base of the tree just in time to see the glint of black feathers disappear into the hillside. She glanced behind her. In the distance, a tiny bright cap of light was all that was left of the moon. A few stars hung above it.

Halley saw a light on the road and heard men's voices coming around the bend. *Well, here goes.* She turned back and crawled into the hole after the bird. Maybe the men would think she fell off the edge of the cliff.

The air was cooler, and it was completely dark. She reached out to the sides, then up. A small tunnel? She groped her way behind the chattering bird and was relieved that the ground under her throbbing knees felt almost soft, like a sandy beach. When the chatter became muffled, she wondered if they'd come to a bend in the tunnel. Then it straightened out again and she realized that it wasn't as dark. She could see the silhouette of the bird strutting and fluttering. When it stopped to preen a wing, Halley smiled. A moment later the tunnel opened out into a large cave.

With a burst of cackling chatter, the bird soared across the cavern between several tall finger-like shapes that climbed up into the darkness. They looked like the jagged towers Halley used to make at the beach when she drizzled wet sand onto the corners of her sandcastles.

"Oh my God," she whispered. "Stalagmites." The lofty, spiraling formations towered over a small, glistening pool of light blue water that reflected a flickering light from across the cavern and several long, icicle-shaped stalactites hanging from the ceiling. The bird circled the cavern and landed with a flourish on the shoulder of a very thin man seated next to a fire. Halley gasped in midbreath, and the man looked up at her.

With the help of a sturdy stick, he stood and struggled toward her, stopping when he was near enough to speak. The bird was chattering and snuggling into his long white beard. His hair spilled down his back. He spoke calmly, but Halley couldn't understand what he was saying and tilted her head.

"Oh," he said in rusty, singing English and smiled. His face reminded her of *Babaji*'s, only he was much taller. "Want tea?" She nodded and tried to swallow. He even sounded like the teacher. "Come." He leaned heavily on his staff and started back. A swath of white cloth was wrapped around his waist and up between his long, dark legs. Parts of the fabric hung down almost to his sandaled feet. He resembled the holy man Kashif had pointed out on the roadside in Bombay.

The bird had turned around and was watching her. "Come," he mimicked.

"Yes, thank you," she said from a few yards behind.

With difficulty, the man sat back down behind an old copper pot that was simmering on a rock in the middle of a small fire. Next to him was an altar with burning incense and candles. There was a painted statue of a seated man on the top.

Maybe one of their gods, she thought. She sat near him and watched him ladle tea into a cup. A curl of steam rose up from it, carrying the smell of earth and bark.

"Looks like Sita brought you through her special tunnel." His English was halting but clear. "Where did she find you?"

Halley looked at the bird and had to smile. She had a bunch of the man's hair in her beak and was gently tugging at it. "Bad men were taking me and some other girls up the mountain on elephants. Sita came screeching out of a tree and knocked me off the last elephant. I almost fell off the cliff. She led me to the tunnel just as the men were coming back, looking for me." She sipped the tea while he filled another cup.

"I don't get many visitors. You're not English, are you?"

"No."

"Those men are very bad. They work for *Laal* Adrik."

Halley was taking a sip of tea. *Laal*, she thought and gasped, setting off a choking fit. She recalled telling Johanna about the two girls who passed her in the hallway at school.

"Laal means red. Laal Baal means red hair."

The man sat quietly, waiting.

When she caught her breath, she blurted, *"Laal* Adrik? Red Adrik?"

"Yes."

He must be the big, horrible man that Lavi told her about. Slivers of anger circled through her, pulsing hot blood into her face, creeping up, prickling her scalp.

The man cleared his throat. "I hear he is Russian and has red hair. He lives like a king in part of the abandoned fort on this mountain. Centuries ago, a faithful *Raja* built the fort around our village to protect the temple and our people. In the center there's a large statue of Lord Shiva. We are devoted to Lord Shiva and care for His shrines. When Adrik and his men invaded, they killed many of our men and forced everyone else to serve him. The day they arrived, I was meditating here in this cave and my students felt it wasn't safe for *Laal* Adrik to know about me. So, they bring me food from the garden and fresh water from the well and study with me here. But I should let you rest. You look exhausted. Here, take this blanket."

"Thank you."

Halley spread her aching body out on the soft quilt, closed her eyes, and listened to the old man's gentle singing.

It seemed like she had only nodded off for a few minutes when she heard voices. Through the gloom from the dwindling candles, she could see the old man. He had another colorful quilt draped over his shoulders. Two men were seated cross-legged in front of him. The man was nodding his head. One of the other men sounded very upset. The only words she recognized were "*Laal* Adrik." Finally, the visitors stood up, bowed to the old man, and left.

When she opened her eyes again, the man was throwing a large, circular patty on the glowing coals. A pungent, earthy odor drifted over to her. *Cow dung*, she thought, pushing herself up. He sat down with difficulty and crossed his legs, ladled tea into two cups, and held one out to her.

Sita was approaching from around the bend behind the old man and was still cawing when she swooped into the cavern and landed on his shoulder. Where had she been? Halley wrapped the quilt around her shoulders and reached for the cup. "Thank you."

The fire sizzled. She watched the flames dance, shrugged farther down into the warm blanket, and blew across the steaming cup. What was going to happen to her? She touched the feather pocket and remembered the time she had asked her dad if he'd ever been afraid. He'd said yes and told her about the time that he and Mom had been traveling in a small boat off the coast of Maine when a dense fog engulfed them. They couldn't see the shore and it was getting dark.

"What's your name?" asked the man.

She looked into the old man's kind, gentle eyes. "Halley Pederson."

"Halley, my students will alert my nephew and his mother. They will bring *chapattis* and rice and boys' clothes so you can walk safely into the village. He'll return when it's dark and they'll take you back with them. All right?

Halley imagined walking into the village disguised as a boy. She felt a surge of gratitude for this kind old man and sighed.

Sita croaked. "All . . . right?"

"Yes, thank you."

They sat silently, sipping tea and watching the glowing fire.

Of course. I'm tall, she thought. Dressed in women's clothing, someone would probably notice her. Would anyone rescue her and the other girls? She pictured Lavi walking down the main road to that house. Would she find someone who would believe her and help her contact Sergeant Patel?

"How long have you lived in India?" the old man asked.

"My father and I arrived in Poona last week from America."

"You've come a long way in just a few days. How did you come to be on the elephant?"

First, she told him about the hunt, about Ganika's kidnapping and how she'd been trying to find her. Finally, she described how when she got too close, the men grabbed her and brought her with them. Then she said, "You speak good English for someone living way up here. Where did you learn it?"

He laughed good naturedly. "I guess we aren't going anywhere, and my students won't be back for hours. So, here goes." He took a sip of tea. "When I was seventeen, my father said, 'My son, you must travel to the city and find work and a wife.' I left the next day with a satchel over my shoulder. When I reached the main road, a kind Hindu nobleman picked me up in his carriage and brought me to his home in Delhi. He insisted that I be educated with his sons. We studied with their teacher in the morning and spent the rest of the day riding horseback and practicing archery. I learned quickly. Two years later my benefactor sent me to the palace of the Maharaja, where I studied logic, Sanskrit, yoga, and began to learn English. When I was twenty-two, I attained the position of teacher and was married. I loved my wife very much. The night she gave birth to our son, they called me into the chamber. She was sleeping. Her beautiful face was framed by her shiny black hair. Her mother sat beside her with her hand resting on my wife's shoulder. She was crying. 'Your baby is dead,' she said and looked at her daughter, '... and so is mine.'"

Halley felt a sharp quiver sweep through her.

"I was very depressed for almost four years. One day the sons of my first patron came to find me and invited me to join the Indian Army cavalry with them. When the Great War broke out, England's King George called on our troops to help them. A few months later we were shipped to France. By the time I returned from the war, I was dreaming in English."

Halley was fascinated by this gentle man. "World War One was a long time ago. What brought you back to this mountain?"

"A short time after we returned from Europe, I heard Mahatma Gandhi speak about non-violent resistance against the British rule of India. I had already seen how little respect the British had for the Indian soldiers when we fought with them during the war. The Mahatma's teaching about the need for peaceful resistance against British domination of India made so much sense to me. I volunteered to help Gandhi and willingly went to prison with him when he was arrested during the Salt March protests against Britain's inhumane salt tax. I continued to work with Gandhi until he was assassinated in 1948, only a year after we won our independence from Britain. At that time I was getting old and decided to return to this village. I had only been here about a year when *Laal* Adrik and his men invaded. I've been in this cave ever since."

Halley sighed. "I remember listening to my parents talk about Mahatma Gandhi. They both read his autobiography. He was a great leader." The old man nodded.

"What's your name?" she asked.

"Arjuna."

A man's voice rang out from around the bend. "*Babaji?*"

"*Darj*," he replied. "Enter."

A young man entered, followed by an old woman in flowing pants and shirt that reminded Halley of the outfit Johanna had given her for the welcome party, but without the mirrors. She had a large bundle balanced on her head. The man set a box down and spoke with Arjuna for a few minutes while the woman removed the bundle and squatted next to the box. She lifted out several round bowls. When she removed the lids, an interesting, unfamiliar aroma reached Halley. Her stomach growled. *I'm sure I could eat almost anything*, she thought.

"Halley," Arjuna said. "This is my nephew, Shankar, and Devina, my sister." They all put their hands together and bowed. "*Namaste.*" Halley did too. Shankar bowed again to Arjuna and left.

15

Sita and the Explorer

After they finished eating, Halley removed the scarf wrapped around her head and was not surprised to see Devina and Arjuna smile at each other.

"You're smart to be wearing the head cover," he said.

Halley laughed. "Sully was the smart one. She covered my head at the *Babaji's ashram*."

"*Ashram*? *Babaji*? When?"

"On Saturday."

He and Devina exchanged a few words. Then they looked back at her and smiled.

"When we were children, we'd have great fun during *Holi*. We celebrated the defeat of evil by the power of good and loved to cover everything in the village with colorful powders, including each other." He turned and spoke to his sister. They laughed.

"One year Devina found some red powder. She managed to sneak up behind me and dumped some on my head. I was so shocked that she'd been able to trick me that I grabbed the rest from her and threw it at her. It landed on her head in one brilliant wave of red. She screamed and ran to our mother, who carefully brushed the powder off her face and demanded that we play nicely. Your red hair reminded us of a joyful time. Thank you."

Devina's wrinkled lips and twinkling eyes continued smiling at her brother. Halley wanted to laugh, too, but her heart was breaking for them. They were so kind, and they didn't deserve to be imprisoned like this. But what could she do? She was bringing them more trouble just by being there. She swallowed a few times to stop the tears she could feel welling up into her eyes. She'd created such a mess. But if she, Hans, and Johanna hadn't followed Mrs. Kaliya, they never would have found Ganika. But now that Halley knew where Ganika was, she couldn't help her. In fact, her presence here might be harmful to these gentle people.

"Halley," Arjuna said, "my sister has borrowed clothes for you from our friend, Sadhu. Tonight, she and Shankar will bring you to him. He and his sons care for our village sheep. Their family weaves the wool into very fine cloth. Sadhu is a kind man."

Devina unpacked a shirt, a pair of rope sandals, and something that looked like it might be pants and held up a brownish red roll of fabric. Arjuna pointed at it. "That's your turban. My sister will help you dress and will carry your clothes out on her head when you leave. We have a few hours before dark. First, she'll help you change your clothes. Then we'll meditate until Shankar comes to tell us that it's safe to leave." After talking with Devina, he handed Halley a lit candle. "Go over there with my sister." He pointed at the nearest stalagmite. "She'll wrap your head later."

When Devina helped her stretch a tight band around Halley's chest to conceal her small breasts, she touched Sundara's pouch. "*Kya?*" she asked. Halley unhooked the cord and removed Sundara's golden feather. Devina nodded. "*Achachha,*" she said and smiled.

When the cord was back around her neck Halley pulled on the tight-sleeved brown shirt, smoothed it over the baggy, white pants, and slipped on the sandals. She felt pretty silly in Sadhu's clothes, but they were comfortable.

A few minutes later her folded clothes were in the sack and they were sitting with Arjuna. Sita was walking around behind him, pecking in the rocks.

"Shankar will introduce you to Sadhu's family," Arjuna said. "Sadhu speaks some English. In the years before *Laal* Adrik came here, he was their family merchant. He'd take their blankets and the clothing they wove to sell at the market in Jaipur and purchase supplies for the village. Now *Laal* Adrik's men take almost everything they make away from them. They will take good care of you. Sadhu will help you figure out what to do. With the turban on, you will look like one of his sons. They believe in giving kindness to strangers, and they share everything. You will like them. Your name will be Sarwan." He smiled at Devina. "Sarwan means 'explorer.'"

Devina knelt behind Halley and ran her fingers through her hair, gently pulling all of it onto the top of her head. She twisted it and wrapped a cord around it.

It must look like a strawberry muffin, Halley thought.

Then Devina stretched some white cloth over her head, tightened it around the muffin, and circled her head with the dark red cloth. Halley ran her fingers over it. "Wow, it's so flat and smooth."

Arjuna translated for his sister. They all laughed.

"Now we will sit in meditation. Did you learn how to meditate at the *Babaji*'s *ashram*?"

Halley nodded, and Arjuna lit a stick of incense. Halley watched its vapor curl up around the flickering flame. She closed her eyes and breathed in deeply a few times.

Babaji is standing in the woods. "Remember the light," he says and bows to her.

The light.

Poor Ganika. What happened to her today?

Light.

That incense smells like flowers. Jasmine?

Light.

How big is the village? Will I be safe?

Light.

Each time she noticed her mind had wandered, she remembered: light.

Glistening black wings pound the air. There is shrieking chatter. Losing my grip. Flying. Falling. Gonna die.

The chatter was getting louder, closer. *"Hailo,"* Sita said from nearby.

Halley peeked over at Arjuna. He was stroking the bird's head. *"Keematee* Sita," he said.

Arjuna spoke to Devina and then to Halley. "Shankar will arrive shortly. I'm wondering if you would like to learn how to say 'thank you' in Hindi?"

"Yes, please."

"The 'thank you' that you will want to use is *'dhanyavaad.'* Try it. 'Dhun-yuh-vaad.'"

When Shankar came around the bend, Devina had the bundle on her head and Halley had repeated *'dhanyavaad'* several times.

Sita was watching her from Arjuna's shoulder.

"*Dhanyavaad*, Sita," she said. "Thank you for bringing me here to Arjuna."

Sita replied. "Here."

She turned to Arjuna. "*Dhanyavaad*, Arjuna. Will I see you again?"

"We shall see."

They both bowed. "*Namaste.*"

Shankar turned on his flashlight, and Halley fell in between him and Devina. Just before they made the turn into the tunnel, she glanced back. Arjuna was standing near the altar, silhouetted by the soft candlelight, surrounded by a golden glow. Sita was on his shoulder.

"Light," she whispered and entered the tunnel.

Shankar cast the beam from his flashlight onto the ground next to his feet. She could only see what was right in front of her. Her skin prickled. The tunnel was narrowing and ascending on a slight incline. Occasionally she heard water dripping. Devina was humming. She touched the pouch through the shirt, breathed in deeply and listened to the crunch beneath her feet.

These sandals are so soft, she thought. *I wonder if they make the cord out* of wool. It was getting warmer. *Why am I shaking? Feel cold. Air is thicker, harder to breathe. Take short breaths, panting. Can't go any farther.*

Just when she thought she couldn't take another step, Shankar extinguished the light. She gasped. Devina's hand gently grasped her elbow. They stood listening. What was it? Why had they stopped? Devina continued to hold on to her. Halley opened her eyes as wide as possible. Was there a little light ahead? She sensed Shankar take a few steps forward and stop. Then he took a few more. Did they do this every time or was there something wrong? They waited. Every fiber in her was at attention. She didn't dare move.

An owl hooted quietly.

"*Theek hai,*" Shankar whispered.

Devina gently propelled Halley forward one step at a time. She felt the air change. Above them was a ceiling of stars surrounded by high, dark walls. Rocks? After a few more hesitant steps, the walls dropped away. They were on a ridge overlooking the village. The owl called again. One step at a time they made slow progress down the hill in the starlight until they reached a road. In the light from the doorways, they made better progress. They stopped outside the clay walls of a house. Shankar tapped on the door and it creaked open. The dim light inside revealed a slender man, flanked by two teenage boys. They were all wearing turbans.

"Welcome," the man said in English. "I am Sadhu Singh." His eyes twinkled with gentle good humor. "Please come in." He stepped back from the door and they entered. "You must be Sarwan."

Shankar closed the door behind them.

"Oh . . . yes," Halley answered, hoping her hesitant response didn't seem strange. It had slipped her mind that they had changed her name. Of course, they knew she was in disguise. After all, she was wearing their clothes. "Thank you."

Sadhu bowed. "*Namaste,*" he said, and she returned the greeting.

He went on. "We have prayed every day for a long time that help would come to free our village. But we had no idea it would be someone so young." His good humor burst through, and she laughed with him. "You could definitely pass for one of my sons."

Devina set the bundle down. Sadhu spoke with them, and they backed toward the door with their hands clasped. Halley remembered "*Dhanyavaad*," and bowed to them, "*Namaste.*"

Once the door was again secured, Sadhu introduced his family. An ancient woman near the hearth and weaving a bright blanket was his mother-in-law. She smiled shyly. Sadhu's wife looked at Halley dressed as one of her sons, smiled, and continued stirring a pot hanging over the fire.

Sadhu went on, "I hear Sita knocked you off a transport elephant last night when they were taking you to *Laal* Adrik, and she led you to Arjuna. Clever bird." He laughed for a moment, then sobered. "Arjuna told Shankar that the New Delhi police are looking for you and the girls and that one of the girls escaped when they were transferring you to the elephants in the jungle. Right?" Halley nodded. "Although it's hard for you, this is very good news for us. We have never been able to get a message to the police about *Laal* Adrik." He invited her to be seated on a cushion near a low table. "Sarwan, soon we will go to check on the sheep and relieve two of my sons who are there. The moon is coming up now and there will be enough light to see where we are going. Would you like to come with us?"

Halley had been watching the lantern light playing over his dark beard. His kind eyes sparkled with inner peace. How could he appear so joyful while living under such oppression? "I'd love to go, but do you really think it's safe for me?"

"You would be as safe as we are. You can't see yourself, but you look just like one of us. If you don't speak, they will never suspect anything. Besides, it would be good for you to get your bearings. This village is not big. It will not take us long to reach the herd."

Halley was excited by the invitation. She felt a new strength welling up inside her.

I am Sarwan, a Sikh boy. Sarwan, the explorer.

"Yes, I'd like to go with you."

"Good. But first, we eat."

Once all the bowls were set down in front of him, Sadhu closed his eyes and musically chanted what Halley assumed was a prayer.

"Thank you, God, for this food," she whispered.

Sadhu poured the tea and handed her a cup and one of the bowls. In it was steaming rice with some delicious-smelling beans and a *chapatti* on top. Like at Arjuna's, there were no forks here. She watched Sadhu tear off a corner of his *chapatti*. He placed it over some saucy beans and rice and pinched it all together. With a swift scooping motion, he swept the small fingerful into his mouth. She tried to copy him but had to hold the bowl beneath her chin to catch the dripping rice. When she finished the last bite, she put the bowl down and sighed. Then she looked up. Everyone else, including the old woman, had been watching her. They were all smiling.

Halley wiped her mouth with the back of her hand. "That was really good," she said and grinned back. Then she helped the boys clear the table. Sadhu's wife handed Sadhu a bulky, flat-bottomed bag that he slung over his shoulder.

A slightly cooler breeze was blowing when they set off down the dark road. Halley tried to mirror Sadhu's calm stride. She held her hands together behind her back and sauntered between the boys as though she'd done this all her life.

I'm invisible, she thought.

Sadhu greeted several men sitting outside their houses along the road. Some wore turbans, others didn't. When they crossed a wide-open plaza in front of the gates of a palatial, laughter-filled compound, they dropped their hands and walked a little faster. She could hear someone plucking a string instrument and men singing a raucous song. A chill ran through her. *These must be some of Laal Adrik's men*, she thought.

They had only gone a little farther when Halley saw the outline of an enormous figure looming ahead of them in the moonlight. She tapped Sadhu's arm and pointed at it. He whispered in her ear, "That's our statue of Lord Shiva, the destroyer of evil. We are walking through the temple grounds."

When they got closer, the dim light revealed a seated figure that looked like it was at least four stories high, with four arms reaching out. As they passed the statue Halley remembered Johanna telling her about

Lord Shiva on the train and thought she could see the crescent of a moon resting on its head and what could have been a snake around its neck. Sadhu and his sons briefly bowed their heads and kept walking.

When they stepped onto a narrower path and started down the hill, she heard murmuring and sensed a shimmer of water next to the path. It appeared to be coming out of the big rocks just above it. A spring? When they crossed a bridge over a small waterfall, she noticed that the tranquil brook had merged into a glassy pond mirroring the celestial canopy above them. They crossed a meadow and stopped at a hut next to a fence on the far side.

From the glow of a small fire beneath a makeshift roof, she saw two turbaned boys. They jumped up to welcome them. Sadhu lifted several bowls out of the bag and removed the lids. They talked while the boys ate. The only word she understood was "Sarwan."

She was enjoying the disguise.

I am Sarwan, the explorer. I am on the top of a mountain with shepherds.

The bleating of several sheep interrupted her reverie, and she heard what sounded like a crow caw, followed by yapping. She looked at Sadhu. "That's the elephants," he said quietly. "We're on the edge of another pond. The elephants love to be in or near the water. So do the sheep. The pond near the temple is only for drinking or cooking water." He turned back to the boys and her eyes drooped closed.

Two men drag her to the elephant and force her to climb the ladder. The animal rumbles and purrs. The fiber mat on top hurts her hands. Can't breathe. She touches the pouch.

"Sarwan."

She jerked awake with a shiver. The boys were standing at the edge of the firelight. Sadhu was beside her. "We will leave now. My sons have exchanged places."

The sheep had circled the hut, and Sadhu called them to move. All except the one next to Halley made a path. That one moved closer, leaning in. The others were laughing. "She won't hurt you. She just wants to say hello."

Halley had never been this close to a sheep before. She reached down to what she thought was the animal's head and attempted to stroke it. When she touched its wooly crown, it felt like a thick sponge. She bounced her hand on it like it was a beach ball. "Nice Sheepie . . . Sheepie," she cooed. They all laughed.

The moon was higher, and in the dim light Halley could see the elephants standing in the water just beyond the sheep. A gentle breeze carried the sound of men's voices from a well-lit structure on the other side of the field. Sadhu followed her gaze. "Those are the men who guard the fort and keep us prisoners here." His sad tone was heartbreaking. A horse whinnied.

On the return trip, Sadhu and the boys stopped at the foot of the waterfall, scooped up some water with their hands, and drank. Halley watched, remembering the edict not to drink water that hadn't been boiled. But this was coming out of a spring at the top of a mountain, and it was crystal clear. She joined them. The water was so cool and fresh. She splashed some on her face and neck and looked up into the stars just as a dark shadow passed over her. It seemed too big to be a bat. A night bird?

By the time they were moving back through the temple, the moon was high enough for her to get a better look at the statue. The legs were folded one on top of the other.

When they passed the noisy compound, Sadhu walked a little faster. This time she heard a girl's voice. Her heart quivered. She could see two men sitting inside the gate, playing cards, but there was no one on the road. They turned a corner and had almost reached the next bend when she heard a snort and hooves clopping in the dust. Horses? Sadhu clearly heard them too. He made a motion for silence and signaled for them to follow him. They ducked around the side of a nearby house just as three men on horseback pranced into view. Many more were right behind them, metal badges glinting on their caps. Sadhu stepped onto the road in front of the horsemen and raised his hands. They stopped. The lead man spoke to Sadhu, dismounted, and signaled for the others to do the same. One man turned on a large light and, using both hands, waved it around numerous times over his head into the sky. Then, with Sadhu in the lead, they all started running toward the compound.

After the men disappeared around the corner, one of Sadhu's sons tapped Halley on the shoulder and motioned for her to follow them. They reached the corner in time to see the men stop at the edge of the plaza. Three men near the front were boosted over the wall. Moments later the gate opened, and the others were quickly out of sight.

Halley and the boys were about to follow when a pulsing, rumbling sound from the temple stopped them. The noise sounded like a barrage of lumber saws and was getting louder. The boys vanished into the darkness. With her mouth hanging open, she watched a giant mosquito rise into the air from behind the statue of Lord Shiva. With bright eyes lighting up the ground, it moved slowly toward her, then hovered over the plaza, whipping a cyclone of dust into the air. It landed in front of the gate. A door opened near the bottom and a troop of men burst out. They ducked under the blades whirling above them and were gone.

A helicopter, she thought, laughing at herself.

She skulked around the edge of the plaza and had almost reached the gate when a large man slipped out through it. He looked furtively around, then lumbered off toward the temple. When he passed near one of the helicopter's landing lights, a blaze of red hair flashed at Halley. *Oh no*. She clenched her fists. *Laal Adrik*. How could he have gotten away unseen? She couldn't let him escape. She felt a surge of hot anger, mixed with cold dread. Staying in the darkest shadows, she followed him.

16

A Midnight Ride

Adrik had almost reached the statue of Shiva when Halley saw something small and dark pass over him. He glanced up at it and kept moving. The shape passed above her, accompanied by flapping and chattering. It circled back. The man stopped, put his hands up, and knelt near the base of the statue. A tall figure towered over him, holding a large bow with an arrow strung on it. The arrow was pointed right at the man. Halley crept forward until she could hear what the tall figure was saying.

". . . and if you move, I'll release this poison-tipped arrow into your heart."

The bird swept over her again. "*Hailo*," it squawked and flew back to the shoulder of the archer.

"Arjuna?" she cried out.

"Halley?"

"I'll get help."

"Hurry."

A few moments later, with Sita careening back and forth over her, Halley ran into the compound entrance, almost colliding into two uniformed men. "Arjuna needs help," she cried, pointing toward the temple. "One of the men got away. Arjuna caught him."

"Needs help?" echoed one of the men.

"Yes, hurry," she said and took off running with the men right behind her.

"Hurry," cried Sita from the air.

Remembering the frail old man in the cave, Halley worried that something bad might have happened during the few minutes she'd been gone. *God help Arjuna*, she prayed.

When she reached the temple grounds the moon behind the head of the statue was shooting bright beams at Arjuna, who was still towering over the cowering man. Lord Shiva's ancient warrior had captured the evil *Laal* Adrik, she thought.

The two soldiers raced around her. They grabbed *Laal* Adrik, pulled his hands behind his back, and escorted him toward the compound.

Halley watched Arjuna carefully climb down. When he reached Halley he staggered, dropped the bow, and grabbed her shoulder.

"Arjuna!"

He was breathing heavily and gasped with a chuckle. "I'm not sure I could have held that bow up another minute." He leaned heavily on her. "Need to sit down."

With all her strength, Halley lowered him gently onto the base of the statue. "I was really relieved that he believed there was poison on the arrow," he said with a feeble laugh.

Sita landed next to him and croaked several times.

"Would you like to lie down?" she asked.

"No, I just needed to rest a minute. We must follow them."

With the bow and arrow balanced on one of her shoulders, Arjuna leaning heavily on the other, and Sita circling ahead of them, Halley left the temple grounds, dreading what they might find when they reached the compound. Had they rescued Ganika and the other girls? Had they caught all the other men?

Arjuna interrupted her thoughts. "They'll be looking for you."

"Oh, right." She'd been so busy she'd forgotten the men would have been hoping to find her too.

A group of men were entering the compound when they reached

the plaza. Some were carrying lanterns and flashlights. "Townspeople," Arjuna announced.

One of the men noticed them limping past the helicopter. "*Babaji,*" he cried out and helped Halley through the gate with Arjuna.

Halley was relieved to see that *Laal* Adrik and his men were sitting in the dirt on one side of the courtyard with their hands tied together behind their backs, surrounded by officers.

In the center, a large, muscular man was barking out orders to everyone. Halley was relieved to see it was Sergeant Patel.

She helped the man assisting them lower Arjuna to the ground. While she was still kneeling in front of Arjuna, he looked into her eyes, touched her forehead, and said, "Thank you, brave warrior. You have saved me and my village. We will never forget you. Now go find your friend."

Halley leaned forward, grabbed his boney shoulders, and kissed his forehead. "It is I, great teacher, who will never forget you. Thank you for saving me." When she clasped her hands together, Sita landed on Arjuna's shoulder. "Thank you, lovely Sita. You are the messenger of light." Then, they bowed to each other. "*Namaste.*"

She walked quickly away, blinking back tears. Sergeant Patel didn't notice her until she was right in front of him. He stopped speaking and looked at her.

"Sergeant Patel." She wanted to laugh. He obviously didn't recognize her and must have been wondering how this village boy knew his name. "I'm Halley Pederson."

"Oh my God, you're alive," he hollered. "We found a few girls. One of them said you were knocked off the elephant. When the guards came back without you, they were sure you'd fallen over the edge of the cliff. But they also said there are more girls here somewhere. We haven't found them yet." He looked closely at her. "Say, where did you get the boy's clothing?"

She pointed at Arjuna. "That man and his bird saved my life and then arranged for my disguise. And you, Sergeant Patel, have rescued not only the girls, but this whole village. They have all been held as slaves by that man," she pointed at *Laal* Adrik, "and his men for several years.

Somehow Mrs. Kaliya has been working with him. But how did you get here so quickly, and where did you find the horses, and. . ." she glanced out through the gate, "a helicopter?"

"We arrived at that house minutes after the truck left with you in it. The Norlin kids told us they saw the men drag you to the truck. They ran toward the house and got close enough just in time to hear Mrs. Kaliya order them to take the girls to the jungle fort. We left immediately for Dr. Fischer's.

"Your father was very upset when he heard that you'd been taken and that Mrs. Kaliya mentioned the jungle. He was sure they were taking you back up the same road those men took you on Friday. Everyone agreed. Dr. Fischer and Dr. Norlin called the Maharaja. He offered his support and asked us to meet him at his country estate near the main road to Jaipur as soon as we could get there. He said he'd call the Indian Army cavalry base near him and ask for help. The helicopter belongs to the Maharaja." He paused to wipe his face with a large handkerchief. "We had barely arrived at the Maharaja's when my Delhi headquarters phoned. They had just received a call from a girl who said she had escaped from the kidnappers and that they had many more girls, including a foreigner. She was calling from only a few miles away. We picked her up right away and she took us to the road that she had walked down."

Just then an officer burst out the front door of the larger building and called out to Sergeant Patel. Halley followed them into a cavernous room. Ornate arches ran down both sides. Candles and incense burned on low tables beneath tapestry-covered walls. She followed the officers to a low, nearly hidden door in the back wall. Girls were crying. She breathed deeply several times and braced herself. Some soldiers held flashlights while others helped a crowd of girls stand up and struggle to the opening. Several had bleeding wounds. They were all crying.

"Ganika!" She called into the darkness.

"I'm here." A flashlight beam lit up Ganika's beautiful face.

"It's me, Halley." She moved around the others.

"Oh, Halley, dear Halley." Ganika's voice cracked. "Great Kali be praised, you're not dead."

Hugging and sobbing, they crawled out the opening. Sergeant Patel was speaking kindly to all the girls as they emerged.

Ganika grabbed her hand, and they followed the others. "Halley, I'm sure now that Mrs. Kaliya was the one who kidnapped them."

Just hearing that name made Halley's mind reel. Her stomach twisted. "Really?"

"Yes. I asked the girls how they were kidnapped. One of them said she was on a trip with her family. They met a foreign woman at the hotel where they were staying. One afternoon she was reading alone in the lounge. That woman hurried up to her and told her that her parents had been in an accident and offered to take her to them. When the car started to pull away, the woman pressed a smelly handkerchief over her nose. The next thing she remembers, she was on a bumpy road in the back of a truck with her hands tied."

Halley's voice trembled. "Did she describe the woman?"

"Yes. The woman wore a *sari* and had a lot of glass bangles and," she paused, "all the other girls described the same woman." Ganika began speaking faster. "Many of the girls have been in *Laal* Adrik's harem, some for at least a year. Several of the girls who arrived yesterday were pulled out to serve with them. The rest of us were thrown into that dark chamber where you found us."

When they reached the courtyard, Halley saw Sadhu and Arjuna's sad faces. They were standing together near the gate, watching the girls. She gasped. Some of the girls were just children.

Halley brought Ganika over to them. "Sadhu, thank you for your help and for lending me your clothes, but it looks like I may be leaving with the girls now and won't be able to give them back to you."

Sadhu's eyes brightened. "Well then, I guess you'll have to keep them."

Arjuna laughed. "Like souvenirs."

Sadhu handed her a bundle. "When my sons told my wife about the helicopter and she realized we were all being rescued, she sent them back with your clothes."

Halley laughed and tucked the bundle under her arm. "*Dhanyavaad*, Sadhu."

Sergeant Patel shouted her name above the other voices, and she realized he couldn't see her in the dim light.

"Over here," she called, waving her other hand. "Sergeant Patel, this is Arjuna, the teacher, and his bird, Sita, who saved me. And this is his friend Sadhu. He just gave me a souvenir, his clothes that I'm wearing." She laughed with them.

"Thank you, thank you." Sergeant Patel said, nodding to each of them. "Is there anything we can do for you?"

Arjuna stepped forward. "Thank you, no. You have already answered our prayers by taking our captors away with you."

Sergeant Patel bowed to them. "You won't be seeing *Laal* Adrik or his men again. They'll be transported through the jungle on the elephants guarded by the mounted soldiers. I'll travel with the girls in the helicopter. We'll be leaving soon."

After more goodbyes, he ushered Halley and Ganika out the gate, stopping several times to holler commands. Flashlights were moving around between *Laal* Adrik and his men, the police officers, soldiers, villagers, girls, elephants, horses, and the helicopter. What a sight! It occurred to Halley that the plaza looked like a strange night bazaar right out of the movies.

When they had almost reached the helicopter, her stomach started to get queasy. Would it be anything like the rides at Coney Island? She loved the roller coaster but had never gotten used to the Ferris wheel and the sideways rocking of her gondola when it stopped at the top. But here went nothing, she thought, and followed the other girls up the steps into the cargo area.

She and Ganika buckled themselves into two of the hammock-like seats along the side. Halley tucked her clothes bundle behind her feet and helped a scared little girl get settle next to her. Ganika was on her other side. The cargo door closed, and it got warm inside. She could hear Sergeant Patel and the pilot talking. When the motor started, several girls cried out. Halley put her arm around the little girl next to her, and Ganika grabbed Halley's other hand. The chilling whine and the flutter of the blades circling above and behind them sent a rush of excitement through her. The flapping pulse got louder. The craft shuddered and rose with a start. For a moment it felt like she'd left her stomach on the ground. Then the helicopter turned around and was soon moving quickly away. The little girl leaned on her shoulder.

Remembering where they had just been, Halley clenched her teeth.

Dark hidden room. Crying girls. Frightened faces.

Ganika squeezed her hand.

Oh God, she prayed, *thank you. Now, please help these girls find their families and bring Rabar Chowdhury to Ganika.*

She tipped her head back against the metal wall and listened to the beat of the blades. And there, buried within the sounds surrounding her, came a deep, hollow, bottomless note. She closed her eyes and settled into it.

The noises got louder. It felt like they were on a plummeting elevator. Several girls cried out. "They're afraid we're going to crash," Ganika said.

"Tell them we appear to be landing."

Moments later, there was a thump beneath them. The shrill howl decreased until all they could hear was a gentle flutter that slowed to a stop. The door opened with a burst of air and dust. Sergeant Patel poked in his head and greeted them cheerfully, then looked at Halley. "Welcome to the *Raja*'s country estate," he said in English and pulled down the steps.

Halley helped the little girl out of her seat belt and grabbed her clothes bag. People outside cheered when the first girls emerged. Ganika said something to the little girl, and they laughed. Halley thought her heart was going to burst with joy.

At the foot of the steps, Johanna and her brother were laughing.

"Halley," Johanna said, "when almost everyone was out, we asked Sergeant Patel where you were, and he pointed at the *Sikh* boy coming down the steps."

Hans chimed in, "From your disguise I'd say that you were a formidable foe for the kidnappers."

Halley saw Dad right behind them. He wiped his eyes and hugged her. "I think that appearing as Romeo at Chapman was good training for the hero in this story. But I'm guessing you've already figured out that I won't be letting you out of my sight anytime soon. Losing you twice in one weekend has given me my first white hairs."

"Yes, Dad." She handed him her bundle of clothes. "I am your shadow now." The lights ahead revealed a stately mansion that disappeared into the darkness in all directions.

Dr. Maria Norlin walked with them away from the helicopter. "After Sergeant Patel helps the girls locate their families, his officers will interview you all in the Palm Room. Then your dad, Gustaf, and I will meet with each of you to record any injuries."

Halley was listening, but her eyes were on a young couple crying and embracing in the moonlight near the side portico. When she had almost reached the entrance, the couple leaned back to look at each other, and she saw the girl's glistening eyes.

"Ganika." she cried.

"Look, Halley, Rabar is here," Ganika called. "Can you believe it? Your friend called him in Poona as soon as she could, and they picked him up at the train station near here."

"Oh, Ganika, this is so wonderful." Halley said.

"Well, this is a happy sight," Dad said, coming up behind them.

"Dad, this is Ganika, the girl we told you about." She threw her arms around his neck and hugged him again. "I'm so happy."

"And stinky," he said, swatting at a mosquito near his ear and grimacing. "The moment Sergeant Patel doesn't need you anymore, there'll be food, a bath, and a cozy bed waiting for you. Kashif will make sure your *chota hazri* arrives on the late side tomorrow. Now, let's get inside, away from this swarm of bloodsuckers."

"Definitely. Say, where are Kashif and Sundara?" she asked, looking around.

He smiled. "They're probably inside with the girls. There's nothing like a talking parrot to help children relax."

Johanna and Hans were waiting inside the doors just past a guard in a military uniform. "Glad you made it in without being eaten alive by those ferocious mosquitoes," Hans said, attempting to scratch his back.

Halley pictured the moment he put his arm over her shoulder when they were hiding in the closet and felt blood rush into her cheeks. *Oh no*, she thought. *I'm blushing like a tomato.*

Johanna looked at her brother. "I'm sure they thought they'd found Dracula's favorite restaurant when they tasted your blood. They barely bothered me at all. Glad I slathered myself with repellant. But Halley, you must be exhausted."

"I am, but also exhilarated and happy."

"Hey kids." It was George Fischer. "Could you come into the front parlor, please? The Maharaja would like to speak with you."

The teenagers were escorted into an opulent room. Intricate mosaics covered the walls. A man on the velvet sofa in the center stood up and approached them. His casual khaki shirt, short dark hair, and clean-shaven chin weren't at all what Halley expected. She had pictured him bearded, decked out in a white uniform, with an ornate medallion hanging around his neck. But of course, she thought, this *was* the middle of the night.

George Fischer introduced them. "Your Highness, this is Hans and Johanna Norlin and Halley Pederson."

The Maharaja laughed. "I understand I'm to believe that this tall Sikh boy is Halley. Am I right?"

"Yes sir." She bowed her head.

"Well, what did you think about your ride in my helicopter?"

"It was fantastic. The very best ride of my life." They all laughed. "But where did you get it?"

"I bought it directly from the engineer who designed it when I was attending a conference in New York City."

"Well, it's far better than anything on Coney Island."

He abruptly became serious. "The Maharani and I have been very upset about the disappearance of all these poor girls and have grieved about it with many of their parents. When the girl who you helped escape told us where you'd been taken, it gave us the clue we needed to activate a rescue plan and mobilize the cavalry troops." His expression softened. "We would like all three of you and your parents to meet with us in the morning after breakfast. But first this young shepherd needs to eat something, get some rest, and be transformed back into a young lady." He smiled. "This has indeed been a great night. Thank you."

17

Majestic

When they reached the Palm Room, Johanna's mother put Hans to work assisting his dad with the medical records and took Johanna to help the Maharani get the rest of the girls settled in their rooms.

Sergeant Patel signaled for Halley to join him at a table across the room. "The tea is for you," he said, directing her to a chair. "I know this has been a long ordeal for you, so I'll keep this brief. The Maharani has arranged for food and a bath to be set up in all your rooms. You'll be able to eat in peace and get some sleep." He glanced down at the papers in front of him, sighed, and went on. "I'm sorry to have to ask, but did any of the men harm you?"

Her mind whirled. *Flashlight. Sharp pain. Climb the ladder. Dizzy tears.*

The room circled around her. She took a deep breath, touched her shoulder, and placed her other hand above Sundara's feather.

He stopped. "Are you all right?" His eyes flitted between her face and her shoulder.

"I'll be okay." She took a sip of tea. "When they were forcing us onto the elephants in the jungle, one of the men clobbered me here with his flashlight. That's all." She pointed to her shoulder.

"I'm sorry to hear one of them hurt you," he said, pointing to the makeshift medical exam station in the far corner. "Dr. Norlin will need to have a look at it for our records."

"Sergeant Patel, thank you for rescuing the girls," her voice dropped, "and for rescuing me."

Suddenly, he stood up.

Halley heard a rustle of fabric behind her and was surrounded by a breeze that could have blown in from a rose garden.

"*Memsaab* Maharani!"

Halley stood up and turned just as an extraordinary looking woman reached them. Elegant and tall, she was encircled in a light-blue *sari*. The end of it floated around her neck to her other shoulder. Her blunt-cut, wavy black hair almost reached her shoulders and framed her fascinating face. She sank into the other chair. "Please sit down," she said, motioning with her hands. "I understand this *Sikh* boy is the last of our new arrivals to get settled into a room." She smiled at Halley and went on. "I heard what you just said and yes, we are all grateful to Sergeant Patel and the forces he rallied to make the rescue, but you are a true hero. If it hadn't been for your perseverance—and your good fortune and wit—we would still be in the dark about these missing girls. Right?" she asked, looking at Sergeant Patel. He nodded.

"The Maharaja already told you that tomorrow morning we would like to meet with you, your father, and the Norlin family. But right now, I understand your bearer and his beautiful parrot are waiting for you just outside this room to take you and your father to yours."

"Thank you, Your Grace," she blurted, not knowing for sure how to address this majestic woman.

Halley found Dr. Gustaf behind an exam screen with his stethoscope around his neck. "Well, Halley, you're my last patient, and I'm sure you're exhausted." He listened to her lungs, checked her pulse, and asked her the same question Sergeant Patel had asked about injuries.

She repeated the incident and showed him her shoulder. "I know it's nothing compared to what the other girls have been through," she said while he examined it closely.

"I suspect that this hematoma is quite painful," he replied.

She raised the bottoms of her pants and showed him the purple welts on her knees. "These happened when a raven flew out of a tree and knocked me off an elephant." She had to smile at his intrigued expression. "If it hadn't been for that, I wouldn't have met Arjuna, and he wouldn't have been there to stop *Laal* Adrik, the leader, when he escaped."

Dr. Gustaf smiled back at her. "I understand from Sergeant Patel that you were also with the man who stopped the troops on the road inside the fort. If he hadn't warned them, their horses would've reached the gate, eliminating the element of surprise and making it impossible to summon the helicopter."

"Yes, that was Sadhu." She stood up. "And these are his clothes."

Dr. Gustaf left her with her dad. Soon she was walking arm in arm with him behind Kashif and Sundara down a long room lavishly decorated along one wall with sculptures, large paintings, and an occasional chair or sofa. Through the floor-to-ceiling windows and glass doors on the other side, she could see stars peeking through the pillars of the colonnade outside.

She smiled. "This is really a palace." They all stopped in front of a tall, elegantly framed mirror. "Wow, I would never have recognized myself if I'd seen me walking down the street," she giggled. "And I had no idea I was covered with so much dirt."

"Dirt," squawked Sundara.

After journeying through the main entry hall and up a wide staircase, Kashif led them along a short corridor to the two doors at the end. He opened the one on the left. "*Memsaab*, this is your room. The Maharani left some clothes for you." He pointed to the other. "And this one is yours, *Sahib*. What time would you like me to bring *chota hazri*?"

"Actually, could you bring it to both of us just an hour before we would be expected at breakfast?" Dad asked.

"As you wish, *Sahib*." Kashif bowed.

"Thank you, Kashif."

When they were alone, Halley's father wrapped his arms around her. "Good night, precious daughter." He let her go and smiled as he stepped out of the room and closed the door behind him.

Halley wandered around the wide, sumptuous room. This was lovely, but how could she be a hero? All she'd done was continually make a mess of things. She ran her fingers over the white, gossamer-thin fabric draped gracefully over a four-poster bed. It was already prepared for the night. *Thank God for mosquito netting*, she thought, scratching an itchy lump on her neck.

The table near the screen doors to the balcony held an array of covered dishes. She lifted one of the lids, inhaled the savory, curling finger of steam, and closed her eyes. "Mmmm," she hummed.

On a brocade couch she found a new yellow robe with matching pajamas and slippers. Beside them were a fashionable lavender-and-silver dress and a pair of strappy sandals. They looked like they might fit. She held up the dress and wondered if the Maharini always had special outfits for guests who just happened to drop in after being rescued from the jungle. She picked up the brush on the dressing table and set it back down next to a crisp, white hair ribbon. Was she this well equipped for all the girls?

One of the doors led to a spacious tiled room with a full, gardenia-scented bathtub in the center. After a much-needed bath and decked out in the soft pajamas, she consumed most of the food and slipped into bed. The bedside clock read 3 a.m.

She was startled awake by the clink of china. "Good morning, *Memsaab*," Kashif said, pouring tea into the cup he was holding. Sunlight streamed through the windows behind him.

"Thank you, Kashif. That was the best sleep I've had since the last time I slept in a real bed." She slipped her arms into the robe and leaned back on the pillows with the cup and saucer balanced on her lap. Through the netting she watched him collect last night's plates onto a tray. He seemed so focused, no wasted movements. She wondered where Sundara was. "Kashif, is our host the same Maharaja who gave you Sundara?"

"No, *Memsaab*." He tied back the curtain of fabric between them.

"I remember that you said you got him twenty years ago. You must have been a teenager." She sipped the tea. "Do you mind my asking why he gave you Sundara?"

"Not at all. But since you need to get ready for breakfast, I'll give you the short version." Kashif's gentle smile emitted a deep calm. "My father was a barrister, a lawyer, for a maharaja in northern India, and I grew up in the palace. When I was twenty, my father and I were invited to a party given by the Maharaja for his son's ninth birthday. My father had business to attend to before the party, so I entered one of the gardens, intending to have a nice walk. I hadn't gone far when I rounded a bend and almost tripped over a gardener quivering on the path. I learned later that the Maharaja's son had just jumped off a wall, landing in front of him. They were both frozen, mesmerized by the broad head of a brown-and-yellow viper uncurling in front of them, hissing loudly."

"A snake!" she said. "What did you do?"

"The gardener had dropped his tool satchel behind him. The handle of his machete was sticking out. Without really thinking about what I was doing, I scooped it up and tossed it at the snake. The machete flipped end over end and crunched into the snake's neck, killing it instantly. We stood there in shock for a moment, then all three of us burst into tears."

"Wow, you saved the boy's life."

"I guess so. At least that's what his son and the gardener told the Maharaja. But I didn't feel like a hero. I just felt lucky and awkward." He picked up the tray. "The Maharaja knew I had visited his macaws ever since I was a boy and was particularly fond of Sundara. When he invited me and my father to his state room to show his appreciation, he gave me Sundara."

"That's so wonderful," she sighed dreamily, imagining how he must have felt when the macaw he loved was given to him for life.

The door clicked shut.

When her dad tapped on the door, she had successfully tied the ribbon around her hair and was spinning around in front of a long mirror, admiring the swirl of the dress.

At breakfast everyone was seated at a long, wide table with graceful, flowering bird-of-paradise centerpieces that towered over the guests all the way down the table. It looked like everyone was there except their hosts. Halley was next to her father and across from Ganika and Rabar.

They waved. The small girl next to Ganika wiped a few tears off her cheek. It looked like some of the girls' parents had already arrived and were happily eating with their daughters. *They must be from New Delhi*, she thought.

Johanna was on her other side. Hans was between her and their mother. "Halley," Johanna leaned confidingly toward her, "the girl sitting next to Ganika is Lavi, the girl who escaped on that jungle road." She paused. "And from what I heard, it sounds like the two girls next to her might have been sold by their families."

"That is dreadful." Halley suddenly didn't feel like eating anymore.

"Actually, it sounded like their mothers were probably destitute. Both of them had heard a woman say that she had a job in the city for their daughter and gave the mothers some money to help them out. Sergeant Patel thinks that if they'd known they were selling their daughter into slavery, they wouldn't have done it. He already has officers looking for them." She glanced across the table. "And Ganika told Mom that Mrs. Kaliya gave her family money when they took her away."

Halley felt like an iron had just been dropped on her chest. Kidnapping was horrible, but a mother selling her daughter was unthinkable. Poor Ganika. How would they ever stop Mrs. Kaliya? Where was that ghastly woman now?

A server set half a papaya in front of her. Barely watching what she was doing, Halley squeezed the lime slice over the papaya, squirting some of it onto her dad's white jacket.

"Oh no," she moaned.

"That's okay," he laughed, blotting it with his napkin. "No matter how hard you try, you will not be able to upset me today. Even though your disappearances terrified me, you are a hero. I'm grateful to have you back and am very proud of you."

Halley didn't feel like a hero, and she wished everyone would stop calling her that. She just felt confused. Maybe this was what Kashif thought when they called him a hero. She hooked her hand around her dad's elbow, leaned on him, and sighed.

Johanna patted her other hand. "I'm sorry, Halley. I shouldn't have told you all that during breakfast."

After they'd finished eating, Ganika and Rabar came around the table. Halley stood. "We have to leave for our train," Ganika said with glistening eyes. "Halley, we are so happy," she glanced at Rabar, "and very grateful." The girls hugged each other. "We want to see you as soon as you get to Poona." Halley felt a happy ache in her heart and watched them head for the doors.

Soon Halley, her dad, and the Norlins were escorted by soldiers in dress uniforms into the meeting with the Maharaja. A magnificent state room stretched before them. Trumpets flourished a ceremonial fanfare. Enormous crystal chandeliers hung from the vaulted ceiling. Large paintings of earlier maharajas covered the walls in gilt frames. The Maharaja and Maharini, regally adorned in silver and blue, were standing before jewel-encrusted golden thrones on a broad, low dais. Turbaned soldiers in white uniforms stood at attention on either side of them with white-gloved hands resting on the hilts of swords that dangled from their belted sashes.

"If you leave your mouth hanging open like that, a fly will get in," her dad whispered. She snapped it shut, horrified that she had been gawking.

Guests gathered at the foot of the steps, dressed in colorful *saris*, smart dress suits, white *topis,* and turbans. When they reached the empty chairs in the front row, Halley noticed George Fischer and Sergeant Patel. The trumpets stopped. A master of ceremonies stepped to the podium and drummed his staff on the floor several times. They waited while the royal couple sat down. With a wave of his gloved hand, the man motioned to the guests. "Please be seated." Halley reached for the arms of the elegant chair behind her and settled into it.

"His Excellency and Her Highness are very pleased that this day has come when many of the families are finally being reunited with their daughters. The disappearance of so many girls has tormented them and our land for far too long."

Halley was listening, but she was watching the Maharani's gentle smile and her dark, glistening eyes. Her gaze was on someone farther down the front row. She was tempted to lean forward and look but thought better of it. *Whoever the Maharani is looking at is none of my business,* she thought.

"They would first like to recognize Sergeant Patel. Sir, please stand." Two soldiers moved to stand on either side of him. "Their Majesties commend you for your stalwart perseverance in your long search for the missing girls and for your flawless command of the rescue. They have a gift for you."

With slow, dignified strides and flanked by the soldiers, Sergeant Patel mounted the steps to the thrones. Another guard approached carrying a purple pillow in his outstretched hands. On it was a long, curved, red-and-gold sheathed sword.

The Maharaja rose. "Thank you, Sergeant Patel." With both hands he lifted the sword from the pillow, spoke to him softly for a few moments, then solemnly presented it to him.

Halley wondered what Sergeant Patel would do with a sword like that. She pictured him carrying it around. Maybe he could hang it over his fireplace or display it in a glass trophy case. When Sergeant Patel returned to his seat, she could see red and green jewels glinting from the golden hilt. His cheeks were flushed.

"Hans and Johanna Norlin," continued the master of ceremonies, "please rise."

Halley watched them ascend the steps between the soldiers. They looked so calm, she thought, trying to ignore the queasy bubbles rising into her chest. They were so brave. She imagined them racing back to that house in the dark. They must have felt so helpless and angry when they heard Mrs. Kaliya order the men to take the girls to the jungle fort. A quake rumbled through her.

The Maharani stood up and moved to her husband's side. Two soldiers approached Hans and Johanna, each carrying a pillow with a thick silver chain draped over the front. After saying something to the siblings, the regal couple lifted the chains over their heads. Halley craned her neck. She could see a flat, silver pendant about the diameter of an orange dangling from each of them. Just before Johanna got back to her seat, Halley caught a glimpse of the front of hers. An animal on its hind legs stood on either side of the medallion. Together they looked like they were holding up a decorated shield. Johanna returned her smile.

"Miss Halley Pederson." She jumped, and her stomach churned. Walking carefully up the steps between the soldiers, she willed herself not to trip. She was sure that her face was as red as her hair. When she stepped into the breath of roses and sandalwood that hovered around the royals, light bounced off their jewels.

The master of ceremonies spoke, "Miss Pederson, their Majesties were deeply touched when they learned that you continued to search for Ganika's captors, even after you had escaped from yours, and that you helped with the capture of that dangerous man."

Out of the corner of her eye, Halley noticed a flash of white. A guard was approaching.

"They have also learned that a holy man, a shepherd, and the villagers of the mountain temple cared for you after your second escape and kept you safe, and that it was the old man who stopped *Laal* Adrik with his bow and arrow."

Halley nodded, watching their gems shimmer in front of her before glancing up into the Maharaja's eyes and then over to the Maharani's. The man continued. "The whole village was enslaved and tormented. Many of their men were killed by *Laal* Adrik, and he will pay. But now, in gratitude and out of concern for the wellbeing of the village, the Maharaja has hired a company to bring electricity and plumbing to the top of their mountain."

Halley's heart leapt for joy. She imagined the villagers happily watching the twinkling lights coming on for the first time.

The Maharaja opened the flat black box that sat on the pillow the guard was holding and held it out to his wife. Her Highness lifted out a dainty gold chain. In the center dangled a polished red gem encircled with gold and diamonds. "Miss Pederson," she said, "please accept this ruby as a sign of our appreciation for your involvement in this historic rescue. You are a remarkable young lady." She undid the clasp and motioned toward Halley. "May I?"

Halley bowed her head. She felt the cool chain and a touch of warmth when the clasp clicked.

"Thank you, Your Majesties," she stuttered. They each shook her hand.

The Maharaja handed her the box. "We hope you will enjoy it and wear it to our celebration."

Celebration?

Once she was back in her seat, the master of ceremonies spoke again. "Their Majesties have an announcement that mingles sadness with a new joy." He continued in Hindi, then translated, "Miss Lavi Anand, please rise."

Halley was watching the Maharani. She followed her gaze to the small girl standing several seats away from her. She was enveloped in a delicate black-and-silver *sari*. The end was draped over her head, partially obscuring her face. A golden band circled her upper arm.

"Miss Lavi, their Majesties know that you were abducted from your eleventh birthday trip a year ago. You have endured over a year of countless tortures. With Miss Pederson's help, you escaped from your captors in the jungle. Barefoot and alone, you bravely struggled through the night to reach the main road to get help. You told Sergeant Patel where the girls had been taken and how they might initiate the assault on *Laal* Adrik's fortress."

The soldiers moved to her side and escorted her up the steps.

The Maharani took Lavi's hand. She led her to stand between her and the Maharaja.

The master of ceremonies continued, "Their Highnesses are saddened to announce that when Sergeant Patel reached Miss Lavi's relatives this morning they learned that Lavi's parents were tragically killed four months ago in a boating accident, leaving her an orphan."

The Maharani handed the tiny girl a handkerchief, spoke quietly to her, and looped her arm around her waist. The Maharaja placed his hand on her shoulder.

"Would you all please rise?" Halley grabbed her dad's hand.

The man waited until the commotion subsided. "Their Highnesses are grateful to announce that, with the blessing of her uncle and in the midst of her deep grief, Miss Lavi Anand has accepted their invitation for her to join their family as their daughter."

Halley's heart jumped. A happy tear slid from one eye. She felt a wave of happiness roll through the audience and wiped her eye just in time to see Lavi smile at the Maharani. George Fischer started clapping. Everyone else joined him, accompanied by an explosion of cheers.

The master of ceremonies hammered his staff on the floor for silence. "You will all be receiving a formal invitation to the adoption ceremony and celebration. Their Highnesses thank you for your presence here today. They look forward to seeing you this Saturday at their palace in New Delhi."

Halley touched the ruby on her neck and watched Lavi walk hand in hand through a doorway behind the thrones with her new parents.

18

Clinking Glass

When they reached George Fischer's home in New Delhi, his wife was waiting for them on the veranda. After joyfully hugging her husband, Mrs. Fischer took both Halley's hands in hers and gently squeezed them. "I don't think I've ever been this happy to welcome a guest." She released Halley's hands and waved toward the door. "Everyone, make yourselves comfortable! Dinner will be ready in half an hour. The family of one of George's colleagues at the lab will be joining us."

Everyone trooped in chatting and laughing. Johanna caught up with Halley. "Do you remember where your room is?"

"Actually, no."

Hans was right behind her. "Well then, let us be your personal tour guides. It's easy to get lost in this place."

Halley blushed. "That would be nice," she said, smiling back at him. "I'm pretty sure it's upstairs. But that's about it."

"After dinner," Johanna said, "the Fischers like a brandy in the living room. They have two lovely pianos and lots of comfy couches and chairs in there. We usually have a Coke, and someone gets the music going. The Fischers love to play piano duets together. Toward the end of the evening, Dad gets us all up singing show tunes around him at the piano."

Hans piped in, "Hey, Halley, your dad is quite a pianist. He hasn't performed for us yet. But we've heard him in there playing the same piece over and over by himself. Mom said it's the 'Tempest Sonata' by Beethoven."

The "Tempest"? Halley remembered standing in the corridor outside the ship's Grand Room on Christmas morning listening to the achingly beautiful notes of the "Tempest" drift through the closed doors.

"Here's your room," Johanna said. "I'm right next door. Hans and your dad are down the hall. We'll come for you in fifteen minutes."

Halley closed the door and leaned back on it, wondering if she was the kind of girl whom Hans might like. She looked around. The room was tidier than it had been when she sat at the dressing table, wrapping her hair in that scarf. Her hunting outfit had been cleaned and was hanging in the closet with the other clothes she had packed. She changed into her mom's sleeveless black dress and pulled the ruby necklace out from under the high bodice before zipping it up the back. She thought about the time she had watched her mother go out the apartment door wearing the same dress and hugged herself in front of the mirror.

After attempting to brush her hair, she tied it into a high ponytail and gazed out the windows into the garden. The pale orange and pink twilight reflected around the silhouette of a solitary duck that was gliding across the Fischers' pond.

There was a tap on the door. "Hey, Halley." It was Hans. "We're here."

"Coming." She slipped into her flat black shoes and joined them.

At the top of the stairs, they met up with her dad. Even with that silly bow tie she thought he looked quite handsome in his white dinner jacket and dark pants.

"There you are," he said and looped her hand under his arm. "After you left, Mrs. Fischer told me that our panther-skin rug is ready. Any chance you kids would want to go with us in the morning to pick it up?"

Halley looked at the beaming faces of her friends. "Sure, Dad. That would be great."

When they turned down the last staircase toward the entrance, they could hear voices. George Fischer's rose above the rest. "Welcome, welcome."

A servant was leading the new arrivals into the main hall.

"Hey, Karl," George Fischer boomed. "This is Dr. Banko Chakma, his wife, Tevy, and their son—"

"Harin," blurted Halley. She couldn't miss Johanna's confused smile or the puzzled tilt of Hans's head.

"Oh my. Is that really you, Halley Valley?" Harin was at the bottom of the stairs, rubbing the back of his neck and grinning.

"Hah," exclaimed her dad. "Small world. I didn't realize we'd be dining tonight with the man I met in the game room on board ship."

Accompanied by the click of high heels on the marble foyer, Tevy Chakma approached. A dark-green taffeta ruffle flounced from the bottom of her pencil-tight skirt. She could have just stepped off the cover of a fashion magazine. "Well, isn't this a wonderful surprise," she said, laughing.

Banko Chakma extended his hand toward Halley's father. "So, it's Karl, is it?"

"My goodness, I'm missing the party." It was Mrs. Fischer. "Come in, come in."

Halley introduced Harin to her friends and noticed Johanna smile awkwardly at him. Then she glanced at Hans and thought his funny, almost suspicious expression made him look even cuter. His tan jacket and blue shirt highlighted his eyes.

"It's great to meet you." Harin was smiling at Johanna. "This evening won't be nearly as boring as I was expecting it to be." Johanna looked awkward but happy.

Dr. Fischer was introducing Gustaf and Maria Norlin when they entered the library. A servant was walking around with a tray of lemonade-filled crystal glasses that were clinking together.

Halley shuddered. Clinking glasses. Tinkling glass bracelets. She clasped her hands together. *Remember the light*. How would they ever find Mrs. Kaliya?

Harin was looking at her. "What brings you and your dad to New Delhi?"

Halley released her fingers and glanced at her dad. "It's kind of a long story."

Dr. Gustaf stepped in. "They came up with me from Poona to help George and Jalil Rabek stop a wounded panther from a killing rampage near Jaipur."

"Hunting a panther with George and Jalil?" chuckled Mr. Chakma. "This definitely has the makings of an interesting story."

An evening breeze filtered through the large screen windows while Dr. Gustaf described the hunt and the rescue of the missing girls. "Then this morning, in front of all of us, the Maharaja and Maharani announced that they're adopting one of the girls. They invited us to the ceremony and celebration this Saturday at their palace."

Mr. Chakma looked at his wife and back at Dr. Gustaf. "Yes, we know about it. As we were leaving our compound just now, a courier delivered an invitation from their Highnesses, inviting us to join them this Saturday."

Halley noticed that Harin was watching Johanna sip her lemonade. He sat down next to her on the couch and said, "Terrific! We'll all go. It'll be great fun."

After a delicious dinner filled with lively conversation, Dr. Fischer invited them into the living room for a brandy and some music. Once everyone was seated with a glass in hand, he stood up. "Geeta and I recently performed the Mozart *Sonata in D for Four Hands* at a piano club concert. If you can endure it, we'd like to open our music this evening with the first movement."

Mrs. Chakma clapped her hands together. "That would be wonderful. But George, you really must tell your guests what happened during that concert."

He looked at his wife. She smiled back at him. "Go ahead, George."

"Well, okay." He glanced around. "There were two ladies on the program right before us. They performed a lovely rendering of a Bach duet. After the applause, they thanked everyone, sat back down at the piano, and opened more music. One of them said, 'Now we have a little encore. The "Allegro" from Mozart's *Sonata in D*.' Then they proceeded to play the first movement of the very same sonata we were about to perform. Geeta grabbed my hand so I didn't throw something at them." He laughed and locked eyes with his wife and continued. "A smattering of applause followed. Geeta moved over to the piano. I remained standing in front of the stunned audience. Tevy, you looked like you were about to throw up."

"Yes, I felt like it," Mrs. Chakma laughed. "Go on."

"To introduce our performance and to lighten the mood I said, 'Let me tell you a little story. There was a large church that was looking for a new minister. The two finalists were invited to give a sermon to the congregation. The church put them up in the same hotel in side-by-side rooms with thin walls. In one room was the bright young minister who had not prepared his sermon yet. In the other was the somewhat slow older man who had been having trouble memorizing his sermon. For half the night he walked back and forth repeating it out loud. In the next room his smart, yet ill-prepared, competitor could hear him.

"'In front of the church the next morning they called on the young priest first and, having memorized the other man's sermon, he proceeded to give it. Of course, the older man was crushed. He wanted to leave by the side door. He had no other sermon. So, when it was his turn, he went to the pulpit and delivered the very same sermon. He was horribly embarrassed and went back to his room to pack and slink out of town.

"'One of the elders knocked on his door and invited him to their meeting. Blushing and shaky, he sat down at the long table, knowing he was done for.

"'One of the elders stood up and said, "Father Kumar, your sermon and your incredible mind impressed us deeply. None of us have ever heard anyone who could listen to a sermon once and repeat it word for word. We would like you to be our pastor."'"

George Fischer paused while his guests laughed, then he went on. "After the audience finished laughing, I sat down next to Geeta, and we played the 'Allegro'...from memory."

Silence hung over their guests. The black, upright surface in front of the Fischers reflected their hands caressing the keys of their grand piano.

Right in the middle of a passionate pause, hands hovering in the air, they glanced at each other and smiled before lowering their hands energetically into the final runs and jumps of the movement.

"Bravo," Mr. Chakma cheered above the applause.

"Now, Gustaf," Dr. Fischer waved at Dr.Gustaf, "how about getting us singing some of those songs from *Meet Me in St. Louis* again?"

Almost an hour later, Hans collapsed on the couch next to Halley. "I don't think I can sing another note." Johanna and Harin fell in next to him.

"Say," Harin leaned forward, "that was fun, and I really liked the songs from *An American in Paris*."

"Yes," said Johanna. "Hans and I always love to sing with Mom and Dad when they croon that song and get that goofy look in their eyes."

Halley's heart was filled with sparkles. Hans had been standing next to her the whole time. She had laughed with Johanna and Harin when Hans sang the high notes of the *April in Paris* theme song in a perfect falsetto. Now she was squeezed in next to him on the couch with his hand resting on his leg less than an inch from hers. She smiled.

Dr. Fischer pulled up a chair across from them. "Hey, kids. The Maharaja's ceremony isn't for four more days. So, your folks and I have been talking about possible plans for the rest of the week. Since the Taj Mahal is just a little over four hours from here by car, we could head out after an early breakfast on Friday, drive to Agra, and be back by dinner. What do you think?"

Halley remembered sitting on the couch with her mother and looking at a picture of the Taj Mahal. She closed her eyes and pictured her mom clapping at the idea.

"Halley." Dad was standing next to Dr. Fischer. "Does a trip to the Taj Mahal this Friday sound good to you?" A puzzled expression hovered on his face.

"Sure, Dad." She sat up and tried to smile. "Especially since we're this close and are probably not heading back to Poona until Sunday, right?"

Mrs. Chakma was nearby. "Harin, your father has a meeting and Mrs. Fischer and I are hostesses for a luncheon at the club. But we can take you out of school for the day so you can go too." They all started walking toward the main hall and she turned to Mrs. Fischer. "Thank you for the lovely dinner."

Harin was walking next to Johanna. "We never tire of the Taj," he said. "I love to see the light that emanates out of the white marble."

"Yes," said Johanna, "the light is so ethereal."

When they caught up with the ladies, Mrs. Chakma took Halley's hand. She looked at Johanna. "Your mother, Mrs. Fischer, and I have decided to go to my dressmaker's shop tomorrow afternoon to select the fabric for new *lehengas* and a *lehenga choli* for the celebration. They require two to three days to make them and would have them finished by noon on Saturday. Would you girls like to come with us and pick something out for yourselves?" She looked back at Halley and dropped her hand. "Halley, we already checked with your dad."

"Oh yes," said Johanna. "Halley, the *lehenga* is a gorgeous, ankle-length skirt. You'll love the outfit. The *choli* is a tight-fitted top that goes with it. You will also need a *duppata*. It's a long, shawl-like scarf. It would be great to have something new to wear."

"Sure, Mrs. Chakma," Halley said. "I only packed for the hunting trip and didn't bring anything dressy to wear. Thanks for including me. Do you think it would be okay for us to meet you there? Dad's taking us to pick up the panther-skin rug in the morning."

"Actually," Mrs. Chakma said. "How about if you all come to our home after the taxidermist for *tiffin*? We can go from there. I'll call my dress shop first thing in the morning."

"I couldn't help hearing your plans." It was Dr. Fischer. "Hans, while the girls are off shopping, would you like to come with us to the club? Harin, you could meet us there after school and join us for some cricket."

Hans glanced at Halley, then back at Dr. Fischer. "Wow, that would be great. Thanks."

Once the door closed behind the Chakmas, Halley looked at her friends. "Could you take me to that screened porch where we sat last Sunday? We need to talk."

"Sure," said Hans and Johanna.

They collapsed into the wicker chairs.

"I'm worried," Halley said. "It's been three days since we saw Mrs. Kaliya at that house. She's probably gone, but what if she's not? She knows *Laal* Adrik. Quite possibly they've been working together for a long time. She's probably still in business and more dangerous than ever."

"What can we do?" Johanna's voice was shaky.

"Probably nothing," said Halley, finding it hard to keep from biting her nails.

"She could be anywhere," added Hans. He looked as worried as Halley felt. "I wonder if our uncle's investigators have found anything. We need to call him. He may have heard something."

"Good idea," said Johanna.

"Thanks." Halley was glad she'd said something.

They were almost to the stairs when they passed the living room. A gentle melody murmured from the piano and out through the closed doors. This was followed by a storm of notes. Strong fingers blew wildly across the keys.

Hans whispered, "It's your dad."

Halley froze, barely breathing, sucked into the tumult of sound. Racing downpours of passion repeatedly interplayed with brief, tranquil, melodic breezes. The notes echoed away into the silence. Her friends had left her alone.

19

Play On

When they reached the taxidermist's in the morning, Kashif and the Fischers' driver stayed with the cars. Halley trooped into the shop with the others. Just inside the door was an enormous snarling tiger perched on a platform next to them, ready to spring. Menacing fierce eyes glared at Halley. She squeezed hers tight.

Blazing sun. Raw, seething power. Hot breath close enough to smell.

Halley gasped, clapping her hands on her icy cheeks. The room spun, and her legs buckled.

"Oh no, she's going down." Hans's voice broke through the descending blackness. Strong, warm hands caught her.

"Halley." She could hear her dad. She felt the hard floor beneath her and a cool, wet cloth gently stroking her forehead. When she opened her eyes, she was gazing up into Hans's worried blue ones, her head resting in his lap.

Dad was unwrapping a hard candy. "Halley, suck on this. Did you eat anything at breakfast?"

She took it. "Sorry, Dad. When I got downstairs, everyone was heading for the cars. I didn't even have time for a sip of tea."

"Well then, that bit of sugar should make you feel better. Hans and Johanna, could you stay with her while we pick up the rug?"

"Of course," said Johanna.

Halley felt Hans helping her to sit up. She popped the candy in her mouth.

"What happened, Halley?" Hans asked. "When you saw the tiger, you turned as white as a ghost and collapsed."

Halley looked up at the preserved tiger looming over her and thought about the numerous times she had gone with her parents to the natural history museum in New York. The stuffed tiger there never scared her. Of course, he was behind a glass wall and very dead. She had never fainted before. Maybe it was just low blood sugar. She really needed to remember to eat breakfast.

She noticed Johanna's concerned expression and realized she hadn't answered Hans's question. Why had she fainted? Her mind jumped to that terrifying moment, cowering in the grass, her eyes glued on the wounded panther crashing down the hillside toward her.

"Well," her voice shook, "this wasn't the first time I was that close to the teeth of a snarling big cat. The first time was on the morning of the hunt when I was in the jungle with Dad and the other hunters." She went on to describe the beaters moving through the jungle and the moment that the terrifying panther burst through the trees and barreled down the hillside toward her. "When Dad's shot hit the beast, it flipped completely over and landed right in front of me on all fours, snarling, eyes glaring, ready to spring on me."

"Oh no," gasped Johanna.

"Then what happened?" blurted Hans.

"She keeled over dead." Halley paused. "Three days later, when I ended up with Ganika and the other girls on top of those elephants crunching along the trail in the moonlight, hanging onto the flimsy *howdah* by our nails, we watched a large panther slinking through the dark jungle beside us for at least an hour. I flashed back to that moment when the crazy panther landed right in front of me. Was this sinister creature pacing beneath us the angry mate seeking revenge? He only turned back when we crossed a wide river."

Hans broke through the stunned silence. "Halley, the more you tell us, the more I understand the depth of the ordeal you've been through."

"Yes, it's a wonder that you aren't just hiding in your closet," said Johanna. "I think I'd be. Actually, this tiger startled me too." She turned to Hans. "Remember Mom telling us about the time when I was a toddler and you were three years old and they took us to that party?" She turned to Halley. "At one point, Hans wandered off down a hallway and managed to open a door leading into a dark room, waking up their big dog. It barked loudly, and Hans screamed, which scared the dog even further. For a while after that, he made our folks check the closet and under the bed every night before he'd go to sleep."

They were standing beneath the tiger, laughing, when her dad returned. "The rug is beautiful and will look great under the piano when our furniture gets here. They'll box it and deliver it to the Fischers' tomorrow. Say, Hans, thanks for catching Halley. She must have been a dead weight. And you, fragile lady, have you recovered enough to head over to the Chakmas'?"

She nodded and smiled at Hans. "I'm sure more than my pride would be aching if you hadn't stopped me from crashing into the floor. Thank you." She noticed his expression soften. He tilted his head and smiled back, and her heart did a little shimmy.

He's so cute. What's he thinking?

When they were almost to the cars, Hans stopped. "Johanna said you play tennis. The Fischers have a tennis court behind the gardens, and we've already tried out their extra rackets. Would you like to play a game with us tomorrow morning, or even just rally a bit before it gets too hot?"

"Sure. That'd be nice." She felt her cheeks get hot.

When they piled into the car Johanna jumped in front with Kashif. Hans got into the back seat next to Halley. "Johanna says you auditioned for the part of Jack in the play and are undoubtedly a shoo-in for it. She's excited about playing the part of Lady Bracknell."

"I hope so. I love that play." She realized it had been a week since her audition and sadly wondered if Sister Jane had replaced her.

"So do I. Your school schedule is a little different from mine. Dad said that if they schedule the play during my spring vacation, I can go with them to see it."

Halley loved the idea that he might be in the audience for the performance and smiled. Then she wondered if she would be able to remember her lines with such a distraction.

Kashif followed the Fischers' car through the Chakmas' prominent metal gate. A guard bowed and waved them on. The drive wound through fruit trees of all kinds.

"Wow, there's a pomegranate tree." Johanna pointed at a spindly dark-green tree with large red balls dangling like Christmas ornaments. "It looks like no two trees are alike."

"That's a mango." Hans was looking at an enormous tree on the other side. Orange and green fruit hung from every branch.

The trees fell away, revealing a pink stucco mansion. Sloping rooftops, gables, narrow towers, and gateways into side courtyards were all frosted with rounded red brick tiles. Iron gates embellished with intricate metal trees and slender vines graced the entrance. They parked behind a red convertible and walked past it toward the house. "Looks like the ladies have already arrived," said Dr. Fischer. "Geeta just loves driving that car."

A servant guided them through the main hall and into a large inner courtyard tastefully landscaped with giant palms, a myriad of other trees, and flowering bougainvillea. The lotus pond behind Mrs. Chakma reflected a large, seated Buddha and a cherry blossom tree. She rose to greet them. "Welcome, my angels. It's so lovely today we decided to eat out here." She guided them to a husky man in a saffron-colored robe. "It is my honor to introduce you to Rinpoche, our teacher."

His compassionate smile and shining silver hair captivated Halley. Resisting the urge to hug him, she clasped her hands together and bowed. He bowed back.

Mrs. Chakma smiled at Halley. "When I was a teenager, my uncle arranged for Rinpoche to come from Tibet to Hyderabad to teach at our temple. When Banko and I married and moved to New Delhi, he came with us. He can speak only a little English."

Once their servants finished passing trays of sandwiches, fruit, and iced tea, Dr. Gustaf looked at Mrs. Chakma, then at the teacher. "Rinpoche, we've been very concerned about China's occupation of Tibet and worried about the safety of the Dalai Lama and the other *lamas*, their holy men. Have you heard from anyone there?" They waited while Mrs. Chakma translated.

"He says, 'Thank you for your concern,'" she said. "'Actually,'" she continued translating, "'we've heard very little since China invaded Tibet last year until a telegram arrived just this morning from Rinpoche's cousin, who is a holy man. Like so many of the Tibetan lamas, he was in danger for his life and escaped from Tibet over the Himalayan mountains this past month. Now he's at a monastery in Kathmandu, Nepal.'"

Dr. Gustaf looked at Rinpoche. "A journey over the Himalayas would be arduous at any time of year, but in the winter? He must be an amazing person." Mrs. Chakma translated, and the conversation turned to their afternoon plans.

Following *tiffin,* the driver parked Mrs. Chakma's limousine in the shade of a banyan tree at the edge of a teeming marketplace, and the girls followed the ladies along a narrow street. Vendors sitting on blankets under brightly colored canopies or squatting in doorways held up large brass cooking pots, blankets, vegetables, or jewelry and hollered as they passed.

They came to a small, impeccably dressed man standing in front of a bright yellow door. He greeted Mrs. Chakma by name and invited them into his showroom. Once they were seated, Halley relaxed and listened to them chatter away in Hindi. Along the walls around them were at least a hundred rolls of fabric sorted by color. The wall across from her was partially covered with different shades of pink. One of them reminded her of the tutu she had worn in a ballet recital when she was a child. One roll of fabric in the green section reminded her of the stairwell up to their New York City apartment.

After what seemed like an hour, the tailor motioned to Halley. Mrs. Chakma said, "Mr. Darjee is going to bring out fabrics for our *lehengas* and our *lehenga choli* and wants to know what colors you would prefer."

"Blue would be nice."

Mrs. Chakma translated. "He says he could make you a beautiful, two-layered *lehenga*. He has a light-blue satin that would shine through from under a delicate blue lace of cascading flowers. For your *lehenga choli*—that's the top—he has a white-and-silver lace that would look lovely with the same blue satin showing through from underneath. Would you like him to show you the fabrics?"

"Yes, please."

A few hours later, after watching the men play a wild game of cricket, they all sipped lemonade on the club veranda and discussed their plans for the trip to the Taj Mahal on Friday. Mrs. Chakma said, "If two of the teenagers were to sit in the front seat with the driver, you would all fit in this Buick. Would that work for you?"

"Thank you, Tevy," said Dr. Fischer. "Taking just one vehicle would be terrific." To determine the seating arrangement, he asked the waiter to bring several straws and a pair of scissors. He cut them into two lengths. "The two with the long straws will sit in front on the way there and the short straws would switch with them on the way back."

Dr. Gustaf laughed. "Great idea, George. You must be an engineer."

"Hey," said Halley's dad, "Maybe we should take bets on who gets to ride shotgun first."

Halley pictured herself sitting in front with Hans. Would the driver speak English? What could they possibly talk about for four hours?

Everyone silently watched Dr. Fischer place the four straws side by side behind his fingers with only an inch sticking out the top. He held them up to Johanna.

"It's a long one," her mother said, laughing.

It was Halley's turn. She held her breath, wished she could sit with Hans, and pulled.

"Whoa," chuckled Johanna. "We have a back seater."

Hans went next.

"Here's the kicker," chimed in Mrs. Fischer.

He inched it out so slowly, everyone groaned and exploded with laughter when the straw got longer and longer.

Halley struggled to hide her disappointment, while trying hard not to look at Hans.

"Another front seater," said Mrs. Chakma. "We have the lineup."

"And what a lineup it is," said Dr. Gustaf. "That is, provided that you two don't fight all the way to Agra."

Mrs. Chakma was called to the phone and returned a few minutes later. "Guess what? Friends of ours are entertaining in their home tomorrow evening and would like us to bring some friends. They've received a surprise visit from a traveling troupe of actors that will perform Shakespeare's *Twelfth Night* in their living room. She needs an audience. Can you all come?"

Mrs. Fischer clapped her hands and held them together at her neck. "I'm up for a good laugh. What do you think, George?" Everyone loved the idea, and it was agreed they would all be at her friend's after tea on Thursday.

Halley's dad caught her eye and chuckled. "Let's see how it compares with the production we just saw in London."

Chatting merrily, they all headed for the cars. Dad was waiting near the Fischers' station wagon for the girls. "Geeta's going back with Tevy to get her car. Maria's going with her. So girls, we have room for both of you to come with us."

The boys had stopped behind them. Halley wondered what they'd been talking about and why they suddenly looked like great friends. "Thanks," Hans said and shook Harin's hand.

Maybe it was during the cricket game, she thought.

Harin turned to Johanna. "I'm glad you'll be at the play. It will be such fun. Also, your brother asked me to trade places with him in the front seat of the car on the way to the Taj Mahal. I hope that's okay with you."

Johanna blushed and dropped her gaze to the ground, then looked back at Harin. He was anxiously watching her. It seemed like forever before she said, "Sure."

Halley glanced over at Hans, who was talking to his father. Did that mean he wanted to sit with her in the front on the way back? Sunshine covered her with a warm glow.

The next day they played tennis all morning. Each set they switched positions. There was always one of them playing against the other two. Most of the time when Halley was on the single-player side against Johanna and Hans, she felt pretty good about her game. But she wasn't used to playing doubles, so when she had to share a side with one of them, she had trouble gauging who was supposed to hit the ball when it landed near the line between them.

In the afternoon they played cards and Clue on the screened porch and chatted. A little while before tea, Halley saw a bent-over old man moving along the edge of the garden. His dark skin glistened in the heat. He was leading a round, blue-black cow with curled horns.

Johanna noticed her watching him. "That's the Fischers' milk man. He comes every day and milks his water buffalo behind the kitchen in back. Sarin said that the cook makes sure the milking bucket is clean before the man starts. Afterward the cook pasteurizes the milk in the kitchen."

"He looks a lot darker than the other servants." Halley watched him trudge out of sight.

"Yes," Hans said. "He's an untouchable."

"That sounds awful." Halley felt a catch in her throat. "What could that possibly mean, 'untouchable'?"

Johanna answered, "Have you heard about the Indian caste system?"

"Yes, but I don't understand it."

"Well," Johanna said, "even though Mahatma Gandhi was particularly outspoken about the racist hierarchy of the castes in India, there hasn't been a real solution. The caste system here is ancient. The British rule of India didn't help, either, because the British are used to their own system. Their countrymen are born into a similar hierarchy: classic lords of the manor, the soldiers, the merchants in town, and the servants. In India, even if a lower caste man makes it to college and becomes an engineer, he never leaves behind his hereditary caste."

"But," Halley held up her hand. Her heart was beating faster, and her voice was higher. "What is an untouchable? That sounds dreadful."

Hans sighed. "They're people who are cast into humble, menial jobs. Outcast. They're not in a caste at all."

Johanna jumped in. "You know, Halley, you Americans have a caste system too."

Hans cleared his throat and looked at the servant standing quietly in the doorway. He announced that tea was being served in the conservatory.

Johanna's last words rang in Halley's mind. "You Americans have a caste system too." What did she mean? America didn't have people with hereditary titles. Halley pictured the difference between the characters in one of her favorite books, Jane Austen's *Pride and Prejudice.* The landed gentry, soldiers, priests, and servants. What about the scullery maid . . . and between Lady Bracknell in *The Importance of Being Earnest* and her butler? Her thoughts turned to the time in New York City when she and her parents went out to dinner after seeing a movie matinee of *Gone with the Wind* for her eleventh birthday. The maître d' seated them right away. A glamorous, young couple in formal attire was waiting for him at his podium when he returned. Halley was particularly fascinated by the silver fox fur the lady was wearing around her neck and her ebony skin that sparkled in the candlelight. The maître d' walked right past them, warmly greeted the couple standing behind them, and immediately seated them at a table by the window. The maître d' noticeably scowled at the first couple and led them past three empty tables to one in the back near the kitchen and slammed down their menus.

All through tea, Halley's thoughts flashed between scenes from *Gone with the Wind* and the couple in the restaurant, between the slave young woman in the American Civil War movie and the beautiful dark-skinned woman in the fur stole.

Johanna is right, she thought. *We do have our own kind of caste system. And it's existed since the colonists first landed in America, the plantation owners, the soldiers, the teachers, and the slaves.*

"Halley, wait," Johanna found her in the hallway. "You didn't say a word at tea." Hans was right behind her.

"Sorry, I was just thinking about what you said about the untouchable man and the American caste system. You're right. I just never thought about it before." Halley told them about the couple in the restaurant. "Did you see the movie *Gone with the Wind* that was set during the American Civil War?"

Hans nodded. "The rerelease of that film finally reached Poona when I was thirteen. Very dramatic."

"Johanna, is that what you meant when you said we have a caste system too?"

"Actually, yes. I'm sorry to have said that without explaining what I was thinking."

Mrs. Fischer was waiting for them in the hallway. "If two of you sit in the way back end of our station wagon, George can drive us to the play, and we can take one car. Any volunteers?"

"I will," Halley and Hans said at once. They looked at each other and laughed.

Mrs. Fischer had arranged for some pillows in the back, and Hans and Halley leaned against them, facing out the back window. Her heart danced helplessly the whole way.

Mrs. Chakma met them in the entrance hall and introduced them to her friend. Within a few minutes they were seated in the living room with an audience of about twenty facing a portable stage.

"This troupe of Shakespearean performers travels all over India," their hostess said. "We first saw them in Bombay. I'm so excited they are here in our home." She stood up and faced the audience. "I'm delighted to welcome you to this performance of *Twelfth Night* by the talented Shakespeareana Traveling Company."

As soon as she was back in her seat and the clapping had died down, two gentlemen entered the stage. A musician behind them began plucking on a guitar-like instrument.

The duke spoke. "If music be the food of love, play on..." Halley felt the words course through her like an old friend, and his British accent fit right in.

Every scene was better than the one before, and the play ended with wild applause.

"I loved the man who played Malvolio," Hans said as they climbed back in the car.

"I laughed so hard," said Johanna. "He seemed crazy, smiling constantly and dressed in those wild yellow stockings."

Halley giggled. "The girl who played Viola gave an excellent performance disguised as a man."

From the front seat, Halley's dad called back. "She reminded me of that young *Sikh* who emerged from the helicopter."

They laughed and chatted all the way back to the Fischers.' Their good spirits carried them through a delicious dinner and on to the usual singing around the piano, punctuated by plans for the trip to the Taj Mahal in Agra the next morning. Halley's dad agreed to play the piano if she would sing "I'm Called Little Buttercup" from the comic opera *H.M.S. Pinafore*.

"Now Gustaf, it's your turn." Halley's dad said, turning the page in the Gilbert and Sullivan songbook. "Please sing 'A Maiden Fair to See' to Maria for us."

Gustaf Norlin smiled at his wife, and they took Halley's place behind her dad at the piano.

20

Crystal Crypt

They set off early the next morning for the Taj Mahal. Almost the moment the limousine doors closed, Dr. Gustaf and Halley's dad started talking about the challenges of malaria research in India. Dr. Fischer, sitting between them on the back seat, interjected an occasional question or an observation. Dr. Maria, seated next to Halley on the middle seat, offered some illustrations. With three of them on the middle seat meant for two people, Hans's head was only a few inches from Halley's. She loved being this close to him and had no problem ignoring the medical conversation behind her.

They had just passed through the Fischers' gate when Hans asked, "Weren't those pancakes great?"

"Yes, and I loved the caramel and banana topping."

"The mango cream sauce was good, too."

"Definitely," said Halley. *Oh no*, she thought, *what do I say now?*

"Hey, let's play Scissors, Stone, and Paper," Hans said, holding his fist in the air in front of him.

"Sure," she replied and held out her fist. That game almost got them out of the city.

"Do you miss New York?" Hans asked.

His question surprised her. "Not the city. It's really noisy. The buildings are gigantic and there are people everywhere. Actually, I've been so busy, I haven't had time to think about it. But I do miss Mom and think about her a lot."

Dr. Maria was listening. "What do you remember most about her?"

Most? Halley thought for a moment. "I don't know," she said. "The first thing that comes to mind was playing piano duets with her. She was always so much fun. She would have loved to go to the dressmaker's, and she was really looking forward to seeing the Taj Mahal."

"Tell us about her," Hans said.

Halley could hear that the conversation in back included her dad and she felt pretty sure he wouldn't hear them talk about Mom.

"She was interested in everything and often took me with her to the museum for lunch and musical programs, even jazz. If it was in the evening, Dad would usually come too."

Dr. Maria put her arm around Halley's shoulder and gently asked, "Do you have a favorite memory of her?"

"I have many favorite memories." She paused. "But the one I'm thinking about happened last August. Mom and I spent the summer with her parents at Meadowcroft, their vacation home north of Boston. Dad would come up from the city on the weekends. One day, she took me sailing on one of Grandpa's boats. The sky was blue. We had a perfect wind. Around noon we anchored in a small cove and swam around near the boat. Then we put our picnic basket in the dingy and rowed to a little rocky beach. We spread out the blanket and set up the beach umbrella. While we ate, she told me about the time she spent a few weeks sailing between the Bahamas and Cuba with some girl friends from Wellesley College, pulling into coves just like the one we were in, grilling fresh fish over open fires."

Halley stopped and gazed out the window.

"Sounds heavenly," said Hans.

She exhaled. "One afternoon they were becalmed on the ocean within sight of Havana. The boat was steadily floating farther away from shore. Some of the girls were really scared; a few started crying. Mom was on the bow messing with the sail when she saw a boat. She hollered at it and started waving. Within minutes a large fishing trawler pulled up alongside them and a man called out, 'Say, would you ladies like a tow?' He hopped aboard. 'I'm Ernest,' he said and tied a rope onto the front of their boat, and his friends began towing them. She said he chatted with them, cracked jokes all the way into the harbor, and even bought them drinks in the hotel lounge. Everyone around them seemed to know him and she could see why. He was gracious, good natured, and handsome with a mustache and strong arms. When he had to leave and was heading out the door, they heard the manager say, 'It was splendid to see you, Mr. Hemingway.' My mom said she and her friends looked at each other and shrieked because they hadn't realized he was the world-famous author Ernest Hemingway."

Hans and his mother laughed with Halley.

"Say, Dr, Maria, how did you end up in India?" Halley asked. "Dad said you're from Holland?"

"My favorite cousin, Michele, fell in love with Andy Patel when he was at the university in Rotterdam. After they married, she moved with him to New Delhi. I missed her so much. We wrote all the time. After I finished my medical residency, I accepted a job at a hospital near her in New Delhi and lived with them. I met Gustaf at a party at their house. A few years later we were married, and we both accepted positions in Poona. Hans and Johanna were both born there."

"That's so romantic. What about you, Hans? What made you decide to go to school up north?"

Hans shrugged. "Mom and Dad knew I loved rugby and playing the cello, and this upper school had great programs in both areas. Since it's so close to my Aunt Michele's, I could stay with her on the short breaks and some weekends."

Dr. Maria smiled. "Not to mention that it's cooler at that higher altitude and is also a prep school for Oxford."

"Hey Mom," Hans leaned forward, "I forgot to tell you. . . Just last week, Iyengar, you know, *Dadaji*'s yoga teacher, came to my school to speak. He also demonstrated. Did you know he can put both his feet flat on his stomach?"

During the rest of the trip to the Taj Mahal, Halley learned that the Norlins had been to Sweden on a recent holiday. They talked about American movies they had seen and that they liked some of the same novels.

On the outskirts of the city of Agra, Dr. Maria told everyone about the Agra Fort and the Taj Mahal. "For about three hundred years, India was ruled by the Mughal emperors. Succession went from father to son. Terrible battles often determined which son would be the next emperor. For a hundred years they ruled from Agra Fort. Soon after Shah Jahan became emperor, his beloved wife, Mumtaz Mahal, died while giving birth to their fourteenth child. Grieving deeply over her death, Shah Jahan commissioned the construction of the Taj Mahal as a memorial to her."

"In 1658," Hans interjected, "one of Shah Jahan's sons seized power, killed all his brothers, and deposed his father."

"Really?" Halley looked at Dr. Maria, then at Hans. "That's awful. What happened to Shah Jahan?"

"I think that's the saddest part of the story," Dr. Maria said. "His ruthless son imprisoned him in the Agra Fort. Shah Jahan spent the last seven years of his life in an octagonal room just across the river from his monument to his wife. Some say he could see it from his room. After he died, his son buried him in the crypt of the Taj with his queen."

The driver parked in a shady area near the gate. By the time they all emerged, he had unfolded a wooden table and covered it with a tablecloth. Harin helped him set up the wooden chairs and opened a huge picnic basket. "Mom made sure we'd have a good lunch." He pulled out numerous dishes wrapped in white cloth, while the driver poured lemonade and set the table.

Johanna smiled. "Harin, this is lovely. Thank you."

He laughed. "I didn't really have anything to do with it, but you're welcome."

Hans helped Halley with her chair and sat down next to her. "Thanks," she whispered and glanced at him.

"Wow," he said, "this all smells fantastic."

They passed around plates heaped with savory fried pastries, skewers of meats, sauces, and fruits.

Dr. Gustaf was holding a crispy triangular pastry. "These spicy beet *samosas* are amazing." He took a bite and closed his eyes.

"And," laughed his wife, "these lamb and mint ones are heavenly."

"My favorite," said Johanna, "are the roasted chicken *tikka* skewers with cucumber slices."

"These are delicious." Halley held up a partially eaten round pastry with a green filling peeking out. "What is it?"

Harin laughed. "Those are pea *kachori*. I love them." He passed her a bowl. "Try them with a little of this yogurt *chutney*."

Dr. Fischer groaned. "I better stop eating or I'll have to take a nap."

Halley walked into the Taj Mahal complex along the market street between Hans and her dad. "This is so exciting," she said. They turned toward a spectacular dark-red building with lots of arches and white caps along the edge of the roof. Hans called them "*cupolas*." White marble panels inlaid with flowers outlined the central arch that rose up higher than a tall house. Through that opening Halley caught her first glimpse of the Taj Mahal hovering in the distance. She blurted, "There it is." She turned back toward Dad and smiled just as he took a picture of her.

They followed a crowd of other visitors under the arch and on through the gateway. A flock of pigeons flew over them. She could hear her father's camera snapping away and was glad he had all those extra rolls of film in his pocket. When they burst into the sunlight on the other side, Halley stopped, soaking in the moment, gazing at the most exquisite monument to love. Its perfect reflection shimmered in the long pool that ran toward them through the garden. Her dad asked Dr. Fischer to take his picture with her and the Taj Mahal. Then there were pictures of everyone. Her dad took one with just the teenagers.

They continued along the walkway beside the pool, Johanna and Harin leading the way. Mesmerized by the light emanating from every arch and minaret, Halley stopped several times to drink in the sight. Everything about the monument was so perfect, from the pristine white dome to the matching vaulted archways. Every time she stopped, the glistening accents of color in the white marble changed. Hans kept pace with her. When they reached the base of the monument, they came to a sea of shoes. Her dad had informed her about the "no shoes inside" policy.

Dr. Maria said, "Let's all put our shoes side by side. Gustaf will give the attendant a nice tip to watch them."

Halley took off her loafers and looked up at Hans. He was smiling at her. *I must have a puzzled look on my face*, she thought. She was worried about finding them in this labyrinth of footwear. Maybe they should make a map.

As though he heard her thoughts, Hans said, "We always check out the area around our shoes and look for landmarks. See these inset arch-like cutouts in the marble. The one above our shoes is three panels from that doorway and across from the steps."

Dr. Maria said, "All right team, we need to really work at staying together. If you get separated from the rest of us, meet us back here at our shoes at two thirty." They followed her through the arched doorway into a large chamber where she pointed to the two marble tombs beneath a magnificent dome that towered above them. One was larger than the other. "Halley, these beautifully decorated sarcophagi are empty. The remains of Shah Jahan and Mumtaz Mahal are in plain marble ones in the crypt on the level below us." She pointed out the precious and semi-precious stones and ornamentation and explained that Muslims don't decorate their actual graves. She sang one high note so they could hear it reverberate between the walls and up into the dome.

After Dr. Maria pointed out the flowers inlaid into the marble, they went down to see the true graves. There, Dr. Fischer described the other parts of the mausoleum and the years that it took to finish the entire complex. "Now, let's go to the riverfront terrace."

Halley was transfixed by the tombs. She barely heard his voice disappear through the entrance to the chamber and closed her eyes. The peaceful silence took her to her mother's graveside. She had kissed the red rose she was holding and placed it next to her father's on the white casket. She had spread her fingers out over it, touching, lingering, wiping her tears and had listened to the priest. "In the midst of life, we are in death: of whom shall we seek for succor, but of thee, O Lord."

Halley sensed someone next to her and looked. It was Hans. He was looking closely at the intricate stone flowers set into the marble.

"Hans, have you ever had someone you love die?"

"Yes." His voice quivered. "We had an older sister. During the dry season two years ago when the river near our house was low enough for us to cross it on an old stone dam, Emma slipped on one of the rocks and fell into the water. When she didn't come right back up, Mom and Dad went in after her. They both tried to resuscitate her. It was awful."

They stood quietly.

"Johanna and I think that's why Mom works so hard all the time. They never talk about Emma around us."

"I'm sorry, Hans. Dad and I don't talk about Mom either. But he plays that music every night. She bought it for his Christmas present a few days before she was hit by the cab. I gave it to him on Christmas Eve on board ship. I felt so sad when I told him she had picked it out for him."

"Halley, what do you think happens to us when we die?"

"At the beginning of Mom's funeral our priest walked in front of her casket when it was carried down the aisle. He was slowly chanting words from our prayer book. Toward the end I remember him saying, 'We shall all be changed, in a moment, in the twinkling of an eye.' When Sita, Arjuna's raven, knocked me off the elephant and I was falling into the black abyss, I said, 'Mom I'm coming,' then crashed into the road. I think that maybe it's like passing through a doorway of twinkling light. What do you think?"

"Yes. A doorway. Ever since Emma's funeral I've felt like she was on the other side of a misty cloud."

A group chattering away in French entered the crypt.

"Well," Hans shrugged, "guess we'd better catch up with the others before they notice we're missing."

"Thanks for telling me about Emma." She'd never known a boy who was so easy to talk to and felt closer to him than she'd ever felt to any friend, except Mary.

They found the others on the terrace. Dr. Fischer was pointing out the types of birds flying around the fishermen on the river. No one seemed to notice they were just arriving. Harin was talking with Johanna about the Agra Fort across the river. They went over to her dad. She slipped her arm around his waist and hugged him.

"Hey, Halley Valley. Pretty amazing huh?"

"It's the most beautiful place I've ever seen."

When they returned to the car, they found cups of tea and shortbread cookies ready for them on the camp table. The driver was closing up a small burner. Once they were seated, Dr. Fischer held his cup up. "Here's to our terrific host. This has been a marvelous day. Thank you." They all extended their teacup toward Harin and he went on, "If we all help the driver put things in the trunk when we're done, we should be back in time for that dinner Geeta has planned."

For the first few hours of the drive back, Halley and Hans chatted away. He wanted to hear all about New York City and what it was like to skate on ice. She was interested in how long he'd been playing the cello and how rugby differed from American football.

"They're both rough sports," he said. "There's a story about a rugby player who goes to the doctor and says, 'It hurts whenever I touch my arm, my chest, or my leg.' The doctor replies, 'That's because you have a broken finger.'" They laughed.

They discovered they were both interested in studying medicine. "Where would you like to go for training?" she asked.

"There are several great schools here, but my first choices are in England. What about you?"

"Not sure anymore. Dad's contract here in India makes it possible for me to go anywhere in the world for college. Before we left for India, my top choices were in the US."

They watched the sun drop into the pink-orange glow on the horizon. A gentle wave of contentment wafted through her. She closed her eyes and barely felt her drowsy head settle slowly onto his shoulder.

21

Royal Races

"There they are," Halley's dad said when he and Dr. Maria found the teenagers playing cards after breakfast. "The Maharaja's secretary just called. In addition to attending their ceremony of adoption this evening, they'd like us to join them at the horse races tomorrow. One of their horses is running. It will be the first purely fun event for their new daughter. They thought it would be nice for you all to be there too."

Dr. Maria must have noticed Johanna's uncertain expression, "In addition to Sergeant Patel and my cousin, the Chakmas, the Fischers, and Kashif are also invited."

"That sounds great to me," Johanna said, closely examining her nails. "I love horses."

Dad added, "So, Halley, the new departure plan is that we'll leave for Poona on Monday."

Anything to have another day here, thought Halley, looking at Hans. He returned her gaze. The evening before had been a whirl of happy moments: waking up with her head on his shoulder, sitting next to him at dinner, singing around the piano together, identifying constellations from the front veranda.

"Great," said Hans.

"Meanwhile," Johanna's mom looked at her and then at Halley, "the ladies need to be leaving for the dressmakers. Hans, we'll see you later."

Halley had been looking forward to getting her *lehenga* and the *choli*. But now she really didn't want to leave and wondered what Hans was thinking.

In their dressing room at Mr. Darjee's shop, Johanna and Halley helped each other with the last hooks on their tight-fitting *choli*s. They swirled their long silk *dupattas* around them in front of the mirrors, then stopped, looked at each other and shrieked with joy. The ladies in the other dressing rooms laughed with them.

That evening Hans helped Halley into the back seat of the Chakmas' limousine. She was glad to sit in the middle and hoped the evening breeze wouldn't ruin the results of the hour she spent struggling to style her hair. She touched the ruby necklace, sensing Sundara's feather beneath it, and straightened the end of her *duppata* that trailed across the outer lace of her *lehenga*. Its ethereal blue matched the satin lower layer of her long skirt. She hadn't missed Hans's appreciative expression when she descended the staircase, or his smile when he climbed into the car next to her. She felt beautiful.

Once Johanna and Harin were settled in the front, Halley's dad had climbed into the back seat on the other side of Halley. Then Mr. Chakma helped his wife into the middle seat and sat beside her. "Well," he said, watching his driver close the door behind him, "you ladies look fabulous."

"I agree," Hans whispered. Halley sensed him looking at her and blushed.

Mrs. Chakma was stunning, as usual. Like a delicious dessert, her embroidered orange *lehenga* contrasted with a perfectly fitted raspberry *choli* and lemon *duppata*. After explaining how things would probably go at the palace, Mrs. Chakma said, "We're also looking forward to the races tomorrow. I love the horses. They're so sensual and perfect. Banko is pretty good at picking the winners. I wonder how the Maharaja's horse will do." She turned to look at Halley. "Do you ride?"

"Yes. My grandfather has horses at his country place."

"Actually," Dad added, "she's been riding since she was a little girl. She's even won some medals."

The driver slowed to pass through an arched gateway. In the distance the lights from the Maharaja's palace glowed in the twilight. Halley's thoughts drifted to Meadowcroft. Even though she had approached her grandfather's estate her whole life, she always got excited by her first glimpse of the gables and chimneys of the house rising above the trees in the distance.

The Maharaja's drive meandered past manicured gardens with intricately shaped hedges and long, rectangular reflecting ponds. Pink-and-white flamingos stood in one of them. In a circular pond, two swans floated past the bronze statue of a dancing man holding a flute to his lips.

"That's Lord Krishna, the Hindu god of love and compassion," said Mr. Chakma.

When they reached the entrance, a glamorous couple emerged from the car ahead of them and were immediately besieged by a torrent of popping flashbulbs. Mrs. Chakma groaned. "Oh dear. I forgot to warn you about the photographers. Sorry."

Halley braced herself. Dad jumped out when they stopped and got around the back of the car just as Hans helped her out. They each offered her an elbow. Together they entered the barrage of lights several paces behind Johanna and Harin. She was still laughing when they reached the doormen. Across the ornate entry hall, she could hear the names of Dr. Gustaf and Dr. Maria Norlin being announced into the Maharaja's state room, accompanied by the sound of more flashing bulbs. Halley figured they must be the Maharaja's photographers.

Still linked with Hans and her dad, they moved together through the doorway. Dad identified them to an official. When their names echoed through the room, a storm of photographers and reporters surrounded them. Flashbulb bursts came from everywhere. Halley was startled by a man who reached toward her with a microphone. "Miss Pederson."

Dad put his hand on her shoulder and started to steer her past the man, but he persisted. "Tell the readers of the *Bombay Express* how you rescued the girl who's being adopted by the Maharaja today." When she shrank back, Hans blocked the next reporter. They moved on into the room.

"Oh, Halley," Johanna was immediately beside them. "Are you okay? Quick, come this way." They all followed Harin across the room toward the seats facing the ceremonial area. Dad and Hans were still on either side of her.

"Thanks for getting us out of there," Halley said when they had almost reached the rest of their group. "It upsets me when people say I rescued Lavi and the girls. Plus, it's horrifying to think that it might be in the paper for Mrs. Kaliya to read. Then she'd know that the police are looking for her." Halley shivered, realizing that Mrs. Kaliya would also know where to find her.

Mrs. Fischer was pointing to the seats next to them in the front row. "These are for you." Sergeant Patel and his wife were sitting behind them next to Kashif.

More names were announced. Halley watched the rest of the guests burst through the shower of lights and find seats. *What if they never find Mrs. Kaliya*, she thought. *She'll keep stealing children.* She was shaking and closed her eyes. *Sundara*!

She touched her *choli* above the pouch and wondered if it was the feather itself that calmed her or just the thought of it.

The stage was covered with flowers. In the center were four white cushions on the floor behind a low table stacked with papers and decorated with strings of gardenias.

Three men came out, two with long trumpets. They stopped in front of the stage. The third man strutted to a podium off to the side and cleared his throat. "Ladies and gentlemen, please take your seats." There was a shuffling of chairs.

The silence seemed to go on forever. Halley wondered what they were doing. The man at the podium looked at his watch. After what was probably just a minute, he nodded to the other men, and they trumpeted a fanfare.

All dressed in white pants and long, white shirts, the Maharaja, the Maharani, and Lavi, followed by a gray-haired man, crossed to the cushions and sat down. The man at the podium announced that because Lavi Anand's parents were deceased, her grandfather would represent the family in the adoption ceremony of "giving and taking."

When they signed the papers, several photographers moved closer. Flashbulbs lit up their ecstatic faces. Lavi stood and faced her new parents. They each placed a string of flowers around her neck and embraced her. Then, hand in hand, they turned to face the applauding guests. Once the clapping died down, they crossed the room to a doorway that opened into the Grand Hall and began greeting their guests. Halley and her father were right behind Mrs. Chakma when they reached the front of the receiving line.

"Your Highnesses, you will remember Dr. Karl Pederson and his daughter, Halley," she said.

The Maharani was standing behind Lavi with one hand on her shoulder. "Very much so," she replied. "Lavi wants you to know she is very grateful to you for sending her out of the jungle to get word to the policeman. That helped her meet her new parents. We are all very happy."

The swirling, sweet aroma of gardenias circled them. Halley hadn't realized that Lavi was so young when she nudged her into the dark jungle behind the truck. "Please tell her that she's a very brave girl. What she was able to do helped to save us all." To the Maharaja she said, "Thank you for including us today and for inviting us to see your horse race tomorrow. What is your horse's name?"

"Her name is Tej Hava," he said. "It means 'strong wind.' She's very fast. Tevy Chakma just told us you're an experienced rider. Would you and your friends like to come to see her before the race when the jockey gets on? Lavi will be there."

"Yes, thank you, Your Highness."

"Good. Banko and Tevy Chakma have joined us before. They know where to go. We'll see you there."

Halley caught up with Hans and her dad, looped her arms around their bent elbows again, and moved with them into the celebration. On the stage, dancers twirled. The musicians were playing instruments she had never seen before. Waiters offered trays of delicious foods and juices. When they found the rest of their group, Sergeant Patel greeted her. "Halley, I hear the newspaper people discovered what you look like tonight. They've been calling every day, wanting a press conference with you. They say their readers would be very interested in learning what happened."

Halley shuddered. "I really don't want to talk to them yet. Mrs. Kaliya is still out there. It would be awful if she realized you're looking for her."

"Uncle Andy," Johanna moved over next to Halley, "maybe she's still in New Delhi."

Halley looked at her dad and then at Sergeant Patel. "I wonder how she connects with *Laal* Adrik. Maybe he works for her. We know she wears a *sari*, but she's European and could easily change her appearance."

"Good thought," Sergeant Patel replied. "She could be anywhere. The girls were from all over the country, although most of them were from around Delhi. We've circulated a description based upon how you and the girls described her. We'll keep looking for her. I'll let you all know if we get any leads."

"Here comes Lavi and the Maharani," Hans said, and greeted them in Hindi. Lavi smiled.

"Thank you," the Maharani answered in English. "Lavi wants you to know that the circus performers have been setting up on the far side of the room. Would you like to join her over there?"

"That sounds fantastic," Halley said.

Dr. Fischer's eyes lit up. "I'd love to see them too. Geeta?" He offered an arm to his wife. They all followed Lavi and the Maharani.

It was late when the Chakmas dropped them off at the Fischers'. Dr. Gustaf asked Johanna and Hans to meet them in the library to go over their travel plans. Dad slipped into the living room and closed the door. Halley started slowly up the stairs.

When she reached the landing halfway up, Kashif and Sundara were coming down. "Good evening, *Memsaab*, the bath is ready for you. Do you require anything else?"

"Thank you, Kashif. The evening was very nice. Except that when we were announced into the Maharaja's state room, the reporters heard my name and surrounded me." She trembled and burst out, "The man from the *Bombay Express* asked me to tell their readers how I rescued Lavi. I hate that. I didn't rescue her. And besides, I don't want to talk to them. Mrs. Kaliya will read the papers, especially the Bombay one. The less she knows, the better. Sergeant Patel has to find her and stop her."

Sundara was moving around on Kashif's shoulder, and Halley frowned. "I'm sorry, Sundara. I'm pretty upset."

"That's understandable," Kashif said. "Ever since the helicopter landed, you've been swept up into a flurry of activity. The reporter's question didn't help."

"You're right. This week has been great, but even so, once in a while a memory startles me and I'm right back there. You were there when the panther came rushing down the hill at us. When I stepped inside the taxidermist's, the tiger inside the door really shocked me and flashed me right back. I fainted. I'm a pretty big mess inside." She tapped her chest. "I still wear the small pouch with the feather. It helps."

"*Memsaab*, when you get swept into the current of troubling memories or fears, the feather only helps you because you notice it. It is noticing that brings you into the present moment, and that is what calms you."

Notes from the piano floated up to them.

"Kashif, thank you for talking to me. I was feeling lonely. Everyone went in other directions as soon as we arrived."

"I'll be driving one of the cars to the races tomorrow. Would you like me to bring Sundara?"

"Bring Sundara," the parrot echoed.

"Yes, please," she smiled. "That would be terrific."

******

Upstairs in the tub, Halley sank her soapy head back into the water. Kashif was right. This week had been such a whirl. Did Hans really like her? She scooped up a handful of water and watched the drops run through her fingers. He was like no one she'd ever met, with his intense eyes and gentle manner. What did he say to Lavi that made her smile? He was so kind.

Swirling water gurgled down the drain. She wrapped a towel around her hair and ran the other one over her body. A night bird called through the window from her balcony. She slipped into her pajamas and crept across the room. It chattered again. The round, white face of a speckled owl was staring at her from the railing. She sat down near the window to catch the breeze and toweled her hair. Several mosquitos buzzed outside the screen.

"You're welcome to all the mosquitos you want," she said to the owl. He lurched forward and snapped at one, then suddenly flew straight at her across the porch. She gasped, expecting him to crash into the screen. Instead, one wing brushed the edge of the window ledge before he returned to his post with a wiggling snake in his beak. "Goodness," she gasped. "Are you my guard owl too? Thanks." He was still out there when she finally curled up behind the mosquito netting. Her last thought before drifting off was that she should wear the ruby necklace tomorrow.

******

Shortly after one o'clock the following day, Kashif pulled through the entrance to the racetrack.

"Look," Johanna pointed past the crowd near the main gate, "there's the Chakmas' car." The Fischers' convertible was next to it. Kashif parked beside them. Sundara was preening one of his wings.

Hans leaned forward. "Say, Kashif, has Sundara been to the races before?"

"Yes. He likes horses. This will be a real treat for him," Kashif paused, "and for me too. It was kind of them to include me."

Kashif and Sundara were right behind Halley when they reached the others. "Great," said Mr. Chakma. "Follow us." He took his wife's hand and led them to a smaller gate behind the stables.

Harin moved over next to Johanna. "This is the way my folks always go in when the Maharaja enters one of his horses." The guard waved for them to pass him. "I like this part almost as much as the race. The jockey riding for him today is really good, and Tej Hava likes him. Look, there they are."

Stepping lightly out of a nearby stall was a handsome horse. Her golden chestnut hair shone in the sunlight, and her sinews rippled with every step. Shadows from Tej Hava's long eyelashes almost reached the white star on her forehead, and her dark eyes focused confidently into the distance. Halley inhaled the smell of straw crushed beneath the horse's hooves and noticed that the jockey's shiny blue jersey matched the blanket that dangled from beneath a little saddle. Both were emblazoned with the number five. The jockey was leading the horse toward the Maharaja's party that was gathering near the track.

Once the jockey had mounted and the cameras stopped clicking, the Maharaja pointed to his shaded box seats overlooking the crowd near the finish line and invited everyone to follow him. The Maharani held Lavi's hand and walked beside her husband toward the stands. Sergeant Patel greeted Halley and started up the steps behind the Fischers.

"Hey, you guys," Harin said looking at the other teenagers, "there are several races before Tej Hava runs. If you don't mind the sun, we can watch the next race from here." Halley's dad said he'd see her in the box and headed up, chatting with Dr. Gustaf about infectious diseases in horses.

Johanna laughed. "Dad is always talking about one disease or another. I'm glad your dad is interested."

They found an open spot along the fence in the brilliant sunlight. Halley was thrilled to stay down near the horses and grateful that Mrs. Fischer had lent each of the girls a hat. The shadow of the white brim on hers helped a little.

In the midst of the horses heading for the starting gates, one jockey struggled to calm a gray filly that was rearing back and trying to turn away. Harin pointed to them. "Dad took me to a horse race in the states. He explained that the American horses are extremely anxious when they go through this parade down the stretch and are unprepared to enter their gate. They each have a pony horse and rider to walk with them and help the racing horses stay calm and focused. They don't use a pony horse in India. Our horses are trained to approach their gate."

The horse was close enough for Halley to see the terror in her eyes and thought that this one didn't look very well prepared. Poor thing. The filly calmed down when she passed close to a couple that was standing in the aisle at the bottom of the stands. The man's jaunty Panama hat and blue plaid jacket complemented the woman's fashionable orange *sari* and yellow hat. Halley wondered if that filly knew them. Had they said something calming to her as she passed? The woman made a sweeping gesture toward the reserved boxes. Sunlight glinted off her arm.

Glass bangles!

Halley turned away. "Johanna, if you look past me to the stands, you should be able to see a woman in an orange *sari* going up the aisle toward the boxes. One of her arms is covered with bracelets. I know that every other woman in New Delhi has glass bangles, and the odds that we'll run into her here are slim. But if it *is* Mrs. Kaliya, we can't let her get away. Can you tell if the man has a dark beard?"

"Oh, Halley. They're getting farther away."

The guys heard her too. "That hat makes it hard to see his face," Hans said. "They seem to be heading for the boxes below the Maharaja's."

Harin scanned the stands. "I see an orange *sari*. Is he wearing a blue jacket?"

"Yes, and a white hat." Halley figured they were far enough away and looked for herself. Johanna's brow creased with worry. "We need a plan."

"Johanna," Halley said. "Could you and Harin go tell Sergeant Patel it may be them?

Hans, I'm hoping you'll stay with me. We need to get close enough to really identify them."

"Definitely," they all replied.

While they inched through the crowd toward the stands Halley kept an eye on the orange *sari*.

Maybe I should just go straight up to that lady, she thought. She could ask if she knew her from the ocean liner. Once she was close enough, she'd know. If it wasn't Mrs. Kaliya, she could apologize and say she mistook her for a friend or something. When they reached the bottom of the stairs, she ran the idea by the others.

"But what if it is her?" Johanna asked.

"I'll think of something. This may be the only chance we have. Ask

Sergeant Patel to come down and stand in the aisle. If it is her and she starts to leave, he could stop her."

"I guess." Johanna was hesitant. "Since there are so many people around, it just might work."

Harin started up the steps. "Come on, Johanna. Let's hurry. And," he looked back at Halley, "can you wait until you see us reach Sergeant Patel before you approach her?"

"That makes sense to me," said Hans. "We'll let you get a head start."

Halley looked back and forth between her friends and the orange *sari*. When she saw them reach the Maharaja's box, she nudged Hans, and they followed. She had difficulty keeping an eye on the woman while trying not to trip on the steps. Just before they reached the entrance into the boxes, she realized that the orange *sari* was moving toward them, followed by the man in the Panama hat. Halley could see his dark beard. She heard the clinking of the glass bangles, thought of Sundara's golden feather, and took a deep breath. Then she stepped in front of them.

"Oh my goodness," she said to the woman, trying to sound nonchalant. "I'm Halley Pederson. My father and I met you on the ship at the captain's table on Christmas Eve. How are you?"

The woman scowled. "I don't know you. Get out of our way," she growled and stepped aside. The man passed her.

"You heard her. Move away if you know what's good for you."

Halley didn't move and cheerfully continued, "Oh, Mrs. Kaliya, don't you remember our conversation? Dad told everyone about the performance of *Twelfth Night* we saw in London."

The man pushed her into Hans, and they fell against the rail. Dragging Mrs. Kaliya behind him, the man made it to the aisle and started down the steps. Sergeant Patel and Dr. Fischer were still several rows away with a crowd between them. Halley darted after Mrs. Kaliya and the man. Hans was right behind her. By the time they got to the track level, the man had pushed an opening through the crowd and was moving quickly toward the stables. People on either side of the path were yelling angrily after them.

Halley and Hans caught up to them. The man wheeled around. "You have stupidly followed us, and you will pay."

Mrs. Kaliya yelled in Hindi into the horse stall behind her. Several men rushed out, grabbed Halley and Hans, and dragged them into the darkness.

22

A Venomous Snake

Before Halley could scream, rough hands stuffed a rag into her mouth. Growling men pulled her arms behind her, bound her hands and feet, and shoved her into the hay on the stall floor. She could hear Hans struggling nearby. "Hey, let go of—" He moaned and dropped to the ground beside her.

Oh no. Poor Hans. Dear God, help us. Don't let them get away.

Tromping feet rushed past the stable door. "There they go," hollered Sergeant Patel. Halley rolled and struggled until she was able to stomp her bound feet against the outside wall.

She was startled by the rustle of straw near the bottom of the stall door. A snake?

In the dim light she could see something moving over the hay toward her. A moment later she felt a stir followed by a crunch of hay right beside her. She was shaking.

"Hello," a voice cackled. Oh goodness, it was Sundara. He squawked and lifted into the air, his wings fanning her face. She banged her feet on the wall again and tried to call out.

"Halley," Kashif called from right outside the stall door. "Are you in there?"

She banged her feet again. In less than a moment she felt a strong hand cradling her head. The rag was pulled from her mouth.

"Help Hans first," she pleaded. "He's near me. I think they knocked him out."

She heard rustling in the straw beside her. Hans groaned.

"You'll be all right, *Sahib*," Kashif said and carried him outside. Halley heard others greet him, and he said, "*Memsaab* Halley's inside."

Voices in the doorway. "Over here," she yelled.

"Halley?" It was Johanna.

"By the wall."

"Quick, Harin. She's over here." In a flash, Johanna was helping her sit up.

Harin lifted her up and struggled with her across the hay. She blinked back tears and sneezed when they reached the bright sunlight. Harin set her down slowly. Johanna untied the rope around her wrists and was almost finished with her feet when Halley's dad and Dr. Gustaf came rushing up.

"Dad, Hans needs help," Johanna called out.

"What about you, Halley?" Dad asked, squatting beside her.

"I felt a lot better when Kashif took that horsey rag out of my mouth. Yuck." She looked over at Hans, who was trying to sit up. "How are you?" she asked.

"Looks like I'll live," he said, rubbing his head. "Did anyone see if Sergeant Patel caught them?"

Johanna looked toward the gate near the entrance where they came in. "I see them. Several security men are with them too."

During a brief lull in the cheers from the stands, they could hear Mrs. Kaliya shouting, "Unhand me. What's the meaning of this? We are paying patrons. You have nothing on us."

"I'll have your badge," the man bellowed.

"I can't stand lying here while she's making such a scene." With Dad's help, Halley stood up. "Please help me go over there."

The crowd near them separated, and the Maharaja, the Maharani, and

Lavi emerged. "Goodness," the Maharaja said. "Are you kids all right? What happened?"

Halley pointed at the gate. "Sergeant Patel and Dr. Fischer caught Mrs. Kaliya and that man. They have them over there." They all followed the Maharaja.

Mrs. Kaliya's voice got louder. "You can't prove anything. I'm a law-abiding citizen."

Halley wanted to scream. *Law-abiding citizen? You kidnap children and sell them to horrible people. But it's her word against mine. What can I say that will prove it?*

The Chakmas, Dr. Maria, and Mrs. Patel appeared behind them.

"Hans," his mother said, "what happened to you?" He put his finger to his lips and nodded toward their Highnesses. The Maharani was bending down, listening to Lavi. The Maharaja looked on anxiously. Lavi was crying and pointing at Mrs. Kaliya. The Maharani had heard enough. She stood up and boomed out. "My daughter says that this is the woman who kidnapped her." Mrs. Kaliya stopped struggling. "Sergeant Patel, they are the ones who have been stealing children for years. Take them away."

Lavi flung her arms around the Maharani. The Maharaja stood behind them. A police car pulled up. Sergeant Patel loaded Mrs. Kaliya and the man into the back seat. Once the sergeant was in the front seat, they pulled away.

The crowd's cheering died down enough to hear the announcer. "Place your bets."

The Maharaja looked at his guests. "We'll need to head back to our seats. Tej Hava is in the race after this one. But you have all been through a great deal and I'll understand if you decide to leave."

Dr. Gustaf put his hand on Hans's shoulder. "How do you feel, son? Should we leave?"

"Not on my account. Halley, how are you doing?"

She marveled at his resilience and said, "Now that Sergeant Patel has Mrs. Kaliya, I wouldn't want to miss seeing Tej Hava's race for anything."

Halley's dad smiled. "Your Highnesses, it would be an honor for us to follow you back to your box. Besides," he waved a ticket in the air, "I put big money on Tej Hava."

Halley hugged him and laughed.

The crowd murmured around them. From the Maharaja's seats Halley could see the horses parading toward the starting gates and located the shiny blue jersey on Tej Hava's jockey. Dad looped the leather strap on his binoculars over her head, and she smiled at him. She raised the binoculars and once she focused, she could clearly see the horse, strong and determined, prancing with confidence. They entered their post.

"They're off!" shouted the announcer, and the horses pounded down the track.

Halley handed the binoculars back to her dad. When the horses were in the backstretch, she cringed. The blue jersey had dropped behind the lead horses. "Run, Tej Hava," she hollered. "You can do it. Go girl." The Maharaja and her dad drowned her out.

As the horses made the final turn, she stopped a groan in mid breath. Yes! The blue jersey was moving up on the outside, flying like the wind. Halley jumped in the air and shrieked. Barely breathing, she clenched her fists together under her chin. Tej Hava passed two more horses and rumbled up beside the lead. "Come on, girl! Come on." Just a foot more. Tej Hava's jockey crouched forward, calling to her. Just inches from the finish line, she pulled ahead.

Their box exploded. "She did it. She won!" Halley was so happy she almost cried.

She could hear Hans laugh. "What a nail-biting finish." When she turned to look at him their eyes met. He smiled back at her.

"On to the winner's circle," announced Mr. Chakma. They all cheered and congratulated the Maharaja. He thanked them and started down the aisle.

They arrived before Tej Hava, but they could see her strutting toward them down the track. Her jockey was riding high, legs straight in the stirrups.

"Isn't she beautiful?" Halley said to no one in particular. Someone moved in beside her. Lavi slipped her small hand into Halley's. Johanna joined them. "Johanna, please tell Lavi that she was very brave today and that I was thrilled when she confronted Mrs. Kaliya. It was a tremendous relief to see Sergeant Patel take her away to jail. Thank you, Lavi."

Johanna translated for the girl, who said something back. Johanna turned back to Halley. "She wants to know how you were able to single that woman out in this enormous crowd."

"We saw her and that man leave the Villante Hotel. My prayers were answered when I got close enough to see his beard and hear her bangles."

The scent of a flowering garden approached them from behind. The Maharani rested her hands on both Lavi's and Halley's shoulders and laughed. "I heard that. It's been said that if you come to this track often enough, you're bound to run into absolutely everyone you know. Although I didn't recognize her, I did notice Mrs. Kaliya when she sat down in the mayor's box. She probably donated to his campaign, like a conniving snake."

When picture-taking was over, the teenagers joked around near Tej Hava's stall. Johanna translated for Lavi. Following one of Harin's jokes, Lavi's delighted laugh stopped abruptly. She gasped. Almost choking, she pointed at an enormous cobra uncoiling right next to Halley.

Halley froze, barely breathing. The viper's head was fanning out, eyes focused only on her. The Maharaja whispered, "Don't move." Then, out of the corner of her eye, Halley glimpsed a furry red animal slinking toward them, tail flashing. Suddenly, it rushed forward and pounced on the snake. In barely a second the battle was over. The viper was dead. The stunned group sighed together.

Tej Hava's jockey blurted out, "Good work, Maanik."

"Good God," said Dr. Gustaf. "A rare red mongoose!"

"Yes," replied the jockey, "Maanik is almost like a pet around the stables. She protects the horses from vermin, especially venomous snakes."

Maanik gazed up at Halley almost like she recognized her. Halley would never have mistaken this mongoose for a cat. It was covered with spikey red fur. A moment later, Maanik grabbed the lifeless cobra's head in her sharp teeth and triumphantly paraded it around in front of them, then she dragged it out of sight behind the stall.

Hans laughed. "Halley, you helped Sergeant Patel catch Mrs. Kaliya, the poisonous snake, like Maanik just did. Maybe we should start calling you the Red Mongoose."

"Don't you dare." Halley playfully punched his shoulder.

When Johanna translated, Lavi exploded in a great belly laugh and hugged Halley.

******

Back at the Fischers' house that evening, they all hurried to the entrance hall to greet Sergeant Patel as soon as they heard that he was pulling through the Fischers' gates in a police car. When he came through the door, his wife hugged him and everyone cheered.

Dr. Fischer jovially slapped his back. "Bravo, Andy. Let's go to the living room for a toast. We have much to celebrate."

Sergeant Patel stopped in front of Halley and placed his hand on her shoulder. "You'll be happy to know that with the testimony of the Maharaja's daughter, there is no way for Mrs. Kaliya to get out of this. As for *Burai* Kaliya, he is a well-known crime boss and has been wanted by the Bombay police for years. We are fortunate that you recognized them in the crowd."

Halley dipped her head and smiled up at him. "I kept thinking she would have disguised herself. All she would have had to do was take off those bangles and wear a dress. I guess it didn't occur to her that anyone could have spoken to Ganika or that we were looking for her." She turned to her friends. "And without you guys, we never would have caught her."

Following dinner, the adults moved back to the living room, and the teenagers slipped away to the screened porch.

"Wow," Johanna said, flopping into a chair. "So much has happened this week. I still can't believe the whole ordeal with Mrs. Kaliya is over."

"Neither can I," said Halley.

"Actually," said Harin, "all I can think about is that it's sure going to be dull around here after you girls leave tomorrow."

"I agree," echoed Hans. "Halley, ever since I met you, things have been more than just exciting."

"Say, Hans," said Harin, "is there any chance you could stay with us the next time you come to New Delhi for the weekend? We could play tennis or rugby at the club."

"I'd like that. I'm pretty sure my aunt wouldn't mind."

Halley felt Hans watching her, and her heart did a cartwheel.

"Say," he stood up. "Would you all like to take a walk by the Fischers' pond? The outside lights should be enough to see where we're going."

"Great idea," said Harin, "and if we keep moving the mosquitos won't get us."

Harin and Johanna started down the steps.

"How's your head?" Halley asked Hans.

"Besides the large egg bulging out of my noggin, it's not too bad."

"That thug really clobbered you." Things had happened so fast, she hadn't had time to worry about him.

"Thanks. I've never been unconscious before. I thought I might get a headache when we went back up to the Maharaja's box, but I didn't."

"I'm sure I would have had a headache when I fainted at the taxidermist's if you hadn't caught me. Being unconscious was strange."

"Hey, Harin," Mr. Chakma called from the veranda. "We'll be leaving in five minutes."

"Okay, Dad. Thanks," he called from the lawn. They started back.

Hans stopped. "Halley, can I write to you?"

"Of course. If you do, I'll write you back," she said, hoping she hadn't answered too quickly. *Stay calm*, she thought.

He didn't seem to notice and went on, "Looks like I'm going to be in Poona for my spring break in April. Maybe you'll even have your play then."

Harin and Johanna caught up with them. "I heard you say something about their play," Harin said. "Johanna and I were talking about it just now too. I should be able to go to my cousin's in Poona on spring break." He looked at Hans. "If that works out, maybe we could take the train down together."

Hans opened the door. "Great idea."

The adults were in the entrance hall. Sergeant Patel and his wife were partway out the door. "There you are," he said to Halley. "Your dad gave me his phone number in case we have any more questions. Have a safe trip tomorrow."

"We were so happy to see you and your father again," said Mrs. Chakma.

Halley saw that Johanna and Harin were across the room, talking quietly. To give them a few more minutes together she turned to his mother. "Mrs. Chakma, thank you for the lovely lunch at your house and for introducing us to the Rinpoche. Has he heard anything more from his cousin since he escaped over the Himalayas into Katmandu?"

"Yes," she said, "but the news is so frustrating. He has to go through the challenges of seeking asylum, and Nepal has procedures. So, it may be a while before he can reach us here. Banko is making arrangements to go there to help him apply for his refugee identity certificate."

Mr. Chakma was listening. "Rinpoche and I may head there next week if I can get us a flight. The Buddhist monastery where his cousin is staying is very gracious and has offered us accommodations too."

"Thank you for asking, Halley," said Mrs. Chakma. "These past few days around you have been exhilarating. Harin is very happy to have met the Norlin kids and to have seen you again."

Halley noticed that Harin and Johanna had moved over next to his father.

"Exhilarating," said Harin. "With you, Halley Valley, there has never been a boring moment. Oh, I forgot to tell you I got your letter yesterday. Johanna says you are a shoo-in for that part in the play, so I'm hoping I'll get to see both of you perform."

Halley looked at Johanna beaming at Harin and hoped so too.

******

The next morning Halley heard the early birds outside her window and was just turning on her bedside lamp when Kashif knocked. It was still dark.

"Looks like *Memsaab* is awake early this morning." He set her *chota hazri* down under the light.

"A little while ago I woke up from a crazy dream. I tried to remember it but couldn't. Dreams are funny like that." She rubbed her eyes. "How much time do I have?"

"Someone will be up in twenty minutes to get your bags." He smiled. "I see you now have two."

"Yes," she sat up, laughing. "Mrs. Fischer gave me that smaller one for everything I've accumulated since we were rescued."

"Two of the Fischers' cars are already at the front door. You may want to head downstairs when your baggage does."

She was dressed and ready when the man arrived for her things. After taking a last look around, she grabbed her purse and followed him down to the front door. Everyone was already there. Mrs. Fischer was the first to see her.

"Halley, we were talking about you. The early morning news announced that Mr. and Mrs. Kaliya had been apprehended and that the police have a clear case against them. They even mentioned Sergeant Patel and you."

Halley smiled weakly. She felt both relief that Mrs. Kalya and her husband had been caught and annoyed that the news had mentioned her name.

Following a breezy conversation, everyone thanked the Fischers. The sky was beginning to get lighter when the cars pulled away.

Halley smiled at Sundara preening on Kashif's shoulder. She scooted forward on the back seat and looked over at Hans and Johanna. "Things would have turned out quite differently if we hadn't all worked together at the races, including you, Sundara. Hans, how's that bump on your head?" She watched him rub it gently.

"It only hurts when I touch it."

"Then don't touch it, silly," chided his sister.

"Touch it, silly," said Sundara. Kashif laughed with them.

The trip to the train station was going too quickly for Halley. Soon she'd be waving Hans off on his train back to school. She scrambled for something to say. "Will you be able to catch up with your homework on the train?"

"I'll be able to do a little. What about you?"

"The only thing I brought with me for school is a story for English, so I'll finish that."

"Which one?"

"Kipling's 'The Man Who Would be King.'"

"That's great. I love that one," he replied.

They were pulling up behind the other car at the station. *Oh no,* Halley thought. *We have to leave just when I'm starting to get to know him. He'll probably forget about me as soon as he gets on the train.*

"We're here," said Johanna and opened her door.

Rather than following her out of the car, Hans grabbed Halley's hand. Joy shot through her as their eyes locked. "I'm missing you already," he said awkwardly.

"Please write," she said and squeezed his hand.

"Hey, Hans," interrupted his dad, "let's go. We need to pick up the tickets and get you to your train."

Halley felt her face blush and dropped his hand.

"Okay, Dad."

Soon they were all watching Hans climb the steps to his train compartment. Dr. Maria called up to him, "Don't forget to telephone us tomorrow night."

Halley waved at him and tried to smile.

Chapter 23

Brimming Bowls

Halley's dad accompanied her to St. Anne's the day after they returned to Poona. The head mistress greeted them warmly. "Miss Pederson, your father called me last week about your disappearance. We were very worried and prayed for you." She turned to Dad. "Doctor Pederson, thank you for calling again when she was rescued. I was so relieved and grateful. But," she paused, pointing at the newspaper on her desk, "it wasn't until I read yesterday's *Bombay Express* that I learned that your kidnappers were led by the infamous mob boss *Burai* Kaliya and his crime ring."

Halley was stunned when she saw her picture on the front page. The headlines read, "American Girl Rescued!"

"Oh no," she groaned. "They used that picture they took at Lavi's adoption ceremony. This is so embarrassing."

When she was excused to leave for her first class, she walked Dad to the main entrance and gave him a hug.

"I'm sorry about the paper, honey," he said. "Now focus on your classes and before you know it, Kashif will be picking you up after school."

The hallway still looked dreary. A group of girls walked by her and cackled, but Halley barely noticed them. She felt new strength welling up inside her and thought of that night on the mountaintop. *I am Sarwan, a Sikh boy. Sarwan, the explorer.*

She lifted herself to her full height, entered her physics class, and walked confidently past her glaring classmates to an empty seat in the back, just as Mr. Rossi closed the door. If the other girls wanted to look like a clan of circling hyenas, they had failed.

Halley was the last one down the aisle after the dismissal bell, and Mr. Rossi stopped her. "Miss Pederson, may I speak with you for a minute?" His benevolent expression intrigued her. Then she saw the *Bombay Express* on his desk. "Congratulations on the capture of *Burai* Kaliya and his wife. Thank you. My family will be forever grateful. My cousin's daughter was abducted from a hotel in Calcutta last year. We've had no word and have all been sick with worry this whole time. She was one of the girls you helped rescue."

Halley was about to say that she hadn't done anything, when she noticed a tear hovering near the corner of his eye and watched it spill onto his cheek.

"When my cousin called," Mr. Rossi said. "I discovered what joy feels like. When I saw your picture, I was grateful that our girl was rescued along with so many others and grateful that I know you and could tell you myself."

Mr. Rossi's words melted away a wall of embarrassment inside Halley and she felt his gratitude flow in.

At lunch Johanna scooped up some rice curry with her *chapatti* and giggled. "In drama class it was hard not to laugh at Martha Miller's expression when Sister Jane announced that she had cast you as Jack."

"But now," Halley groaned, "I have to learn all my lines in a week."

After school when Kashif pulled up at the Royal Palm Club, Halley saw Padma walking past the veranda toward the tennis courts and jumped out of the car. "Kashif, could you please take my books to our living room?"

Padma smiled. "Oh Halley, I was hoping I'd see you. Ganika and Rabar are so happy. She said you were abducted, too, and helped that girl escape and that you fell off the elephant. But it wasn't until we saw the paper yesterday that we learned of the capture of Mrs. Kaliya. What a despicable woman."

Halley was relieved to see that the burn on Padma's face was almost unnoticeable. "Yes, Mrs. Kaliya is a horrible person. But Padma, I've been hoping to see you too. On my first day at St. Anne's, when I was changing for tennis, I overheard some girls in the locker room mention you and a girl. They suspected her of attacking you because you were seen talking to her boyfriend. I wanted to tell you about it, but we left the next morning."

Padma tilted her head. "That's okay. The next time I went to the hospital I had a different doctor. He knows Kavita's family and told them that if she went anywhere near me again, he would tell the police that she attacked me. I haven't seen her since. Besides, her boyfriend, Radhesh, is my cousin, one of the Royal Palm gardeners."

Halley's eyes widened. "Just a few hours after Johanna and I first met you on the tennis court and you called Rabar, I saw a gardener watering in the twilight beneath my balcony. He stopped and pulled an envelope out from under one of the bushes. Could he have been your cousin?"

"Yes," Padma said, laughing, "that envelope was from me. Ever since we were children, we've left notes for each other under special bushes in the garden. He'd left one for me that afternoon that said, 'I hate what Kavita did to you and I'll never speak to her again.' My note that you saw him pickup said, 'Thanks.'"

Kashif was dusting the furniture in their living room when Halley walked in. Sundara was on his stand by the window. She dropped onto the couch next to her books. "Kashif, do you think dreams mean anything?"

"Sometimes."

"This morning I woke up from a dream that I think was the same one I had on Monday morning. Only this time I remembered part of it."

"How did you feel when you woke up?"

"A little uneasy, but peaceful. Just like the other day," she said, moving over to the table. "Could you sit with me?"

Once they were settled, she went on, "In it there's a skinny little girl. I'm happy to see her. I reach for her hand. I realize her hands are full and look at them. In one is the handle of a pot of rice, in the other a basket of *chapatti*s. Then I wake up."

"Do you recognize her?"

"She's Lavi, but all dirty."

"Where were you and what did you feel when you saw her?"

"We were on the street. I felt hungry."

They were interrupted by the doorbell. Kashif went to answer it.

"Is *Memsaab* Pederson here?"

"Yes."

"Tell her there is a couple in the tearoom who would like to see her, a Mr. and Mrs. Chowdhury."

Halley sprang up, beaming. "Ganika."

******

The tearoom was bustling. A beautiful lady was crossing the room, her lavender *sari* dancing around her. "Halley," she cried.

Halley barely recognized Ganika. They laughed and hugged. Rabar came up behind her and hugged them both together. "Come sit down with us, please," he said.

While the tea got cold, Halley answered their questions. Ganika cried happy tears when she heard about Lavi's adoption.

"Now, Ganika, what have you been doing since you left the Maharaja's?"

Ganika glanced lovingly at Rabar, then back at Halley. "After a few days, Rabar returned to his work. I met with the servants each morning to go over the household business and plan the menus. But the rest of the time I missed Rabar and thought about Lavi and the other girls. I felt so small and useless. We didn't know what happened to Mrs. Kaliya until we saw the newspaper yesterday." Rabar patted her hand encouragingly. His eyes were moist.

"One evening, Rabar suggested that our bearer drive me to the Royal Palm Club to visit Padma," Ganika continued. "I went the next day. She was devastated to hear about the other girls and those awful men. I cried and told her I needed to find a way to make a difference. I couldn't just sit back and watch. I knew from experience what could happen to all those begging children. She told me about a group that had started a school to help children get off the streets. In addition to housing and feeding them they also have classes, including Hindi. They needed teachers. She gave me the address and phone number. I practically floated out the door. The possibility gave me hope and a new purpose. That night I told Rabar." She looked at him.

"It turns out," he said, "I know one of the project supporters from my mosque. He's been helping to raise money and involve his friends. Also, one of my Jewish colleagues engaged his friends. It occupies a former school at a church near here."

Halley felt goosebumps ripple down her arms. Feeding the children? She was on the edge of her seat. "Have you gone there yet?"

"Rabar took me there on Saturday." Ganika was glowing. "Oh, Halley, it was amazing. I guess it could be called a foundling home or orphanage. But they have dormitory rooms with bunk beds, toilets, classrooms, a gymnasium, and a large dining room, all full of happy children. Volunteers were everywhere, men and women, working together. It's called *Prem Makaan*, which means 'Love House.' We went back on Sunday, and they put us right to work. Rabar served food and I helped in one of the classrooms."

Halley thought of the children surrounding the car, begging. "That's wonderful. I'm going to ask Kashif if he can take me there too."

The rest of the week Halley caught up on homework and memorized her lines for the play. Sister Jane coached her on her British accent and how to pitch her voice like a man's. Johanna came back with her after school each day, and they had tea on the veranda. When Halley wasn't pumping Johanna for news from Hans, they helped each other rehearse their parts. Johanna was interested in going to *Prem Makaan* with her on Saturday, but she had a violin lesson.

Halley had asked Kashif for early *chota hazri* on Saturday. When he arrived, she told him that her dream had changed. This time the child was a little boy. He had an empty bowl in one hand. The other was outstretched toward her, also empty. They were next to the road, surrounded by honking car horns.

"What do you suppose the dream means?" she asked.

"Why are you going to *Prem Makaan*?"

"To help the children."

Kashif came into *Prem Makaan* with her. Just as they opened the office door, a group of chattering children passed behind them. They were all dressed in white shirts and white pants that were tight at the ankle, some were laughing.

"This seems so much like a normal school," she said.

"We try to make it that way," said a turbaned, dark-bearded man who was approaching them from behind the desk. "You must be Halley Pederson. We are pleased that you want to help. I am Mr. Suhaan, the director of *Prem Makaan*." He bowed to them. "*Sahib*, will you be staying too?"

"I have to leave soon," Kashif said. "But when I come back to pick her up, I could bring Sundara, my macaw. Do you think some of the children might like to meet him?"

"They'd love it. I hope you can stay long enough now for a tour."

After Kashif learned where to pick her up, he left Halley chopping vegetables in the kitchen. In the afternoon he found her helping some children make clay bowls in a classroom. The children clamored around him when they saw Sundara. Kashif sat on the floor with them and told them about macaws. At least Halley thought that was what he was saying, since he was speaking Hindi.

Each day after school Halley checked at the front desk for a letter from Hans. She tried not to worry, but the taunting thoughts weren't far from the surface. She chided herself. *Don't be silly. My letter to Harin took a week to get to New Delhi. Maybe he sent it by water buffalo.*

She'd close her eyes and picture him gazing into hers when he said, "I'm missing you already." She'd think repeatedly about the moment she first saw him on the Fischers' veranda, felt his protective hand on her shoulder in their cramped hiding place, or when she woke up in the Chakmas' limousine with her head on his shoulder.

One afternoon she and Johanna were lounging in the big chairs at the end of the Royal Palm veranda. After they agreed to volunteer at *Prem Makaan* the next Saturday, they began rehearsing their lines from a conversation between their characters, Lady Bracknell and Jack, whom she thinks is named Ernest.

Johanna as Lady Bracknell started out, "Are your parents living?"

Halley as Jack pretending to be Ernest said, "I have lost both my parents."

In her stuffiest voice, Johanna replied, "To lose one parent, Mr. Worthing, may be regarded as a misfortune; to lose both looks like carelessness."

"There you are." Dad was walking toward them. "Johanna's parents have invited us to dinner tonight. Kashif will drive us over there in an hour. And Halley," he handed her a blue airmail envelope, "this is for you."

She sprang up. "Thanks, Dad." She stared at it for a moment, then noticed Johanna's inquisitive expression. "Oh," she said, trying not to sound disappointed, "it's from my friend, Mary, in New York City." She read it quickly. "She says her family went skiing in Vermont for Christmas and that school has been all right."

Halley loved both the Norlins' monkey with a natural part down the middle of his hair and the French doors leading into the dining room. Savoring her last bite of delicious, curried chicken, she heard Sarin summon Dr. Gustaf to the phone. Moments later, he returned. "Halley, there's someone on the phone who'd like to speak to you."

Halley listened to Hans's excuses for not writing: rugby practice, tests, orchestra rehearsals, and visiting Harin on the weekends. He had finally found the time that morning to write her a letter. "That's nice," she said flatly, wanting to get off the phone before she exploded. "Well, I've got to go," she said, trying to think of an excuse to get away. "It looks like dessert is being served. It was nice to talk to you. I'll get your mom." She thought she heard him saying something else when she put the receiver on the table.

Her cheeks were hot. *I shouldn't have wasted all that time worrying about him*, she thought. *He's obviously been too busy to think about me. Well*, she decided, approaching the table, *I'm too busy to think about him too.* "Dr. Maria, Hans is on the phone."

******

The date for the play was fast approaching. Following Sister Jane's daily afterschool rehearsals, Halley would nonchalantly wander past the front desk at the Royal Palm. Two weeks before the day of the show, the attendant stopped her. "*Memsaab* Pederson, you have mail." She took it right up to her room and out onto the balcony. It smelled a little like tree sap when she pulled the letter out of the envelope. Her heart was pumping loudly.

"Dear Halley, I trust this letter finds you well."

What a silly way to start a letter, she thought, and took a breath before continuing.

"I'm pleased to say that our spring break coincides with your play, and I'll be in Poona then."

She wondered if he still wanted to see her after she practically hung up on him.

"It will be great to see you."

She hoped so, but maybe she'd be too busy.

"Just this morning I sat down at a long table in the school library next to a copy of the Bombay Express. *There you were smiling right at me from the cover."*

Halley groaned. That stupid newspaper again.

"Although I've been very busy, I think about you all the time and can't wait to see you."

Really?

"Until then, I remain yours truly, Hans."

Halley's heart fluttered and she read the letter again and understood that, although he wasn't much of a letter writer, he thought about her all the time.

On the day of the play, Halley was relieved that Sister Jane expected all the actors to be on stage for their final check at the same time Hans and Harin's train was scheduled to arrive. She was nervous enough as it was. Her character had a carefree attitude. Being sidetracked with anxiety about seeing Hans could mess her up. She pleaded with Dad not to let anyone see her until the play was over.

When she was in her costume and makeup was finished with her, she stood in front of a long mirror. *I am Jack*, she mused, pointing at her reflection. *I am a complicated gentleman.*

At the end of an almost perfect performance, Halley, as Jack, pronounced the last lines of the play, took a deep breath, and watched the curtain close.

Sister Jane congratulated the cast on an outstanding performance then said, "Now go out there and find your fans."

Still in costume, Halley and Johanna entered the lobby amidst cheers and another burst of applause.

"Well done, Jack," Hans said as he lifted a garland of fragrant white flowers over Halley's head and handed her a box of English chocolates.

She was glad to see him and laughed. "These are the same brand I bought from the gift shop on the ship. I love them. Thank you."

She glanced at Johanna just as Harin laid a circle of pink flowers on her shoulders.

◊ ◊ ◊

The following morning, after a great evening at the Norlins' house, Hans helped teach the children in one of the classrooms at Prem Makaan and Halley helped the cooks make lunch. Then, without a break, she started serving it. She was tired but pushed herself to keep going. There were more children to feed.

Hans tapped her shoulder and picked up a pair of tongs from the spot next to hers. "Lots of kids in the math class," he said, laughing. "Some came into the room with their bowls full of food and sat down in front. They looked more interested in learning than eating."

Halley looked up at him and smiled. "Thanks for coming with us today. It sounds like the kids really like you."

Hans dropped a *chapatti* onto the bowl of rice she had just filled. "I think they're really hungry to learn."

A small girl hugged one of Halley's legs and tugged her hand.

"Go ahead with her," Hans said. "I can dish the rice and the *chapattis*."

The child led her to a veranda overlooking a garden with a small pond and crawled up on the couch next to her. Halley reached around her bony shoulders and saw there was a *chapatti* in the girl's other hand. The child tore it carefully in half, handed Halley a piece, then took a bite of the other. Halley sniffed at the warm fragrance. She bit into hers and chewed.

Together they watched a pair of squawking ducks splash down onto the pond. Halley looked deep into the cascading spray that shot up behind them. In the center of the spray, she saw a shimmer of sparkling light.

Glossary of Indian Words

Achachha. Good
Aiya. Takes care of the children
Ashram. A place for religious retreat
Babaji. A highly respected or elderly man.
Bombay. Bombay returned to the name *Mumbai* after liberation from the British
Burai. Evil
Chup raho. Shut up
Chota hasuri. An early, small breakfast of tea and fruit or toast
Chutney. A sweet or savory topping of fruit or vegetables
Cupola. Large, often hollow, dome topped enclosure on a decorative roof
Dadaji. Father figure
Darj. Enter
Dhanyavaad. Thank you
Dharma. Higher truth
Dhoti. A men's garment made of cloth wrapped around the waist that covers the legs.
Dupatta. A long, delicate scarf or shawl worn with the *lehenga*.
Hailo. Hello
Howdahs. A platform, carriage or thick woven matt on the back of an elephant
Jaldi . Hurry
Kachori. A crisp, spicy filled pastry
Keematee. Precious
Kya. What?
Laal. Red
Laal Adrik. Red Adrik
Laal Ball. Red Hair
Lama. A title of respect applied to a spiritual leader in Tibetan Buddhism
Lehenga. An elegant, ankle length skirt
Lehenga Choli. A fitted blouse worn with the Lehenga
Riken. Stop
Maanik. Ruby, a precious red stone

Maharaja. King or ruler - During British rule if India, the maharaja's territory became part of the British Empire.
Maharini. Wife of a maharaja
Main Hoon. I am Lavi
Memsaab. Mrs. or Miss.
Namaste. I bow to you or I bow to the divinity within you.
Pice. Very small amount of money
Poona. City returned to the name *Pune* after liberation from the British
Prem Makaan. Love House
Punjabi. Someone who lives in the Punjab region of Northern India
Raj. When the British controlled India
Raja. King or prince
Riken. Stop
Sahib. Mr.
Sari. A garment of yards of fabric wrapped around the waist and then up over the shoulder
Sarwan. Explorer
Shikari. A guide for hunters
Sikh. A follower of the Indian religion Sikhism
Theek hai. It's all right
Tiffin. Lunch
Topi. Hat